Maybe This Time

Maybe This Time

KASIE WEST

SCHOLASTIC PRESS
NEW YORK

Library of Congress Cataloging-in-Publication Data

Names: West, Kasie, author.
Title: Maybe this time / Kasie West.
Description: First edition. | New York: Scholastic Press, 2019. | Summary: Sophie
    Evans works for the local florist and party planner in her small southern town, so
    she attends all of the big "events," all the time sketching and dreaming of applying
    to design school; but this year there is a fly-in-the-ointment of her life—Andrew
    Hart, son of the fancy new chef in town, who is also at all the local events, and
    keeps getting in her way, making her life more complicated.
Identifiers: LCCN 2018053895 | ISBN 9781338210088
Subjects: LCSH: Man-woman relationships—Juvenile fiction. | Interpersonal
    relations—Juvenile fiction. | Special events—Planning—Juvenile fiction. |
    Dating (Social customs)—Juvenile fiction. | CYAC: Interpersonal relations—
    Fiction. | Dating (Social customs)—Fiction. | Love—Fiction. |
    Parties—Fiction.
Classification: LCC PZ7.W51837 May 2019 | DDC 813.6 [Fic]—dc23
LC record available at https://lccn.loc.gov/2018053895

10 9 8 7 6 5 4 3 2 1   19 20 21 22 23

Printed in the U.S.A.   23

First edition, July 2019

Book design by Yaffa Jaskoll

To my beautiful bridal
bouquet, which was thrown
away by my husband.
"The flowers were dead!"

R. I. P.

Valentine's Day Retirement Home Dinner

TULIP

Grown from a bulb, tulips blossom in the spring, yet one day somebody thought, "Hey, let's sell them on Valentine's Day," and everyone else apparently went along with it. Still not as popular as the rose, but cheaper. And therefore requested by the old folks' home.

Chapter 1

The cafeteria had been transformed into a red-and-pink extravaganza. Like Hello Kitty herself had decorated for the occasion. The flowers, my contribution to the party, sat in the center of each table.

I walked around one centerpiece, trying to pinpoint why it looked off—aside from the vase, which was wrapped in metallic cellophane and adorned with pink hearts that I wished would disappear. The thick stems of tulips were my favorite, and a bit more green would have been good for the aesthetic, but it wasn't up to me. My boss had decided on the cellophane. As if the red confetti hearts sprinkled on the tablecloths or the pink and red balloon hearts tied to the chairs weren't enough. But as Caroline always said when I tried to give suggestions: *You're preachin' to the choir, honey. This is for the clients.*

She was right; the clients would love this. And, honestly, I didn't care enough to fight it. Working for the town florist was never my dream job. But money was money, and I needed it if I wanted to go to design school in New York. And I did. With all my soul.

"There." I spotted a pink tulip that was throwing off the balance of the arrangement. I pulled it out and traded it with the red one next to it. "Much better." Looking at the flowers, an image sprang to mind of girls in brightly colored sundresses marching through a field of tulips.

"Sophie," Caroline said as she came into the cafeteria with another bundle of balloons. "The flowers look great."

I blinked, and the girls in dresses disappeared. "Thanks."

Every Occasion was mainly a flower shop. But in a town as small as ours, Caroline took on the role of party planner as well. People would come into the shop for centerpieces and walk out with a minute-by-minute itinerary for their event. She could sell honey to bees, Caroline always said.

"Were you just at the van?" Caroline asked me.

"No, I've been in here for a while."

"Can you check and see if I left the gift bags in there? They're in two cardboard boxes."

"Sure." I wiped my hands on my apron and gathered the buckets and supplies to put away.

Outside, I opened the back doors of the van and swung the buckets inside. I untied my apron and tucked it into a bin. I didn't see the gift bags Caroline was talking about. What I did see was my backpack, with my design journal—its leather cords barely holding its bursting pages closed—sitting on top. I'd pulled the journal out earlier in a bout of inspiration but Caroline had called me away in the middle of a sketch.

I picked up the journal and untied the cords, flipping past drawings and material samples and pressed leaves to the sketch of a blouse I'd been working on. A scowl came over my face. Where had I been going with this? The lines were rushed and sloppy. As always, I wished I had more time to devote to this journal. I was hoping to use its contents to convince schools they wanted me. Especially since I had no design experience.

"Sophie!"

I turned to see Micah, my best friend, rushing out of the retirement home.

I smiled, then tucked my notebook back into my bag and faced her. "Hey! When did you get here?"

"Holy crap you cut your hair!"

I reached up and pulled on the ends. I'd cut my long dark hair to a choppy shoulder-length style the day before and was still getting used to it. "I told you I was going to."

"I know, I just didn't think you would."

She didn't think I would? "So you hate it?"

"What? No! It's awesome. It makes your eyes look huge."

"Thanks."

Micah wore her cater waiter outfit—black pants and a white collared shirt. She tugged at the collar, which was obviously bothering her neck.

"You know, if you let me alter that shirt a little, it would feel a million times better." I pinched a section near her waist. "And while I was fixing the neck, I could take it in here . . ."

"Yeah, yeah." She pushed my hands away. "I'm sure my dad would love you messing with his uniforms." Her dad was a caterer, the only one in this small town. Micah pointed at her tight black curls, which I could tell at one point had been gathered on top of her head but now spilled every which way. "Speaking of uniforms, my hair tie broke."

"It looks cute. Leave it."

"Because hair in food is so appetizing."

"I'm sure you have another hair tie in your *just-in-case*." That's what I liked to call Micah's plastic case of sectioned squares that she kept in the trunk of her car. Her *just-in-case* mainly covered hair, makeup, and clothing emergencies, because the bin wasn't big enough to include things like road flares or neck braces.

"You mock me, but that case has saved your butt on multiple occasions," she said.

"So true." I followed her to her car, where she removed the case from her trunk. "I wonder what the makers of your squares actually intended them for," I mused. "Tools, maybe? Nuts and bolts?"

"This, Sophie. This." She smiled, then pulled out a hair tie. "Do you need anything?"

I surveyed the selection—earrings, nail polish, Q-tips, Band-Aids, lip gloss—all in their own little spaces. It was the perfect representation of how Micah liked to live her life, everything in its proper place. "I'm good." I nodded back toward the van. "I'm supposed to be getting gift bags."

"Is that why you were sketching?"

"I was not sketching!" I cleared my throat. "I was looking at something I'd sketched earlier."

"Uh-huh." She shut her trunk and we walked back to the flower van together. "How did your date with Kyle go last night, by the way?"

My stomach flipped at the mention of Kyle. "Not great," I admitted. "Gunnar hid in the back seat of Kyle's car as we were driving off to get dinner, and he jumped out after five minutes to scare us." I frowned, remembering my little brother's antics. "Kyle nearly wrecked his brand-new Mustang. And then he talked about nothing else the rest of the night."

Micah cringed. "First dates are always weird. You need to give him a second chance."

"I don't know that he'll give *me* a second chance." I sighed. "My brother nearly ruined his baby. Or so I heard . . . all night." I scanned the back of the van again and finally spotted a couple of cardboard boxes behind the passenger seat.

"*I* would give you another chance," Micah said. "Besides, Gunnar is adorable."

That reminded me. I pulled my phone out of my pocket and sent my brother a text: *Is your homework done?*

Yes. Wanna see a spider? I found a spider under the cupboard.

Yuck. No.

"So that's it?" Micah asked.

"What?" I turned toward her. She was giving me her impatient eyes.

7

"You're done with Kyle after one date? You can't be done. I gave you a compatibility quiz. He was your match." After Kyle had asked me out last week, Micah had made me take some online quiz she'd found and we'd laughed over every question.

I rolled my eyes. "Really? You're going to claim that as gospel now?"

"Whatever it takes." Micah thought I had a habit of not giving guys a chance. She wasn't wrong. But Kyle was different. I'd been crushing on him for a couple of months now. So despite having to sit through his detailed descriptions of what a V8, 435-horsepower engine could do, I was willing to agree with her that first dates could be aberrations.

"Fine, one more date."

She smiled. "Good. Will he be here tonight?"

"Could you see his band playing at this thing? The old people would riot."

"I meant with his grandma. Doesn't his grandma live here at Willow Falls now?"

"Does she? She wasn't at last year's event. But maybe. I can tell you who doesn't live here: his car. I know everything about his car."

"I got that." Micah tugged on the hair tie to make sure the curly bun on top of her head was secure. "Okay. Better get back to work, love."

She kissed the air by my cheek, then headed toward the building. I walked around to the side door of the van and slid it open.

"Oh!" Micah turned and walked backward for a few steps. "I have to tell you something later! Something really big!"

"What do you need to tell . . . ?" Before I finished my question, she was through the door and it swung shut behind her.

Something big? Good big or bad big? Why did she do that to me? She knew I couldn't sit with information like that.

Chapter 2

I slid Caroline's boxes full of gift bags toward me. Unassembled gift bags. Great. I now knew what I'd be spending most of my night doing. I stacked one box on top of the other and carried them back inside.

I made it halfway down the hall when I heard a voice call out from behind me.

"Excuse me?"

I turned. A guy around my age, dressed in fitted jeans, a pastel collared shirt, and a tailored sport jacket stood there, a smile on his handsome face. He clearly wasn't from around here. He was citified.

I offered him a polite smile, hoping this wouldn't take long. "The event doesn't start for fifteen minutes," I said. "But you're welcome to wait in the lobby. Families are already gathering there."

I knew every school-aged kid in my town (and most of their living and dead relatives). So this guy had to be here visiting for the event. I tried to place him with a grandparent in my head—Betty or Carl or Leo or . . .

"You're not from around here," he said, as if voicing my thoughts.

I shifted the boxes in my arms. They weren't heavy but they were bulky. "What?"

"You're not from Rockside," he said.

"I am, actually. Born and raised."

"Ah. There it is. I didn't hear your Southern accent at first."

I straightened with a bit of pride. I worked very hard on making my accent as minimal as possible so that when I went away to college I wouldn't stick out like a sore thumb.

The guy took several steps forward and pulled his hand out from behind his back to reveal he'd been holding a pink tulip. "Something beautiful for someone beautiful."

My brows dipped down. *Seriously?* I wasn't sure what to make of such a brazen romantic gesture. If that's what he was going for. Was it?

I looked at the boxes in my arms, transferred them awkwardly to one hip, and reached out for the flower. With my hand halfway to its destination, I noticed a small green wire wrapped up the stem and supported the bulb.

I paused. "Where did you get that?"

The question seemed to surprise him, his smile faltered a bit, but he recovered with, "It doesn't matter where it came from, only where it's going." He extended his arm farther.

I set the boxes down on the floor and took the flower to inspect it. Sure enough, the wire was wrapped exactly the way I'd done it on over a hundred tulips that very morning. Hours and hours of my life were spent with that wire, in fact.

"You took this from one of the vases in the cafeteria?" I asked, incredulous.

He nodded. "Yes, I rescued it from its tacky prison. It looks happier already."

My mouth dropped open.

"No worries. There were hundreds of them. Nobody will be able to tell."

"No worries?" I turned and marched back to the cafeteria.

"I sense I've offended you," Mr. Obvious said, following me. Or Mr. Entitled? Maybe I'd go for a hyphenated last name since both applied.

I stood in the doorway and scanned the centerpieces.

"You're telling me that you're going to know which one of these flower arrangements I found *this* flower in," he said.

"*Found?* Yes, I'm going to tell you exactly which flower arrangement you *stole* this flower from, considering I've spent the last eight hours putting them together."

He coughed. "Oh. Did I say tacky? I meant . . . uh . . . festive."

I rolled my eyes.

I saw him glance my way, as if sizing me up. I was wearing a silky green blouse with a floral knee-length skirt. My party attire. But even outside of work events, I liked fun colors and classic styles.

"These centerpieces aren't your design anyway," he pronounced, "so I don't know why you're upset."

I scowled. "There is no way you could possibly know that."

He shrugged like he disagreed, then said, "I still don't think you'll be able to tell which one I took it from."

"I will."

"Without counting the flowers?"

"You're adding rules to this made-up game?"

"Yes!" he said proudly. "If you can't tell which arrangement is missing a flower just by looking, then nobody else will be able to tell either and you must accept my gift."

"Can something that was stolen really be called a gift?" I asked, and began weaving in and out of tables.

"Deal?"

Leo's grandson sure was annoying. Maybe he was John's grandson. John was known for being demanding. But I could've sworn I'd met all John's grandkids at the town's Fourth of July barbecue the previous year. "And if *I* win?" I asked.

One side of his mouth lifted in a half smile. "If you win, I owe you a dozen flowers that I must pay for."

"A dozen flowers arranged by me."

"Only if they don't involve foil."

I narrowed my eyes at him. "It's called cellophane. And they won't."

"I sense this is going to be expensive."

Based on his appearance, I was more than sure he could afford it. "I sense that you need to make restitution for dozens and dozens of past stolen flowers."

When he didn't argue, I knew I'd guessed right. I wasn't the first girl he'd tried to impress with a flower, acquired without any forethought. My eyes moved from studying him standing there in his arrogance to studying the flowers again. It didn't take me long to see the lopsided arrangement. He'd taken the flower from the right side, throwing off the entire shape. I sighed, made my way over to the table, and tucked the tulip I was holding into its rightful place.

"Orange calla lilies are my favorite," I said, walking back toward the hallway.

"Did you see me take it?" he asked as I passed him. "Is that how you knew?"

"No, I told you. I arranged all of these. It was obvious."

"Well, I'm impressed."

"Don't be. And seriously, don't steal my flowers again." I left him standing there in the cafeteria, staring after me.

In the hallway, I pulled out my phone and sent a message to Micah: *PSA, there's an entitled guest roaming the halls. Engage at your own risk!*

A train of wheelchairs rounded the corner and blocked my way for a moment as several nurses escorted their patients toward the lobby.

"Sophie," Mr. Washington said as he was being wheeled

by. His nurse, Kayla, stopped. "I think my wife once owned a skirt like that."

"Is that a compliment or a statement, Mr. W?" I asked.

"Always a compliment, Miss Sophie. You look stunning."

"Thank you."

"Do you know how to tie a bow tie?" He held up the bright red material.

"I do."

"Could you help out an old man with arthritis?"

"Of course." I stepped forward and draped the tie around his collar.

"My nurse doesn't know how to tie this," he said, as if everyone in the world should have this skill.

"Guilty," Kayla agreed. "How do *you* know, Sophie? This town doesn't really have any black-tie affairs."

"I watched some YouTube videos when I was like ten and practiced on one of my dolls," I said, looping the tie. "My mom wasn't exactly thrilled with my new skill because I'd cut up one of my skirts to make the bow tie."

"That's funny. I forgot you were into fashion," Kayla said. "You want to go to design school or something, right?"

When she said it like that, it sounded like a passing thought and not my everything. "Yes."

"Have you applied for my scholarship?" Mr. Washington asked. "You're a junior this year, right?"

I tightened the bow tie and stepped back. "I am. But you

haven't changed the rules of your scholarship, have you? I
thought it was only for students who want to go to college in
Alabama." Mr. Washington had more love for Alabama than
anyone I knew, and he had been bribing students to fill its colleges for over twenty years now.

"It is."

"I'm going to school in New York."

Mr. W's wrinkled brow became even more wrinkled.
"But your mother told me you couldn't afford that."

"I've been saving, and my dad is going to help some."

He must've heard the defensiveness in my voice because he
said, "That's great, but it doesn't hurt to apply. There's nothing wrong with a backup plan."

My mom liked to use that phrase a lot too—*backup plan*.
She had me failing before I'd even begun.

I nodded. "I'll think about it." I'd think long and hard
about how I wasn't going to do that at all. In a year and a half,
all my dreams were going to come true.

Chapter 3

When I brought the boxes of gift bags back into the cafeteria, Mr. Entitled was nowhere to be seen. Thank goodness. But Caroline was there, messing with speakers she had set up by two potted plants.

"Oh, good!" Caroline said, coming over to me. "I was worried I left them at home." She peeked into the top box I carried. "Aren't these adorable?" She picked up a cellophane bag with little red hearts on it. "They match the centerpieces!"

"Cute," I said, trying to sound sincere.

"Now," Caroline said, "if you'll fill each of the bags with a large pinch of pink grass and a handful of these wrapped chocolate hearts, they'll be the perfect little take-home favors for the guests. There's some ribbon to tie the bags in there too." She looked around like she was searching for something, then put her hands on her hips. "You can't put the bags together in here. That's not very professional. Do you think you can find a room somewhere?"

"I'll do it in the back of the kitchen," I said. "Mr. Williams doesn't ever mind if I take over a counter."

"Hmm. I don't know if that will work today."

"Why not?"

She looked at her watch. "Oh, it's nearly time. Just tuck the boxes in that storage closet and you can get to them later. Right now, will you go to the lobby and see if they have all the guests gathered yet? If so, you can lead them inside."

"Okay." I found the supply closet outside the kitchen, pushed the boxes under the bottom shelf, and walked down the hall. The entire lobby and part of the hallway was filled with chatting families.

"Good evening!" I tried to say above the voices, but nothing changed. I scanned the group, curiosity getting the better of me and wanting to place Mr. Entitled into a family. But I didn't see him anywhere. I did see Kyle, though, standing next to his grandma. So she *had* moved into the home sometime in the past year.

Kyle was wearing a tie, which he'd already loosened, with a collared shirt and jeans. His blond hair was rumpled and falling into his eyes, as always. He smiled at me and I smiled back, my face getting warm. Maybe my brother hadn't ruined things after all.

Finally one of the nurses let out a loud whistle and a "Quiet down, y'all!"

I turned my attention back to the group. "I'm glad you're already having fun," I said. "If everyone is here, we'd like to welcome you into the main event. Please follow me."

I led the large group back down the hall, acutely aware

that Kyle was probably watching me. But I was here to work, not get distracted.

Inside the cafeteria, soft music poured from the speakers. "Welcome!" Caroline beamed.

I held the door open while the group filed inside, so I heard their first *oohs* and *aahs*. Caroline was right; they loved the over-the-top setup.

Kyle was one of the last to enter, and he paused right next to me. "I didn't know you were going to be here," he said.

"Every Occasion did the flowers."

"Oh, yeah. That makes sense," he said.

"You didn't get asked to play?"

Kyle and I went to school together, but we'd also been at a couple of the same events since I'd started working at Every Occasion last year (after I'd been turned down by the one place in town I *wanted* to work at: Minnie's Alterations).

"You think my band would've gone over well here?" He nodded to the speakers with a grin. Kyle's band played mostly loud and unintelligible music, but somehow they made it work.

"Your grandma doesn't like your music?"

He laughed, and the sound made me smile.

"See ya around, Evans." He joined his grandma at a center table.

Just as I was about to shut the cafeteria doors, a man wearing a white chef coat and a sour expression swept out of the kitchen. He grumbled something and angrily marched to the end of the hall, where he shoved open the door leading outside and stepped through. He looked vaguely familiar but I couldn't place him. Had Mr. Williams hired an assistant chef? I didn't think he could afford that. He already employed Lance Ling (a guy who went to school with me and Micah) to help out at events.

Micah was suddenly at my side. "Where did he go?" she asked.

"Um . . ." I pointed and she raced after the runaway chef.

I started to shut the doors again. Then I hesitated, looked behind me once, saw that Caroline was occupied with some guests, and followed after Micah.

When I made it outside, I pretended to head to the van, my eavesdropping not subtle at all. Micah and the man in the white coat were standing on the sidewalk.

"He's more than honored to have you here," Micah was saying. "Anyone would be. You're Jett Hart."

Jett Hart? I held back a gasp and did a double take. Sure enough, it was him. Jett Hart, the host of a now-discontinued show on Food Network called *Cooking with Hart*. He looked much older than I remembered him from back in his television chef days, but it had been at least ten years since then. Where had he been for the last ten years? Here? In Alabama? What was he doing at the Valentine's Dinner? How did Micah know him? So many questions flooded my brain, none of them with ready answers.

"That's correct. Anyone would be," Jett said with an air of self-importance.

"Please just come back," Micah said. "He'll listen. He's just old and set in his ways."

"Old and set in his ways does not sound like someone willing to listen."

"He will," she promised.

I realized I had stopped on the path and was gawking so I resumed my walk toward the van.

As I passed her, Micah reached out and grabbed my arm, pulling me to her side. "Mr. Hart, this is Sophie Evans. She's a big fan."

That wasn't true. I was in second grade when his show went off the air. I'd seen a few reruns over the years. He was bossy, mean, and arrogant, albeit talented. But I knew Micah needed me to agree with her statement, and I always backed her up.

"A huge fan," I blurted. "The things you do with fish, sir, are inspiring."

Micah elbowed me in the side and cleared her throat. "I think the timer on the appetizers is about to go off. Let's go back in before my dad burns them."

Her dad would never burn appetizers. He was a great chef as well. Sure, he wasn't famous (and he wasn't famous ten years ago either), but everyone loved his food.

Jett let out a huff and headed back for the building.

I held on to Micah's arm to keep her from following him.

"What is going on? Why would your dad burn his appetizers? He's been cooking them for years."

"Because they're not my dad's appetizers. They're Jett's."

"Jett made the appetizers? You changed up the menu for the retirement home Valentine's Dinner? Tell me he's not doing something extra fancy for them. They literally just got excited over heart balloons."

"It'll be fine," she said. I knew when Micah felt out of her comfort zone, like her carefully organized life had thrown her for a loop. And she was feeling that now. "It'll all work out."

"Yes, it will." Since I had no idea what was going on, I wasn't actually sure this was true, but I knew she needed to hear it. "Is this part of the big news you were going to tell me?" I asked.

"Yes," she said. "I'll fill you in later. I need to go play referee."

"Okay. Good luck." I gave her my best smile and she ran back inside.

I was so confused. Jett Hart was in Rockside, Alabama, a town where nothing out of the ordinary ever happened. I wanted to think this was a good thing—a sign of exciting things to come—but my gut was telling me it might be the exact opposite.

Chapter 4

You had to stay in case of a flower emergency?" Mr. Entitled asked me when I reentered the cafeteria. He stood next to the punch bowl, holding his phone and studying the mingling crowd.

I replenished a stack of napkins. "I was informed there was a flower thief on the loose so . . ."

He smirked.

"Are you bored?" I asked.

"How could I be? This must be the most excitement this town sees all year."

Before I could voice my indignation yet again, Micah came by with a trayful of food. Apparently the appetizers hadn't burned after all.

"Quick," Micah whispered. "Eat one of these."

"Why?" I asked, studying the tray. A square made of an unknown substance (bread?) was topped with a red-and-white cream and finished off with a sprig of green.

"Because nobody is eating them. They taste good to me, but maybe I'm wrong."

Mr. Entitled picked one up and ate it in one bite.

I continued to study Jett's appetizers. A surge of irritation sparked in my chest at the person causing my friend this much stress.

"I knew this would be the wrong crowd to try a new menu on," I said to Micah. "They just want pigs in blankets, or those amazing mac-and-cheese balls your dad does. They don't want fancy crap from some washed-up chef."

"Um . . ." Micah started.

"What?" I said, trying to reassure her. "Your dad is awesome. He doesn't need help from some has-been. What is Jett Hart even doing here? He obviously disappeared for a reason. And if it wasn't because of his absolute arrogance and lack of common decency on his show, I'm guessing it had a lot to do with whatever this . . . *thing* masquerading as an appetizer is." I picked up the offending square of food and sniffed it. It actually didn't smell half-bad. Then I stuck it in my mouth. It seemed to melt on my tongue, awakening all my taste buds.

Mr. Entitled cleared his throat. "He actually disappeared because he wanted to live a quieter life with his family and help struggling small-business owners find their footing. But some might describe that as *washed-up*." He gave a small nod, took the tray from Micah, said, "Let me try for a minute," and left.

I stood there trying not to choke on the food in my mouth.

"I thought you knew who he was," Micah hissed.

"How would I know who he is? I still don't, but I'm guessing he's somehow related to Jett?"

24

"That's his son," she said. "Andrew Hart."

Oh.

"I'm a jerk."

"Yeah, kind of."

I hit her arm. "This is all your fault. Why didn't you tell me about this . . . whatever *this* is, I still don't know—before today?"

"Because I didn't know until last night!" Micah exclaimed. "And I didn't want to text you and bother you on your date."

I glanced around to see if Kyle was nearby, but thankfully he was still sitting with his grandma at the table across the room.

"My dad applied for this program Jett Hart does," Micah continued. "Jett mentors small-business owners and then they get to use his name on their business."

"Sophie!" Caroline called, waving me over to where some balloons had come untied. "I need you!"

I started toward Caroline but glanced back at Micah. "You are going to tell me all the details later," I said.

"Absolutely. For now, I better go learn how Andrew is selling the appetizers. His tray is half-empty."

"Andrew Hart," I mumbled, annoyed at just the thought of him. At least I wouldn't have to see him again after tonight.

"A year? What do you mean a *year*?" I cried.

"Shh." Micah was scraping the remains off dinner plates into the garbage can and then sticking them in the trays that would later be transported to their industrial dishwasher. I was standing at a side counter, finally assembling the gift bags.

I looked over my shoulder, but we were the only ones in the kitchen. Mr. Williams and Jett were circulating the cafeteria, listening to feedback. I assumed it was mostly complaints that her dad hadn't made his famous mashed potatoes and instead had tried to force balsamic-dressed arugula down their throats.

"That's the program," Micah explained calmly. "A year of mentoring, which then allows us to use Jett's name on our business."

"Does his name hold any power anymore?" I kept my voice low.

"You'd be surprised."

I grabbed a bunch of pink grass to scatter in a bag. "But what's in it for Jett?"

"I think he really *does* want to better communities and help small businesses thrive," Micah said with a shrug. "Well, that and he'll own a percentage of our business after a year."

"What?"

"Shh."

"Sorry. It's just, I thought you said you were already struggling. How is giving Jett a percentage of your business going to help?"

"He promises he'll grow our business by at least thirty percent, and in return we'll give him ten percent."

"Has he ever worked with someone from a town this small?" I asked, still not convinced. "There is no way you are going to grow your business by thirty percent living here." I added a handful of chocolate hearts to another bag.

"That's the beauty of his name," Micah said, reaching for another plate. "It's going to give us the recognition we need to expand into the surrounding areas. We'll travel a little more, but we'll make more money. Plus, Jett Hart is a famous white chef. His name could get us past the barrier of people who otherwise wouldn't hire a black caterer."

"Oh," I said, humbled. There were a couple of families in particular that I knew she was referring to. But I was sure I didn't know everything Micah had to deal with, even though we'd been friends since kindergarten. "You're right."

"Andrew is going to help my dad put together a website too."

I curled my lip. "He is? Doesn't Andrew have to go to school? How old is he anyway?"

"He's seventeen. And no, he works with his dad. He does independent study."

"How do you know all this?"

A piece of lettuce clung to the plate she was holding, and she shook it until it fell into the trash. "I read through the entire contract last night when my dad told me he'd actually won. And then I spent hours on the internet compiling every bit of information I could find from past participants."

Of course she had. Micah would want to know every detail of everything to help her process this news. Which was probably why her dad hadn't said anything until he actually knew if it was happening or not.

"And what did you conclude?" I asked, still not able to tell if she was fully on board with the whole plan.

"I think it might actually work. Jett *has* turned other businesses around."

"And *you're* okay?" I asked, studying her. "You seemed upset earlier."

"I'm good. I was just stressed because Jett and my dad were arguing."

"I don't get it. If your dad applied for this, how come he is fighting the changes?"

"I think he thought Jett would show up and be like, 'Wow, you're already amazing, here's my name and a million dollars.'"

"Really?"

"Well, no, not exactly, but something like that." She turned to face me. "I thought *you'd* be more excited about this."

"Sorry, you're right, I am. I wasn't sure if you were, so I was hesitant. But this is cool. I hope it works out for your family."

She waved a dish at me. "No, not excited for us, but thank you. I mean, excited for *you*."

I frowned. "Why would I be excited for me?"

"Do you know how many connections Jett Hart must have?" she said, her brown eyes sparkling. "He's worked in Hollywood; he's lived in London and New York. New York, Sophie! This guy could be an in for you."

My mind spun. Jett Hart would definitely have connections to the food industry, but to the fashion industry? Hmm. Maybe he'd cooked for some big-name designers or fashion-magazine editors. Maybe he could score me an internship or, at the very least, a contact. "I hadn't thought of that. You might be right."

"You're welcome," she said.

I grabbed the spool of ribbon and scissors as my mind replayed the events of the evening. "Do you think Andrew is going to tell his dad what I said about him?"

Micah shook her head. "I doubt it. He might be a spoiled pretty boy, but he doesn't seem like the type to go running to daddy."

"Spill," I said. Micah had been researching for hours the night before, so she'd obviously discovered some things about Andrew too. If I had to put up with this guy for a year, I wanted to know exactly who I was dealing with.

Micah put another plate in the tray and straightened up. "Not much to tell. He and his dad have lived in seven different places in the last seven years."

"Is that the excuse he uses for his personality?"

The door pushed open and Jett Hart and Mr. Williams stepped through, cutting our gossip session short.

"Sophie!" Mr. Williams said, pulling some mixing bowls out of a box on the island. "It's good to see you."

"You too."

Jett Hart went over to the fridge and began collecting ingredients. I watched him skeptically. Was Micah right? Could he be the key to both the Williams family's future *and* mine? My heart doubled its speed as my brain tried to think of something clever and memorable to say to him. Jett, holding an armful of food, headed straight for me. I froze, my mouth halfway open.

He paused at the counter, which was strewn with the gift bag materials. "What is this?" he demanded.

"Favors?" I responded unhelpfully.

A carton of whipping cream tucked under his left arm began slipping. "Well, move it," he growled.

I jumped into action, sliding the completed bags down the counter to make room. Micah came to my side and helped me transfer them into the boxes on the floor.

"I don't have all day," Jett barked, using his foot to shove my box out of the way.

The tension on Micah's face and the thought of my future kept a rude response from spilling out of my mouth. I had a year. An entire year to win him over.

Chapter 5

Events were often spent putting out mini fires. Tonight, that meant helping Mrs. White deal with the sauce she'd spilled all over her blouse and making sure that Mr. Langston didn't eat the confetti he sprinkled onto his food because he thought it was some sort of topping.

But my favorite part of the Valentine's Dinner was happening right now.

Caroline stood at the front of the room with a microphone. "Ladies and gentlemen!" she began. "Before dessert is served, it's time for the eligible bachelor auction. Get your Willow Falls bucks ready. You can purchase a date to share your dessert with, or perhaps to dance with, tonight."

I helped some of the older men form a line next to Caroline, then stepped back to watch the auction start. It didn't take me long to realize there were going to be more eligible men than women. Some women were bidding on more than one man, which I found both fun and funny. But when the last man, Mr. John Farnsworth, went to the front, I knew he'd be a hard sell. John was notoriously grumpy, and the women in the audience were already talking with their new dates, men they'd probably known for over a decade. This was a tradition, though, and this town was crazy about their traditions.

I found myself raising my hand to enter a bid, even though I had no fake money to back me up. Nobody called me out on it and Caroline gave me a beaming smile as I walked to the front of the cafeteria to collect my date. *Happy customers are future business*, she always said. From the corner of my eye, I saw Kyle smirking at me across the room, and I glanced away.

"Mr. Farnsworth," I said, hooking my arm in his and leading him to a far table. "How has your night been?"

"Aside from no mashed potatoes and some sort of fish paste on my crackers?"

"Sure, aside from that."

"There've been better years."

"But not years when Jett Hart has come to an event," I said. Everyone over thirty in this room would know who Jett Hart was. And Mr. Farnsworth was well over thirty.

"Jett Hart? Is that who the old man talking about salad was?"

I couldn't help but laugh as I nodded.

"Well, that makes more sense. I don't think he's aged well."

I disagreed. Jett Hart may have been grumpy, but with his thick head of hair and classic good looks, it was obvious why he'd once been selected to be on TV.

"I do like him, though," Mr. Farnsworth added thoughtfully. "I enjoyed his show. He never took any crap."

Huh. Maybe Jett's name *would* do something for Mr. Williams's business. "Is your family here tonight?" I asked Mr. Farnsworth as we took our seats.

"My family can't be bothered to come visit me on normal days," he grumbled. "Do you think they're going to fly to Rockside for Valentine's Day?"

"I'm sorry."

"I didn't ask you to be sorry."

"You're right, I did that all on my own."

"Where is this dessert I was promised?" Mr. Farnsworth asked, looking around.

As if by magic, Andrew appeared, holding two of the smallest desserts I'd ever seen. They were some sort of pudding or mousse in shot-sized glasses, each topped with a berry and a dollop of whipped cream.

"What's *that* supposed to be?" Mr. Farnsworth asked, voicing my exact thoughts. Mr. Williams usually served a healthy slice of berry pie.

"This will be the best thing you've ever tasted," Andrew said.

"That's a lofty promise," I said.

"I stand by it." He set one glass down in front of each of us.

"The best two bites I'll ever taste?" I said. I needed to stop.

This was Jett Hart's son. Plus, I'd told Micah I'd stop being so negative. I needed to do just that.

Mr. Farnsworth seemed to appreciate my comments and gave a small chuckle. He picked up his spoon and took a tentative taste, then grumbled about how it wasn't half-bad. Coming from him, that was a very high compliment.

I almost didn't want to try the dessert. Then *I'd* be forced to compliment Andrew. No, that wasn't true. Andrew's dad had made it, not Andrew himself. I took my own bite. The chocolate was light and fluffy and just the right amount of sweet. It contrasted perfectly with the tart flavor of the raspberry.

I nodded. "I'm not sure it's the best thing I've ever tasted, but it was a good choice for tonight's theme of . . . what was that word you used again?" I shot a look up at Andrew. "Tacky?"

He raised an eyebrow. "And here I thought you'd be a little more apologetic, considering what you said about my father earlier."

"Just like you apologized for what you said about my decorations earlier?"

"What I said was true."

"Same." I bit my lip, hard. That was uncalled for. Andrew was right about the centerpieces. They *were* tacky. What was wrong with me?

I opened my mouth to apologize when he said, "It's more than obvious by your outfit and your hair and your accent that you're trying to come off as some seasoned city girl. It's not working for you."

A wave of anger followed by a wave of embarrassment swept through me. How did he know exactly which sore spot to jab at right away? When I got to New York, was it going to be obvious that I was some out-of-place small-town girl? My face went hot.

"You're just mad that I rejected your pathetic attempt at a pickup," I said, getting to my feet. "I wouldn't have thought my rejection was your first, but your inability to lose gracefully is making me think otherwise."

Andrew took a step back. "Grace? Is that what you're demonstrating so well?"

"Young man," Mr. Farnsworth said, surprising me. "This is the face of a woman who wants you to move along. Study it because I sense you see it a lot and are oblivious to what it means."

I wasn't sure what my expression had looked like before, but now I was on the verge of laughing.

Andrew seemed to come back to whatever small amount of sense he possessed and offered Mr. Farnsworth a charming smile. "You're right, I have seen it a lot today." He gave a little bow. "Thank you for the life lesson." And with those words, he was gone.

"Thank you," I said to my date, slowly sitting back down.

Mr. Farnsworth patted my hand. "I will always stand up for a lady, but you were throwing some pretty good punches of your own in there. I don't think you needed my help. Just be careful, Ms. Evans. That one seems to bite back."

I cursed my inability to control my tongue. I had let this Andrew person bring out my worst . . . again. I had known him for barely three hours, and I had lost my cool three times. My way to Jett Hart was definitely not going to be through his son. I shook out my hands and took a deep breath. I was a professional. At work. And despite Andrew's comments, I was good at what I did and I would make sure it showed.

"Sophie!" I heard from across the room, so loud that I was positive everyone had heard it.

I looked over to see my little brother standing next to the double doors, holding on to the handlebars of his bicycle.

Oh no. I rushed across the cafeteria, avoiding stares. I was sure Kyle was watching. My brother was not redeeming himself with this performance.

"Gunnar," I whispered, taking the handlebars of his bike and directing it out of the room and toward the exit. "What are you doing here?" I pushed through the heavy glass door and leaned his bike against the outside of the building.

"Mom said she had to work a double shift, and Taryn had to go to work, so she told me to come here."

"Taryn told you to come here?" Taryn was our neighbor and sometimes babysat my brother.

"No, Mom told me to come here."

"*Mom* told you?" That was worse. I was at work, which my mom always thought of as a fun side hobby and not something real.

"She said maybe I could sit with Mr. Fenell or Ms. Pinkston."

Of course she did. "Come on, maybe you can draw in the lobby or something." I opened the door.

"Can I play on your phone?"

"Once we get home. I need my phone."

His lower lip jutted out.

"I know, totally unfair," I said. I tried to remember this wasn't his fault and put my arm around his shoulder. He was getting tall. He was only ten, but I was sure by the time he was fourteen, he'd outgrow my five-five frame.

The receptionist in the lobby smiled at us when we walked inside.

"June, do you think my brother could sit in here until the event is over?" I asked hopefully.

June wanted to say no, I could see it on her face, but her Southern hospitality wouldn't let her. "Sure thing, Sophie."

I turned to my brother. "Gunnar, be good," I told him in my most serious tone.

"I'll put on a show for him," June said, turning on the ancient television in the corner.

"Thank you so much. I'll stop in to check on him, and if he is any problem whatsoever please come tell me."

"I will."

I felt so stupid asking her to watch my brother for me, as if it were her responsibility.

As I walked back toward the event, I pulled out my phone to text my mom, but my phone buzzed in my hands before I could. It was Caroline.

Are the favors ready?

Almost, I responded, and ran to the kitchen. Caroline might've thought assembling a hundred bags was a thirty-minute job, but it really wasn't, and I still had to cut, tie, and curl all the ribbon. This was something she should've given to me a week ago.

Micah must've seen the panic in my eyes because she immediately stopped loading cups in a tray and said, "I'll help."

"Are you sure?" I asked. I knew she was methodical in her cleanup routine.

"Yes, and tell Caroline she doesn't understand this thing we call time. She keeps doing this to you."

We retrieved the boxes from against the wall. "I shouldn't have eaten dessert with my date."

Micah's eyes widened. "With Kyle?"

I shook my head, feeling flustered. "No! With Mr. Farnsworth."

Now Micah frowned. "Mr. Farnsworth was your date?"

"It's a long story."

She laughed and gave my shoulder a shove. "Come on, let's take these to the lobby."

"Good idea. My brother can help us."

"Your brother is here?"

I sighed. "Another long story."

"I get it," Micah said. "Your mother. Another person who doesn't understand other people's time."

There were a lot of things my mother didn't understand— pretty much anything that happened outside of herself.

Chapter 6

Micah and I finished all the gift bags just in time to send them off with the happy guests as they returned to their rooms. A lot of them took the tulip centerpieces too, still loudly admiring the pretty cellophane.

Slowly, the visiting friends and family departed—Kyle among them. He waved to me as he walked outside, but he didn't say anything. I wondered if there really would be a second date.

In any case, I had more work to focus on. Back in the cafeteria, I turned the music to something livelier and spun around a few times as Micah cleared small cups off the tables.

Caroline was busy in the office talking to the director of the home, getting her final payment and probably already selling next year's event.

Gunnar bounced around next to me as I loaded the few remaining vases into a box. "Can we go home yet?" he asked. "How are we going to get my bike home? Will it fit in your trunk?"

"I'm driving the flower van."

"Oh, good! It will fit in the van. I like the van; it's fun. I didn't eat dinner tonight. Can we get food on the way home?"

"Of course. I just need to get all these tablecloths and load them into the van, and then we can go," I said.

"Can I help?" he asked.

I nodded. "There should be a box of black trash bags by the door. Will you grab a bag for me?"

"Okay!" He ran over to the box and yanked on a bag, unraveling at least three before he freed one.

"Thanks," I said when he brought it back.

"Can I put the tablecloths in the bag?"

"Sure, that would be helpful. Only take the ones that have already been cleared off."

He nodded.

"Sophie!" Micah called out. "It's our song!"

I listened for a moment—she said this about a lot of songs and we didn't actually have a song. "Our favorite," I replied.

Lance, her coworker, sang the wrong lyrics and Micah laughed. When I walked past her to pick up a discarded tulip, she whispered, "Where did Kyle run off to anyway? Did he already leave?"

"Yep."

As if she knew exactly what I was thinking, which she probably did, she said, "I'm sure you didn't say goodbye to him either."

I crinkled my nose at her and she smirked.

My brother had filled the big black trash bag with table-cloths and was carrying it in his arms and walking precari-ously toward another table.

"Gunnar, that's enough for that bag, start a new one." I went to grab one for him, but when I turned around I was too late. Gunnar and his bag of tablecloths went toppling.

"I'm sorry, Sophie!" Gunnar said.

"It's okay. Are you okay?"

"Yes, I dropped all the tablecloths."

"Good thing they aren't made of glass," I said. "Let's just pick them back up." We loaded the bag back up, and I went to take it to the van when I saw Caroline standing in the doorway.

"Sophie, is that your brother?" she asked, nodding toward where Gunnar stood, talking to Micah and Lance.

"Yes."

"Has he been here all night?"

"No, he came toward the end. My mom had a childcare mix-up." And by *mix-up*, I meant she hadn't planned childcare at all.

"He can't actually do any of the work. If he got hurt . . ."

"You're right. I'm sorry."

I turned to look back at Gunnar and Caroline added, "And Sophie, don't bring him to work again."

My stomach tightened. "No, it won't happen again." I wanted to have confidence in that assertion but I knew I wasn't the one who had any control over that.

"Thank you. And good work tonight. I'll see you at the shop this week." She smiled and left to go to her car. Caroline never did any of the cleanup. That's what I was there for.

I hefted the overfilled trash bag into my arms and headed for the van, grumbling internally about how much design work I could've been doing if I worked at Minnie's Alterations instead of at a flower shop. As I passed the lobby, I heard June talking to someone. I stopped, shifting the weight of the bag to my hip.

"June, thanks again for your help with my brother tonight." As I fully adjusted the bag, I noticed the person talking to June was Andrew. He sat in a chair with an open laptop and June was looking over his shoulder at whatever he had pulled up there.

June glanced at me. "No problem, hon. You tell your momma I said hi, okay?"

"I will." I paused, almost expecting Andrew to say something snarky, but he didn't say anything at all. "Okay, well . . . I better . . ." I nodded toward the bag.

June hit Andrew on the shoulder. "Go help the young lady with that bag."

"Oh, no, that's okay," I said. "I have it."

"She has it," Andrew said.

June hit his shoulder again and he reluctantly rose, putting his laptop aside. I started walking, bag and all.

"It's fine," I said when he was at my side, reaching out for the bag. "I'm nearly there."

"I'm here. Give me the bag."

"Wow. Your words inspire immediate obedience." I kept walking.

"Should I get the door or do you have that too?"

I turned my back to the door and pushed it open with my butt. "It's like I did things by myself before you arrived."

He held up his hands in surrender. "Yes, you're proving you're much more capable than you look."

I smiled a fake smile at him. "Can't wait until this year is over."

"And you read minds too," he said, then backed away.

I continued grumbling as I opened the van and deposited my armload in the back.

The clicking of bicycle spokes sounded next to me, and I looked over to see Kyle on Gunnar's bike, his knees up at his elbows. He rode in slow circles.

"Hi," I said, surprised. "I thought you left."

"I didn't."

"That bike is the perfect size for you."

"I thought so." He stopped beside me, the back tire skidding, then put his feet on the ground. "It's almost as nice as my other ride."

I tapped a finger to my lips. "Your other ride?"

"My Mustang." He nodded toward the car parked thirty yards away, at the back of the parking lot, probably so other cars wouldn't scratch it.

I tilted my head, wondering if he was serious. "I was kidding. I know what car you drive . . . Remember?"

"Right. Yeah." He stood up, swung Gunnar's bike out from under him, and loaded it into the back of the van.

"Thanks," I said.

"You're welcome. I'll see you at school," he said.

"See you." My heart was racing. Now was the time I should ask if he wanted to go out again, prove to Micah that I'd meant what I said. But instead I watched Kyle walk away. I didn't need to ask him now. We had time.

The voices in the lobby were even louder when I went back inside. I told myself to walk past without looking but I didn't listen to my own advice. Micah, Lance, and Gunnar had joined June and Andrew around the laptop. What was so interesting about Andrew's laptop anyway? My pride kept me from asking. But it didn't keep Micah from seeing me.

"Soph, come check it out. Andrew has already started the website for my dad."

I walked over to give the computer a polite glance, but my gaze froze when I saw the screen. A gorgeous picture of brightly colored plated food was the backdrop, and the business name stood out in big, bold letters. There were tabs along the top and Andrew clicked on the one marked *Events*. Pictures from tonight's Valentine's Dinner were already uploaded. Really good pictures.

"Those are cool," Gunnar said.

They *were* cool. A lot were of the food, but then there were some of the guests, old faces wrinkled with happy smiles and young faces shining with laughter. There was even one of a tulip. It was a close-up, just showing the pink edges, and I loved it.

"Who took pictures tonight?" I asked, trying to sound casual. I hadn't seen a photographer.

"I did," Andrew said.

"How?" How could a person as thoughtless as Andrew take pictures with so much life?

"With my phone," he said. "It has this thing called a camera on it."

"It's just . . ."

"It's just that they're really good," Micah said when I didn't finish. "My phone doesn't take pictures like that."

"Maybe it's the operator," he said, giving Micah a smirk.

"I have no doubt that's true," she said, smiling.

I rolled my eyes. "Give me a break."

"Show us some of your other photos," Lance said.

And then it was the Andrew Show. Destination after destination of all the places Andrew had been in the last several years. Most were big cities—New York and San Francisco and London. But there were quieter towns as well, with pretty hillsides and remote cottages.

"You sure travel a lot," Micah said. She hated to travel. All the variables involved in the process made her anxious. If she had her way, she'd stay in Rockside working for her dad forever.

"My dad loves traveling," Andrew says. "And he usually takes me with him."

"What about your mom?" Gunnar asked.

"No mom," Andrew said simply. "She left when my dad's career dried up."

"Oh," I said, almost without meaning to. Andrew looked at me quizzically.

"What?" he asked.

I shook my head. "Nothing," I said coldly. Andrew did not need to know the details of my life, that my dad had left as well, even if his reasons weren't quite as shallow.

Andrew was still clicking through his photos on the screen. One of them was of an airplane, soaring through a cloud-filled sky.

"Wow," Gunnar said. "One time we drove to an air show in Birmingham and I saw an airplane," he added, sounding very much like the country kid that he was.

"Wait, you haven't been on an airplane?" Andrew asked. He met my glance, a mocking glow in his eyes.

Micah, who was changing out of her work shoes and into some boots, said, "I have. We went to a food show in Vegas last year. Airplanes are the worst."

Lance nudged her arm with his. "It wasn't that bad."

An uncomfortable feeling churned in my stomach. "Let's go, Gunnar," I said. "It's getting late."

Lance looked at Micah and Andrew. "You guys ready to load up the rest of the catering van?"

"Yes," Andrew said. He shut his computer, tucked it under his arm, and left without a backward glance.

I collected my brother and went to get the last few things still in the cafeteria. As Gunnar and I walked through the parking lot, I watched Micah, Lance, and Andrew carrying large trays of dishes to the open van.

"I'm sorry I made it so you can't hang out with your friends," Gunnar said.

"You didn't, buddy. They're heading home too."

I had always felt out of place here in my small town. Like the odd person out. I thought it was because I didn't belong here; I belonged somewhere full of action and creative energy. When I went away to college, I had convinced myself, I would finally feel like I'd found my place, my people. But as I'd looked at all of Andrew's pictures, as I talked with him, as I watched him in all his world-traveler confidence, I realized all these years, maybe I had been fooling myself.

Mother's Day City Park Brunch

SUNFLOWER

While growing, sunflowers tilt their faces to follow the sun throughout the day. So if a mother is like the sun and her child is like the flower . . . Well, the analogy speaks for itself. Mothers are super important.

Chapter 7

I leaned against the side of the flower van, my notebook open in my hands, my pencil furiously scratching away. I was attempting to sketch a skirt. I wanted a variety of pieces for my design portfolio, and so far I felt like I only had one or two really strong options.

I paused and studied what I'd drawn. It wasn't good. I growled and scribbled through it, making it completely impossible to fix later. I hadn't designed anything useful in the past couple of months. It felt like my inspiration had dried up somewhere between Presidents' Day and Easter. I slammed the book shut and threw it on top of my backpack just as Caroline came back to the van for more centerpieces.

"Is your mother coming today?" she asked, lifting out two tin watering cans filled with sunflowers. "You should take a break to sit with her at some point. I think I can spare you for an hour."

I grabbed two centerpieces as well. "She picked up a morning shift at the diner so she might be a little late, but she's coming."

"Oh, good."

I carried the centerpieces across the park to the tables set up between two big oak trees. I set the flowers down and stared at them. I wasn't a fan of the tin. If it had been up to me, I would've arranged the big yellow flowers with small white daisies and white roses in painted mason jars. Or maybe clear jars filled with water and sliced lemons. But as Caroline had said, the organizer of the annual Mother's Day Brunch, Ms. Jewel Jackson, would *love* the watering tins.

I spotted Micah standing at a long table, lighting the fuel can under a chafing dish. I wondered what was on the menu. Last Mother's Day it had been muffins, apple-cinnamon French toast, fruit, sweet tea, and lots of bacon. If Jett Hart was in charge, which he was, I had a feeling there wouldn't be any bacon under those silver lids today.

I walked across the grass to join her. "Hey, friend."

Micah twirled the lighter around her finger once and clicked the trigger.

"Looks like you're feeling better," I said. She'd missed school on Friday with some stomach bug that I was glad I hadn't caught because we'd shared a drink at lunch the day before.

"Because my lighter-twirling skills are back?" she asked.

"That was the main clue."

She smiled. "I feel so much better. Thanks for bringing me history notes last night."

"Of course. I mean, once I heard your dad made cookies, I was going to use any excuse to come over."

"And here I thought you were just worried about me."

"Right. That too." I ran a hand through my hair, which had grown long past my shoulders.

She tilted her head. "What's on your hand?"

"What?" I looked and saw the smeared pencil from the sketch I'd been drawing. I rubbed at it. "Nothing. Absolutely nothing."

"Caroline," I heard a guy's voice say from behind me. "The decorations are even better than last time."

I turned to see Andrew carrying a dish to the table. I hadn't seen Andrew Hart—or his dad—since Valentine's Day, and in the intervening months I'd convinced myself that I had overreacted. That Andrew probably wasn't nearly as bad as I'd made him out to be.

"Thank you," Caroline said, arranging another centerpiece.

"What?" Andrew asked when he noticed me staring. "Can't a guy give a compliment? For example: Nice skirt."

My skirt was black with little oranges on it, and I'd paired it with a short-sleeved orange cardigan that I'd sewn lace along the bottom of and buttoned all the way up to wear like a shirt.

"Did my dad tell you to try to match a menu item today?" he continued.

Or, I hadn't overreacted at all.

"Does your dad actually *talk* to people he thinks are beneath him? Or only growl at them?" I shot back.

After the Valentine's Dinner, I'd gone home and Googled Jett Hart. Micah was right; he had connections. He'd been photographed with plenty of celebrities—from movie stars to models. Then I'd rewatched some episodes of *Cooking with Hart* on Netflix and was reminded of how gruff and obnoxious the chef could be. So my hopes were pretty low that he would actually use those connections for me.

Andrew didn't take my bait but his jaw tightened, so I knew it had bothered him.

Micah waved the lighter in the air like a flag. "Really? Are you two going to be annoying at another event? Can we live in peace, please?" Unlike me, Micah had seen Andrew at three private catering events in the past few months. Events that hadn't required flowers. She'd been the one to tell me he was nicer than I was remembering. She was wrong.

"I'm busy working," I said. "I will keep to myself."

"Promise?" Andrew asked.

Micah elbowed him and he let out a grunt followed by a "What?"

I shook it off and went back to the van for the last couple of centerpieces. *You can handle Andrew Hart today*, I told myself. *You're a professional.*

As I set the last sunflower centerpieces on their tables, Caroline handed me a piece of yellow paper. "The game!" she said, her voice full of excited anticipation.

Right. I'd forgotten that the Mother's Day Brunch always included a game of some sort. At the top of the page were the words: *How strong is your mother/daughter bond?* That title was followed by a list of questions, from favorite foods to favorite movies to nighttime rituals.

"So you answer one side for yourself and the other side for your mom, or daughter," Caroline explained. "Then you match up answers. The team who gets the most right wins our annual prize."

"Hank's Barbecue gift certificate?"

"Of course."

Because nothing says *mother* like a gift card for barbecue. But I couldn't be too harsh. While my pick would've been a gift card to a spa, we didn't have a spa in town. The closest thing we had was a nail salon and even that was a thirty-minute drive.

"Fun, right?" Caroline asked.

"Yes, that should be fun." I handed her back the questionnaire.

She did a last-minute sweep, taking in the tables and flowers. "We have extra flowers in the van, right?"

"Yes," I said.

"Good, because the food table could use a little something. Will you take the stems off a dozen sunflowers and place them strategically around the chafing dishes?"

I nodded.

The tall sunflowers sat in a big bucket in the back of the van. I pulled one out and turned it bloom down to cut off the stem, then set it off to the side. I retrieved another flower. I flipped it and smoothed the petals down. I twirled the stem, watching the petals extend like a little flower ballerina. An image twisted through my mind: a dozen ballerinas flitting across a stage in airy, bright yellow tulle skirts with yellow ballet slippers, ribbons twisting up their legs, the stage blanketed with flower petals. I shook my head; I was so easily distracted.

I finished the flower-beheading assignment and carried the fifteen sunflowers over to the food table, where Andrew and Micah were laughing about something.

"You did not," Micah said.

"I did," Andrew returned.

"Prove it."

"What, you think I took pictures?" he asked.

"You take pictures of everything," she said.

"Are you mocking my picture-taking skills?"

"No, your skills are solid. I'm mocking the sheer number that you take."

"For work," he protested.

"Whatever," Micah said. "Soph." She turned toward me.

I had laid out three flowers and was trying to decide if this was going to look good or cheesy. "What?"

"Vote."

"On what?" Did she think I'd been following their conversation?

"Andrew said he stuck his tongue in one of these fuel canisters when it was lit."

"Yes," I said.

"Yes, what? You think he did? These things are like a million degrees. The fire is blue!"

"Yes," I said again.

"See, she believes me," Andrew said.

"I believe you are that stupid."

Micah laughed but then sucked in her lips and said, "Soph, that was mean." But then she laughed again.

"Thanks," Andrew said to her. Then to me he said, "Is this what you call keeping to yourself?"

"Believe me, I'm trying."

"How'd your mom like the gift?" Micah asked, changing the subject. She was excellent at avoiding conflict.

Micah and I had gone shopping the week before and thought it would be fun to pick out dresses for our moms to wear today. My mom wasn't exactly a dress kind of woman so I'd picked her one that seemed more her style—not too fancy, but comfortable.

"She hasn't opened it yet," I said. "I left it on her bed with a note that she should open it before coming here."

"Fun! I'm sure she'll love it."

"Hopefully." I couldn't say why, but I felt anxious about it. "How about your mom?"

Micah grinned. "She was so happy with hers. She choked up when I gave it to her, but then tried to cover it up by saying she had a cough."

I smiled. Mrs. Williams was so sweet.

"Cute necklace, by the way," Micah said, leaning over the table to look at the pendant around my neck.

"Thanks, I got it at Everything."

"What's Everything?" Andrew asked.

Micah gasped. "You haven't been to Everything?"

"No."

Micah looked up as if she was trying to figure out how to explain the unexplainable. "It's a store next to Sophie's work that sells—"

"Mostly crap," I said. "Other people's crap."

"Not just other people's crap! You can also buy a gallon of milk there. Or a brand-new shovel."

"So everything?" Andrew asked.

"Exactly!" Micah said.

I loved browsing through Everything. It was where I found half my jewelry and almost all the scrap material I used to design or embellish clothing. Because we were such a small town, the items there were never too picked over. People emptied their attics into Everything, and that's where their attics stayed.

"Mom!" Micah called out, then went running around the tables and across the grass to throw her arms around her mom. Mrs. Williams was a short, curvy woman who Micah had shot past in the seventh grade. She had copper-brown skin and kept her black hair just an inch long, accentuating her strong cheekbones and brown eyes. She was wearing the dress Micah had given her—a knee-length green one. She looked beautiful.

I turned my attention back to the table and placed another sunflower. I tried to ignore Andrew, whose gaze I could feel on me. I also tried to keep myself from messing with my overgrown bangs.

"What?" I finally said.

"Is your brother coming today?"

"To a Mother's Day brunch?"

"Why not?"

"This isn't for sons. It's a mother-daughter thing."

"Ah. I see how it is around here."

"It's tradition. That's how it is. You'll learn more about tradition when you witness the reaction of fifty women deprived of bacon."

He lifted the lid off a chafing dish. "I know I'm not from Rockside, but is this not what you guys call bacon?"

My eyes shot down to see the dish nearly overflowing with crispy bacon. "Oh, well, I'm glad your dad learned after last time."

"Pretty sure this town didn't invent providing bacon at brunch."

I placed the last few flowers on the table, ready to escape.

"Do you know what your problem is, Sophie?"

I stiffened and glared at him. "What answer would I have to give for you not to continue?"

"Your problem is that you have a chip on your shoulder. I'm not sure what about, but I'm trying to figure that out."

"A chip on my shoulder?" I snapped. "Do you hear yourself talk? Who says that? I'll tell you who says that: self-absorbed guys who don't live in the real world and have no idea how to truly relate to people. If I have a chip on my shoulder, it only exists for you."

Jett Hart walked up to the food table carrying a foil-covered platter, and I practically jumped out of my skin in surprise.

"Good morning," I said cheerily. Probably too cheerily considering my nostrils were still flaring with irritation.

He set the platter down right on top of three sunflowers. When the dish didn't sit right, he furrowed his brow and lifted it back up to see what the problem was. "Son, move those," he barked. Andrew collected the three sunflowers as Jett walked away.

I gritted my teeth. Great, my memory of *him* wasn't wrong either. I sighed and held out my hands for the squashed flowers.

Andrew dropped them in my hands. "They are kind of big and very . . . yellow."

I held his gaze for a moment in disbelief. "The chip on my shoulder seems to be getting heavier."

He laughed, which I hadn't expected. Normally he was ready to meet my snark with his own. I must've caught him off guard with that comment. I rolled my eyes and couldn't collect the rest of the flowers fast enough before I was able to hurry away.

Chapter 8

The brunch was in full swing. Jett Hart and Mr. Williams were hovering protectively around the food like their presence would make it taste better. I wasn't hearing any complaints so maybe it was working. Micah and Lance were helping with drink refills and questions. Andrew was socializing with guests, but actually, I realized, taking pictures. And my mom still wasn't here.

I stood watching the parking lot and checked my phone again. There were no *Sorry I'm going to be extra late* texts.

I tucked my phone back in the pocket of my skirt and peered down the road. Maybe she'd gotten stuck at work. I mean, her job didn't save lives or anything, but the owner of the diner where she worked sure acted like it did. Maybe it was better that she wasn't here; then I could just do my job and not worry.

"Where's your mom?" Micah asked as she passed me, holding a pitcher of orange juice.

I shrugged, pretending I hadn't noticed her absence.

"She'll be here," Micah said.

"Who will be here?" Andrew asked, walking by at that moment with his phone in hand. *Ugh.*

"Sophie's mom."

"Speaking of moms, yours is trying to get me to eat with her because you can't," Andrew said to Micah.

"Don't fall under her spell. Sophie can never resist my mom."

"It's true," I said. "Mrs. Williams has power over me."

"That's because she loves you," Micah said.

"And here I thought I was special," Andrew said, putting his hand on his chest.

"Nope," I answered back.

Micah waved her hand through the air. "She loves you too, Andrew, don't worry." Then Micah hoisted her pitcher and left.

"Mrs. Williams loves everyone," I assured Andrew.

"You know, you really should be the one refilling glasses with *orange* juice."

"You already made one swipe at the skirt today. Get some new material."

His eyes lit up with amusement. Had he found me funny for the second time today? I didn't like this change. I liked the shot-back insults better. I avoided his gaze and scanned the parking lot again.

"You should just text her," Andrew said.

"What?" I asked, then realized he knew who I was looking for. "Shouldn't you be taking pictures?"

He held up his phone and snapped one of me, then smiled and left. I scowled at his retreating form.

It was time to distract myself with work. I found Caroline standing under a tree, scrolling through her tablet. "Should I get the game started?" I asked her.

She looked up. "No, not yet. Gloria and her daughter are going to sing for us again this year. Will you go and see if they're ready?"

"Yes. Um . . . Did they bring a keyboard or some music?" I had suggested both at our pre-event meeting. It wasn't that Gloria and her daughter weren't good singers . . . Well, it was sort of that. They were decent. They could definitely carry a tune. But I knew they'd sound better with some background music.

"I think they're going a cappella again. But the guests seem to love it. I always get positive feedback. They're sweet."

"Okay, I'll go talk to them. If they're ready, you want them to go on now?"

"Yes. Thank you, Sophie. And tell your mother I said hi."

My mom? I turned just in time to see her car pull into a parking space. She stepped out wearing tight jeans, a black T-shirt, and heels. Not what she'd worn to work that day, but obviously not the dress I'd bought her either. Her long, bleached-blond hair was down and straightened.

I took a deep breath and went to find Gloria. She was sitting at a table and waved when I approached. "Hi, Sophie, good to see you!" she called. "I just adore the flowers this year."

"Thank you," I said. They weren't my design or preference, but I supposed I *had* put them into their holders so there was that. "Are you ready to sing?"

"Nearly," she said.

"Okay, just head on up when you are." I pointed to the microphone set up by the big tree.

Gloria nodded happily.

I looked over and saw that my mom was approaching. I hurried to meet her halfway.

"Hey, honey," she said. "Sorry I'm late."

I gave her a hug. "It's okay. I'm glad you made it."

"Well, don't you look colorful today," she said.

"Yes. I do." I looked down at my outfit then back up at my mom. "Did you get my present?"

"Yes, it was so cute. Thank you."

I swallowed. "I thought you could wear it today."

"Oh! Well, you know I don't really wear dresses to casual events."

She was right, I did know that. I wasn't sure why I'd gotten her one at all. I should've gotten her a pair of cute shoes . . . or a gift card. A gift card was safe and didn't take my taste into account at all.

"Maybe I can wear it around the house," Mom added.

I nodded, as if I didn't care. "Well, come eat," I said. "There's lots of food."

She looped her arm through mine and we continued across the grass. "Is Jett Hart here?" she whispered.

"Yes, he is."

"Will you introduce us? I've always wanted to meet someone famous."

"I don't really know him, Mom." Or rather, he didn't know me except as the girl who always got in his way. "And he's not really famous."

She let out a puff of air to disagree, then said, "You've worked two events with him and you haven't introduced yourself? Why are you so antisocial?"

"I'm not antisocial."

"You are. You know if you practice more, you'll get better at interacting with people."

"I'm fine at interacting with people." At least, the ones I liked.

"I guess I'll just have to introduce myself. Is that him?" She pointed to Jett Hart, still standing like a sentinel by the food.

"Mom, just wave or something. He's really busy."

"He doesn't look busy."

"Let's dish up our food and then we can tell him how nice it looks when we get to the end of the line."

She didn't listen. While I retrieved a plate, my mom marched straight up to Jett, her hand extended.

"*The* Jett Hart," she said. "We're so honored to have you in our little town."

He shook her hand and presented her with the first smile I'd seen him give. "Happy to meet you."

"I hear you're trying to bring us culture with fancy food."

I cringed. "Mom, I have your plate," I called.

She didn't budge.

"I'm trying to bring you variety with bold flavors," he said, like he was suddenly in a commercial for international coffee or something. So this was where Andrew got his speaking skills from.

Speaking of variety and bold flavors, I was now staring at what looked to be green peppers cut in half and filled with cooked egg. I glanced down the row of dishes to see if there was a different egg dish. I saw a very colorful quiche and wondered what was in it.

"I like bold," I heard my mom say. I could tell Jett was done with her. He'd crossed his arms and was looking over her head. I thought about dragging my mom back to the food line, but the less attention I drew to myself in this moment, the better.

Finally, Jett rescued himself. "Excuse me, I need to go check on something."

Mom came to my side and picked up a plate. "He's not nearly as bad as you made him out to be," she said.

"Shh," I responded.

She looked around. "Who are we worried about hearing?" Then her gaze landed on Andrew Hart. "Who's that?"

"Who?" I knew exactly who she was talking about so I didn't know why I was putting on an act.

"Broad shoulders, great hair, and handsome as all get-out, that's who."

"Mom, he's seventeen."

"I wasn't lookin' to date him, child. I just asked who he was while appreciating his finer qualities."

"That's Jett's son."

She tilted her head and looked back at me. "Jett has a son? How come you didn't tell me about him before?"

"Didn't I?"

"No, you didn't. That means one of two things: You like him or you hate him."

"Or maybe I just don't think about him at all."

"Nope. Which one is it?"

"Neither, Mom. Can we eat now?"

Suddenly, Gloria and her daughter were singing, and I silently thanked them for the interruption.

My mom moved down the row of dishes, taking a little bit of each. "Ugh," she said after a moment. "Why does Caroline still let them sing at this?"

"Mom. Shh." They actually sounded good. They'd gotten better.

"I *was* quiet," she whispered. "It's just I've been puttin' up with Gloria since high school. That woman can't carry a tune in a bucket. Do you know she sang the national anthem at nearly every football game? And you thought *I* liked attention."

"I never said that," I mumbled.

"Here, hold this," she said, handing me her plate.

"Why?"

The song ended and my mom marched straight up to Gloria. By the time I realized what she was doing, I had to scramble to find a place to set our plates.

"Good afternoon, everyone," Mom said into the microphone. "How y'all doin' today?"

There was only one whoop back. I cut through tables, heading toward her.

"I'd like to sing you a song now called 'Jesus Take the Wheel' by the lovely Carrie Underw—"

I snatched the microphone from her hand. "She's just kidding. My mom, isn't she funny? Enjoy your brunch, ladies. Can we give a hand for this lovely spread provided by Mr. Williams and Jett Hart?"

I turned off the microphone to a smattering of applause.

"Oh, don't look at me like that, it was fun," Mom said, and left me holding the microphone.

Micah appeared at my side. "It's okay," she said, squeezing my arm. "You smoothed it over."

"You think?" I asked, grateful for her assurance even if I knew she was lying through her teeth.

"It's all good. Do you want me to hide that somewhere?" She nodded toward the microphone.

I handed it to her. "Yes, please."

"And you should probably go rescue Andrew."

"What?" My head whipped over to see my mom holding her plate and heading straight for Andrew.

"Mom!" I called. "Our table is over here."

She didn't listen. She tromped across the grass, me trailing behind, and paused in front of him.

"Young man," Mom said to Andrew, "follow me."

And he did.

Chapter 9

If I had to hear my mom laugh at some stupid thing Andrew said one more time, I was going to lose it. After sitting down with my mom at our table, Andrew had already shown her several scrolls' worth of pictures (including the one of me giving him the look that I imagined I directed at him all the time), and they were now discussing the food. It was mostly my mom asking, "And what's in this?" and pointing to things on her plate. He had the standard mocking twinkle in his eye, so even though he was being polite, overly polite, I knew he was silently judging my mom.

I noticed Caroline walking over to where the microphone had been. She looked around, probably for the microphone that Micah had hidden. Then she cleared her throat and said loudly, "I have a game for y'all to play!"

I thought I was in charge of the game. I started to stand up and Caroline waved her hand at me as though she anticipated my reaction.

"I want all the mothers and daughters to play it." That was directed at me. "You know what's on the line: Barbecue."

"Barbecue?" Andrew asked as Caroline began handing out the yellow paper and pens.

"Hank's Barbecue," Mom answered. "The best barbecue in town."

"The only barbecue in town," I said.

"Which makes it the best," Andrew said.

"Exactly," Mom agreed with a smile. I tried not to let out a huff. How was Andrew winning over every person in my life?

"You should try my dad's barbecue," Andrew said.

"I'd like to try your dad's barbecue, honey," she said.

Andrew raised his eyebrows at me.

"Mom," I said darkly.

"What? It was a statement. If it's as good as his fancy eggs, then I'm sure I'll like it." She waved her fork over the quiche she had barely touched.

"Don't they have quiche at the diner, Ms. Evans?" Andrew asked.

"Call me Larissa. And, no, they do not. The diner specializes in greasy eggs and lots of added cheese."

Caroline handed both me and my mom sheets of yellow paper. "Have fun," she said.

I sighed and took the paper and pen. Andrew tilted his head to read my mom's sheet. She moved the paper in between them.

"You should help me answer some questions about Soph," my mom said.

"He really shouldn't," I said. "He knows nothing about me."

Andrew picked up the pen and said to Mom, "I'll be your scribe." He scanned the questions, then started. "What's her favorite book?"

I lowered my eyes, realizing this was actually going to happen, and the more I fought it, the more he'd enjoy it. I pretended like I didn't care and tried to focus on the sheet in front of me. Mom's favorite book. She hated to read. When she wasn't at work, she was out with friends or watching a movie or bingeing a television show. I left it blank.

"Easy," Mom said. "She loves Harry Potter."

I did love Harry Potter, but it had been several years since it had been the top on my list.

"Favorite music?" Andrew asked.

I wrote down *classic rock* for my mom.

"She likes poppy stuff," Mom replied. "Like Taylor Swift and those guys who dress like they're from the eighties. There's something about a moon in their name."

"Walk the Moon?" Andrew asked.

"Maybe?" Mom said.

Again, she was a couple of years behind on my tastes.

"What's the most embarrassing thing to happen to her?" he asked.

I raised my hand. "Right now is winning at the moment."

Mom laughed. "No, no, no. I can do way better than this moment. When she was twelve, we were at the town Fourth of July celebration up at the lake—"

"Mom, seriously?"

Andrew leaned back in his chair like he was ready to be entertained.

"And she threw up all over Charlie, who she had a big crush on at the time."

I put my head in my hands.

"Poor Charlie," Andrew said.

"Poor Charlie?" I looked up, furious. "He'd put a worm from his fish bait in my sandwich! He deserved it."

"Yes, Andrew, be careful." Mom laughed. "You do not want to get on Sophie's bad side."

"I fear I am too late," he said.

"You are," I assured him.

Mom's mouth fell open and then she rolled her eyes. "She's just kidding."

"I'm really not."

"Back to the questions," Andrew said, bending over the sheet of paper once more. "What does Sophie like to do on a rainy day?"

My mom squinted her eyes in thought.

I liked to drive. That's what I liked to do. I liked to listen to the sound of the rain pounding on the metal roof of the car. Sometimes I would park at the lake or the canal or the historic house downtown and watch the way the drops pelted the water or poured off the eaves.

"She hates the rain. Thunder scares her."

I looked at my mom in surprise. Thunder didn't scare me.

Not anymore. But then I realized my mom wasn't just a couple of years behind in her knowledge of me. She was five years behind. She was still living in the summer my dad left. She'd stopped paying attention after that. It shouldn't have surprised me. It didn't. But I hadn't had proof until now.

Andrew was staring at me and I relaxed my face to neutral.

"Are you?" he asked.

"Am I what?"

"Scared of thunder?"

"Are you trying to cheat? Hank's Barbecue is on the line." I wrote down the answer for my mom on the paper: *Drink coffee and watch black-and-white movies.*

When I looked up, Andrew's gaze was moving between me and my mother. "You two look nothing alike," he said.

Of course he was right. My mom was pale and blond with blue eyes. I had olive skin, brown hair, and dark brown eyes.

"Sophie takes after her father," Mom said. "He was Italian."

"Is, Mom," I said.

"Is what?"

"Dad *is* Italian."

"Was, is." She waved her hand through the air like those two words conveyed the exact same meaning.

"Your dad is from Italy?" Andrew asked me.

"His parents. He grew up here," my mom answered for me.

Perhaps it was the ominous tone in my mother's voice that kept Andrew from asking for more information, but he looked back at the paper and said, "Okay, Ms. Evans, another question. Name one of Sophie's bad habits."

I wondered what she'd say for this. Five years ago my bad habits consisted of leaving dirty clothes on the floor or art supplies scattered all over the table. I put my pen to the paper and almost wrote: *My mom only thinks about herself.* But I stopped and chose instead: *Habitually late.*

"Maybe you should answer this one," Mom said to Andrew.

I crossed my arms and looked at Andrew in a silent challenge that said: *You better not.* But I already knew Andrew's bad habit was *not listening*, so of course he answered.

"Bad habit?" He bit the inside of his cheek and squinted his eyes. "Too judgmental. Or stubborn," he said. "Or closed off."

"You were supposed to pick *one*," I said.

"I couldn't help myself."

"You never can." I plucked the paper from his hand. "I think we're done. We can't win anyway, since I helped make this game." I hadn't at all, but I was so over this.

"That's too bad," Mom said. "We totally would've won." She picked up the paper I'd been writing on and looked over my answers. "Yes, we would've won. My daughter knows me well." She handed the paper to Andrew as if he was interested in the minutiae of her life. "You didn't fill out my most embarrassing moment, Soph."

"I didn't know that one." I often wondered if my mom ever got embarrassed. I knew she was humiliated when my dad left her to open a surf shop in Southern California, his lifelong dream that apparently didn't include her (or his kids). They'd gotten married too young, both of them said often. They had barely known who they were. But humiliation wasn't the same as embarrassment. Either way, I didn't think that needed to be written on a bright yellow paper for a chance to win barbecue.

Chapter 10

"Sophie!" a cheerful voice called out.

I turned in my seat to see Janet Eller approaching our table. She had a petite frame and big messy curls. She'd lived down the street from us since forever.

"Janet!" I said, cheering up. "Hi. How are you? Getting ready for the big day next month?"

"Janet's getting married next month," Mom said to Andrew.

"Congratulations," Andrew said.

"Thank you," Janet said, running a hand through her curls. "And no, I'm not ready. I feel like a chicken with her head cut off. I'm running around with no direction."

"It will all come together," I said.

"I was hoping you would do my bouquet."

"Isn't Caroline doing the flowers?"

"Yes, but I want you specifically for my bouquet."

"Me? Why would you want me?" I didn't design flowers. Well, I did in the shop, but only because I had to.

"I've seen some of the arrangements you've done for the store," Janet explained, her eyes wide. "They're so good. You think you could draw up some samples for me to pick from?"

I shifted in my chair. "Oh. I really think you should stick with an experienced florist for an event as big as your wedding."

"Sophie," Mom said. "The girl is asking for you. Have some confidence, child."

Janet put her hand on my arm. "Listen to your mother."

My mother had just proven in writing that she knew nothing about me. I wasn't sure she was the right person to listen to. Plus, I didn't have a lot of extra time; I had my own designs to work on, and putting energy into designing a bouquet could zap my creativity. But Janet's face looked so hopeful that I found myself saying, "Do you have any idea what you'd like?"

"No. That's why I'm asking you. I want you to design it the way you think would look best."

"What does your dress look like?"

"It's traditional. Fitted bodice and full skirt."

"White?"

"Of course. Do you want my mother to murder me before I can even walk down the aisle?"

I smiled. "Okay, I'll draw you some samples."

She pulled out the chair next to me and sat down.

"I meant . . . later," I clarified.

"Can you just quickly do some rough sketches now?" She opened her purse and produced a notebook and a pencil for me.

"Now?"

"Please. I feel this heavy weight hanging over me, and I just want this off my plate."

"Okay, I guess I can try . . ." I took the notebook and flipped through page after page of wedding notes until I found a blank one. I stared at the white paper. This wasn't how inspiration worked for me, with three people staring at me expectantly. "You said it was a traditional dress?" I asked.

She nodded.

I sketched an outline of a dress. "Kind of like this?"

"Yes," Janet said. "That's the right shape."

What flower shape would look good with this dress shape? My eyes took in the lines, and I thought about the symmetry. "I think you should go with a globe-style bouquet. I would do blush roses, tightly placed. Then maybe some ribbon wrapped around the holder and some pearl accents tucked into the flowers." I drew as I talked, then stopped to look at the design. I flipped the page as another shape came to me. "Or you could have a more elongated shape by leaving on the stems and gathering the roses into a bunch. The stems could be wrapped with a string of pearls or a sheer ribbon." When I was done, I showed her the sketches. "I need a little more time to fully develop the ideas but it's a start."

Janet's face was all aglow. "How did you do that?" she asked. "Those are great."

"Yeah?" I felt a warm glow myself. "I can think of another design."

"No, really. These are beautiful. I love them."

"Which one are you leaning toward?"

"The ball one."

"Okay. I'll work on it."

"You will?"

"Um . . . yes."

Janet gave me a hug and then headed straight for Caroline, as if she was going to inform her that moment of these plans.

"Look at you," Mom said, standing. "Drawing and everything."

If my mom was at all observant, she would've seen the design journal I toted around everywhere. How had she *not* seen it? I tried not to be hurt over this fact, but I felt the unwanted emotions bubbling just beneath the surface.

She threw her napkin onto her plate, then wiped her hands on the back of her jeans.

"Where are you going?" I didn't mean for that to sound so desperate, but it did, I realized.

She showed me the time on her phone. "I told Taryn I'd be back for Gunnar at noon."

Her phone said eleven thirty. *Now* she was worried about punctuality?

She squeezed my shoulder. "I'll see you at home. And Andrew, it was great meeting you."

"You too, Ms. Evans."

"It's Larissa." She took the long route to her car, talking to a few people but really meandering her way toward Jett Hart.

Andrew sighed. "Your mom is nice."

I studied his expression. Was he ever sincere? I just nodded.

He jerked his head toward Janet. "That was impressive, Soph."

"Don't call me Soph. And don't mock me."

He shook his head a little like he was confused. "Who says I was mocking you?"

"Your face says it."

"Those bouquets you drew? That's what you want at your wedding?"

"See, I knew you were mocking me."

"Just a question."

"Of course it's not what I want at my wedding."

"Isn't that what she asked you for, though? What *you* thought would look best?"

"That *is* what I thought would look best at her event with her dress. My tastes don't matter."

"Kind of like these arrangements?" He plucked a petal off one of the sunflowers and let it drop onto the white tablecloth. "I'm sure you gave zero opinions about them as well."

"What's your point?"

"You want to be a designer, right?"

"Not that it's any of your business, but yes." Micah must've told him. I was going to kill her later. "A clothing designer, not a florist."

"A real designer puts a piece of him- or herself in everything," Andrew said thoughtfully. "So that when people see it, they say, that is a Sophie Evans design. You're going to have to stop holding on so tightly to all those pieces."

I couldn't believe it. "You think because you throw a few pictures up on your computer that you are the expert on design and style?" I asked. "Right now, I *don't* have a name for myself. People want something that fits who *they* are. That's what they're asking me for. And I'm really good at figuring out who people are and what they want. Really good." I stood up and walked away.

I marched straight up to Micah, who was chatting with Lance by the food table. When she saw me, she stepped closer to me, a look of concern on her face.

I shook out my hands and then my whole body. "Ugh."

"Is someone bothering you again?" She peered over at Andrew with a small smirk. "It's like he knows exactly how to get under your skin. I need to ask him for pointers."

"Funny." My eyes locked onto my mom, who was still talking to Jett. She had one hand on his arm and was leaning toward him, saying something. "Seriously?"

"What?" Micah asked.

"My mother. I'm going to die of embarrassment. Jett's

now met most of my family and he'll never take me seriously."

"Your mom is not you," Micah said.

"She may not be me but we are a reflection of each other, right? Good or bad, Micah, our family defines us."

Chapter 11

The text came in from my dad as I was walking toward the tree where Micah sat, waiting for the last of the guests to leave.

Hello daughter of mine. Haven't heard from you in a couple of weeks. How is everything?

I shared a weird relationship with my dad. Was I angry that he could up and leave his family just like that? Yes. Did I understand his desire to escape such a small town and pursue his dream? Also, yes. So I went back and forth between being bitter and empathetic.

I texted back: *Earned another fifty bucks for college.*

Nice. I'll match that by adding fifty to the savings I have for you here.

Thanks, Dad. I'm at work. I'll chat with you later.

OK, honey. XO.

I gently tossed my phone onto the grass and sat down next to Micah. "Do you think Mrs. Perkins could walk any slower?" I asked. "One day we might get to leave this park."

Micah giggled. "Yes, just in time for next year's Mother's Day event."

I began picking dandelions and stringing them together into a chain.

"What did you think of the food today?" Micah asked. I could hear the worry in her voice, the hesitation. It was the first sign in months that she still hadn't completely incorporated this new Jett Hart development into her well-organized life.

"It was great," I said, meaning it. Good thing Jett's personality didn't get in the way of his ability to cook. "Jett's pretty talented."

She smiled a relieved smile. "I thought it was good too."

"And your dad? Is he still resisting this?"

"He seems to be coming around. He's been learning some new things, so no matter what I think this has been good."

"What do you mean, 'no matter what'? It's still the first half of the year. There's lots of time left for lots of good things to happen."

"You're right." She nodded resolutely. "You're right."

I bumped her shoulder with mine. "Of course I'm right."

Lance turned on some music, like we always did for cleanup. The guests had all cleared out and Micah's parents swayed between tables, sharing a dance. I averted my gaze. I held up the string of dandelions, circled it into a crown, and handed it to Micah.

She smiled and placed it on her head. "Remember when we used to make these as kids?"

"Yes," I said.

"I heard Jett saying something about putting them in a soup or salad or something."

I crinkled my nose. "Dandelions? Really? That might be a little out there for these parts."

"Yeah, one recipe past normal." Micah squinted her eyes. "Is that . . . ?"

I followed her gaze. Kyle in his convertible Mustang rolled into the parking lot. Last month, Kyle and I had gone on exactly one more date that was slightly less awkward than the first one, but not awkward enough for me to write him off completely. There was something there; I just couldn't figure out what.

Kyle's bandmates, Bryce, Jodi, and Lincoln, were in the car with him. Jodi sat in the passenger seat, and Bryce and Lincoln were in the back. But there was someone else too. A leg stood straight up from the back seat, in between Bryce and Lincoln. Bizarre.

Kyle slowed down and lifted a hand in a wave. "Sophie! Micah!" he called out.

Micah and I stood and started walking to the parking lot. Lance beat us there, and he was taking a lap around the Mustang when we arrived. I was sure Kyle appreciated it. Lance and Kyle weren't in the same group at school. Lance was into sports, while Kyle was more artsy.

"Hey, y'all," Micah said.

"Hi," Jodi said.

"Who is . . ." That's when I realized the leg sticking up from the back seat wasn't a person at all. It was a mannequin. "What are you doing?"

"Veronica here has been stuck in the window of Everything for at least seventeen years. We thought it was time she saw the town," Kyle said.

Micah laughed.

"She's not seeing much of anything with her head on the floorboard," I said.

"What?" Kyle turned around. "Bryce! Veronica fell, help her."

Bryce sat Veronica up. I noticed she could use a new wardrobe. I wondered if Mr. O'Neal, the shop owner, would let me dress her.

Lincoln put his arm around Veronica and pointed to the park behind us. "This is the city park," he told the mannequin. "One day you can come to the annual Mother's Day Brunch here."

"Did you even ask her if she wants to be a mother?" Kyle said. I smiled. He was different when we were alone. Was it nerves?

"She may not want to be a mother, but everyone *has* a mother, Kyle, so she's welcome," I said.

Lance laughed. "You're all a bunch of weirdos."

Micah patted the door of Kyle's car. "We have to clean up. Have fun with whatever this is." She circled her hand at the car and then left with Lance.

I lingered. "Where are you taking her next?" I asked.

"The Stanton Estate . . . or the Barn," Jodi said.

"Have fun." I backed up a few steps.

Kyle gave me his lazy smile. "We will." He drove away.

The first thing I noticed when I joined the cleanup crew was that all the centerpieces had been claimed and carried away by guests. (Caroline really did know what she was doing.) So I gathered tablecloths and carried them to the van. I opened up the back doors and a short scream of surprise escaped my lips when I saw someone sitting on the floor.

It took my brain two seconds to process that it was Andrew. His computer was open on his lap, but my design journal was in his hands.

My stomach dropped to my feet. "What are you doing?" I asked, throwing the tablecloths on the floor inside and yanking my book away from him. "Did you go through my backpack?"

"What? No, it was just sitting there."

He hadn't even untied the cording, but still. "And so you thought that meant you had free access to it?"

"No," he said, defensive. "I didn't even open it. What is it?"

"Not yours," I barked.

But he seemed to know what it was without me having to tell him because he said, "You know, they have these really cool electronic notepads now that you can draw on and take pictures with. They help keep things better contained."

Did he have to practice to sound so condescending, or did it just come naturally to him? I looked at my book nearly bursting out of its seams and once again felt like a backwoods country girl. Heat crept up my neck. I slid the book into my backpack and zipped it shut. "Technology can't replace everything. Some things have to be felt—" I stopped myself. Why was I explaining this to him? "What are you even doing in here?" I asked again.

"I needed to get some work done. I have a review packet due at midnight. Finals are coming up."

"And the back of the flower van was the only choice?"

"The dark floor of a windowless van was the best I had to work with."

"Couldn't you just go home? Do you have to be here for some reason?"

Andrew sighed. "Yes, actually. I didn't bring my own car. Plus, my father requires me at all events."

"It's like you're trying to annoy me."

"I really am just trying to get this done. The annoying you part is an added bonus." He gave a small smile and pointed at his computer. "Give me five more minutes."

I opened my mouth, not sure why I was ever surprised at his nerve.

"Please," he added.

"You have until I'm done loading this van."

He held out his arm and pulled up the sleeve of his shirt to his shoulder, revealing his toned bicep. "How well do you know the male body?"

"Excuse me?"

"For my anatomy review," he said. "What did you think I meant?"

I shook my head. "You knew exactly what you were doing."

He laughed. "Five minutes."

I picked up the stem of a sunflower I'd left on the floor of the van earlier and flung it at him. "Hurry." Then I went to finish cleaning up.

Caroline approached me. "Thanks for another great event, Sophie."

"I'm glad you think it went well," I said.

"So Janet asked you to do her bouquet," she said. It wasn't a question.

Like a wake-up call, I realized I shouldn't have committed to Janet without talking to Caroline first. It was her flower shop, after all, and she was offended. I could tell. "Only if you want me to," I said, trying to salvage this. "You have much more experience than I do. I could really use some training on this, if you want me to do it at all."

That was the right thing to say. She nodded slowly. "She probably thought someone younger might have more modern ideas. But I'm current."

"You are."

"I'll walk you through a few sample bouquets in the next couple of weeks."

"Thank you. I appreciate it."

Caroline headed to her car and I stacked a few chairs. The rental company was there loading them into a trailer.

I picked up the three remaining tablecloths from the grass next to the food tables and turned around, nearly face planting into Jett Hart's chest. I stopped just in time.

I opened my mouth to greet him when he said, "Did I see you hanging out with my son earlier?"

"No . . . Well, I mean yes . . . sir. Not by choice."

"He has a job to do at these events and I'd like him to focus on that." He waved his hand at me. "Without distractions."

"You'll need to talk to him about that."

"Right now I'm talking to you, who could obviously use a lesson on professionalism."

I could feel my face burn up, which immediately made my eyes water. I hated that when I was angry it looked like I wanted to cry. "I am very professional."

"Just like your mother?"

My mouth dropped open and I snapped it shut quickly.

"These events aren't social hour," he continued. "Understood?"

I feared if I spoke too much, my anger-stung eyes would fill with actual tears. "Understood perfectly."

Jett turned to leave, and Lance, a chair tucked under each

arm as he passed me, said, "He's just a bucket of sunshine, isn't he?"

"Pretty sure he's a steaming pile of something else, but I won't go there."

Lance laughed and continued walking. I thought, not for the first time, that I should find a different job. One that was more than just a paycheck.

Chapter 12

By the time I got back to the van, my jaw hurt from clenching it so tight. I threw open the doors, where now Micah was sitting with Andrew. He was pointing out some bone on her forearm.

"Did you honestly fall for the *help me study for anatomy* line, Micah?" I asked darkly.

"It wasn't a pickup line," Andrew said, and Micah gave me a look that said she wasn't falling for anything.

"Whatever. It's been five minutes," I said to Andrew. "Get out."

Micah tilted her head and studied my face. "What happened? You look like you're going to kill someone."

"It's going to be him if he doesn't leave," I said, nodding toward Andrew.

Micah moved to her knees, took my hand, and pulled me into the van. Then she shut the doors and said, "Spill."

The front windows let in some light so it wasn't pitch-black. But it was dim enough that my eyes were now in shadows, I was sure. Still, that didn't mean I wanted to talk. I just wanted to go home. Or better yet, to a big city somewhere,

where I could sit on a bench downtown and nobody would know who I was for hours while I listened to life bustle around me.

"Don't shut down," Micah said, pulling me out of my head. "What happened?"

"Nothing happened. Oh"—I looked at Andrew—"except your dad is a huge jerk, but that's not new."

"Excuse me?" Andrew asked.

Micah seemed to realize that maybe now, with Andrew in the van, wasn't the time I should be venting about his father. She tried to backtrack. "We'll talk about this later."

"What did my dad do?" Andrew asked. "Look at you funny? No, wait, did he insult your centerpieces?"

I gritted my teeth. "He insulted my work ethic . . . and my mother."

"Because she was throwing herself at him today? He gets that a lot, so he has zero patience for it."

"Get out of my van," I said coldly.

"Gladly." He closed his computer and stood, immediately whacking his head on the ceiling. He sucked in a breath of air. I probably shouldn't have thought that was instant karma, but I did.

"Wait," Micah said, grabbing Andrew's arm. "Don't leave like this. There is some misunderstanding between you two and we need to figure it out."

"No misunderstanding," I said.

"None at all," Andrew agreed.

"Sit," Micah said. Andrew was still hunching, his hand on the back of his head. He sat. I sighed.

Micah looked at Andrew. "So your dad *is* kind of a jerk sometimes." Then at me. "And your mom does flirt with men she thinks might be a means to security. Can we at least all agree on that?"

I took a few deep, angry breaths then reluctantly nodded. Andrew let out a grunt.

"There. See, don't we all feel better when we find common ground?"

Andrew and I both started talking at once, me saying exactly how uncommon our ground was and him saying that his dad was under a lot of pressure or some other stupid excuse.

Micah put up her hands and yelled, "Stop!" Then she looked defeated. "It really sucks that you two can't get along."

She was good at making me feel guilty. I noticed that Andrew looked a little ashamed himself. That was a new look.

"Is that what I think it is?" Micah asked, pointing to a yellow piece of paper that was folded next to Andrew's leg. She picked it up and opened it.

"It's everything you'd ever want to know about Sophie," Andrew said. "According to her mother."

"And why do you have it?" I asked.

"Thought you might want it."

"Because I need a study guide on myself?"

Micah started laughing and I realized she was reading it. "Walk the Moon? Scared of thunder?"

"I know," I said.

She hummed a tune I didn't recognize at first. Then she sang out, "'Don't you dare look back, just keep your eyes on me.'" Walk the Moon's most popular song. "Remember how much we loved that song?"

"Yep."

"You have some blank answers here."

"We didn't finish."

"Okay, challenge," Micah said. "We each have to answer one of these remaining questions honestly. I pick who gets which one."

"You get to pick your own question?" I asked. "How is that fair?"

"Because you know I'd answer any of them. I'm an open book." She held up the page. "What do you say, you in?"

"What are the questions?" Andrew asked.

"You're either in or you are out," Micah said.

"I'm in," I said, mostly because Andrew was hesitating and I was petty enough to want to do the exact opposite of what he was doing.

"Fine," he said.

Micah smiled big. "Okay, Andrew first, then." She read and reread the questions and apparently figured out who would get each one because she finally asked, "What, my friend, is your biggest fear?"

"Answering personal questions," he said.

She kicked his foot with hers. "Nope. I reject that answer. Try again."

He drummed his fingers on his leg. "If I answer this honestly, you two have to do the same."

Micah held up her hand. "Scout's honor."

"That's not the sign, but whatever," he said. "My biggest fear: making friends."

"What?" she asked, like he had answered it with a throwaway answer again.

A stray sunflower petal stuck to my palm and I picked it off and rolled it between my thumb and forefinger. When nobody said anything, I asked, "Because you move so much?"

He met my eyes and gave the smallest of nods.

"So you're scared to let yourself get close to people?" Micah asked as though she hadn't suspected this about him at all. I wasn't surprised.

"Yes. I mean, I'm really good at being friendly with people."

I let out a single laugh.

"Well, most people," he amended. "But getting close to people when I know I'm just going to leave? What's the point?"

"The point is," Micah said, clutching her hands to her chest, "everyone needs to bare their soul from time to time."

"I never need to bare my soul," he said. "My soul is pretty surface level."

I smirked. "Micah has all her soul barings scheduled."

"I probably *should* do that," she said. "It might help. Well, Andrew, your biggest fear has come true. You have friends."

I pointed to Micah. "Just the one, really."

He laughed.

Micah shoved my shoulder and shook her head. "No, really. I've already added you to the friend column on my spreadsheet, so it's set in stone."

"Spreadsheet?" he asked.

"Yes, it helps me keep track of people. There are a whole one hundred fifty-three students in the ninth through twelfth section of our school. I like to keep them organized." She smiled. "There's the friends-only category. Then there are students who are good at certain subjects and willing to take notes. The guys I've already dated and the ones I can't date because my best friend has dated them."

I was 99 percent sure this spreadsheet didn't exist and she was just being funny.

Andrew turned his gaze on me. "In a town this small, you still have the best-friend's-exes-are-off-limits rule?"

"Of course." Micah looked back to the yellow paper and then at me, and I was suddenly wondering why I had agreed to this.

"Soph, how do you react when angry?"

Andrew let out a scoff. "I got biggest fear and she gets *that* question?"

"Everyone reacts differently when they're angry," Micah said. "It can say a lot about a person."

"I think I've seen her angry enough to know exactly how she reacts," Andrew said. "I say she has to answer the fear question too. Both of you do."

"No," I said at the same time Micah said, "Okay."

"Traitor," I shot at her.

"He's right. It's fair. Biggest fear, Soph."

"Yes, spill it, *Soph*," he said.

There was a pounding on the back of the van door and I jumped. The doors were flung open and Jett Hart stood there. First, he gave me the coldest look in the history of looks, then he said, "Drew, let's go."

Andrew didn't argue or try to score an extra few minutes. He just slid out of the van and walked away.

As they got into an expensive black car and drove off, Micah sighed. "Is he your biggest fear?"

"Jett Hart?"

"No, the younger one."

"Absolutely not. He's my biggest pain." I stared out at the now-empty parking lot. "My biggest fear is that I'll never get out of this town." That I could never make it anywhere else but here.

The Eller-Johnson Wedding

ROSE

Hands down the most recognizable and popular flower. Maybe it's its intoxicating scent or velvety texture that inspires hundreds of poets to compare it to love and beauty, but whatever the case, it's overrated, just like its comparisons. People seem to forget about the thorns.

Chapter 13

I stood in the master bedroom of an old colonial-style house. The Stanton Estate was the only wedding location in town that wasn't a church . . . or a barn. I watched as Minnie made a last-minute alteration to Janet's wedding dress while Janet sat on a chair in her white silk robe. Minnie was sitting at the desk with her sewing kit and the classic white gown spread out before her. My fingers itched to do the alteration myself, because I would've been a lot faster. But instead I gripped the box that contained Janet's bouquet and waited my turn.

"Are you giving Minnie a dirty look?" Micah whispered from next to me. She was also waiting her turn. She had a question to ask about the menu and we'd realized quickly that Janet couldn't focus on more than one thing at a time. Considering the ceremony was supposed to start in less than two hours, I understood. But also, Minnie wouldn't let us get a word in edgewise. She was talking and talking about whatever seemed to pop into her brain—the tractor that had been sitting on the side of Holiday Road for days, the graduation ceremony at the high school two weeks ago, how the Harris boy who'd received Mr. Washington's scholarship was going to Alabama State, and how good of a football team they had.

"Yes, I am," I said.

"She's like seventy," Micah said.

"There's an age requirement for who I can give dirty looks to?"

"Yes. Besides. I thought you were over that."

"She is the only person in town with any clothing-design experience and she wouldn't give me a job. I will *never* be over it."

Micah laughed, and then threw her hand over her mouth when Minnie looked back at her. "Sorry," she said, and Minnie got back to work. Micah lowered her voice again. "She already has an employee who has worked there for a hundred years and it's not like she does anything more than alterations. You can do those in your sleep."

"I know . . . but it would've looked good on my applications." I sighed. And I could've sat at a sewing machine all day instead of staring at flowers. I lifted the bouquet box. "It would've given me inspiration. I need inspiration."

"Is your portfolio giving you issues? Maybe if it wasn't a huge mess of jumbled pages and random pieces of trash, you'd have a freer mind."

I gasped. "Trash? There is no trash in my notebook. And that's how I work best. In chaos."

"Sophie?" Janet said when Minnie paused in her talking. Janet was staring out the window into the backyard, where workers were scurrying about, preparing for the event. "I think it's going to rain. It's not supposed to rain. The sun is supposed to be setting, the heat is supposed to be evaporating, and this is supposed to be the perfect wedding day."

"It's not going to rain." I was 70 percent sure of that. Or at least the weather app on my phone was. It claimed 30 percent chance of rain, but the sky wasn't supporting that prediction. The sky looked straight out of a horror movie.

"We could use some rain," Minnie said. "The heat is stifling. Last time it was this hot, there was a five-city-wide power outage and poor Mrs. Frieson, bless her heart, lost her entire fridge full of meat for her party."

Janet's eyes became panicked.

"The power is not going to go out. It's not that hot," I said. "And these overcast conditions will make for beautiful pictures."

"But rain does not make for beautiful pictures. It makes for drippy, soggy, wet pictures." Janet pointed to her hair. "These curls took two hours to perfect."

"You look gorgeous."

Minnie stood, hung the wedding dress up on the wardrobe door, and tucked her supplies back into her bag. "You're all set." With that she headed toward the door.

Micah elbowed me in the ribs; apparently I was still scowling.

"Nice to see you, Ms. Baker," Micah sang.

"And you as well, ladies." Minnie let herself out of the room.

I set the box I was holding on the white lace coverlet on the bed. Janet needed a major distraction and I was glad I had it.

"I have your bouquet!" I announced. I pulled it out of the box. Between thinking about the bouquet, being trained by Caroline, doing several practice versions, and finally picking out the best roses and placing each one perfectly into the foam holder, I had spent basically the entire month on it. I had added zero designs to my sketchbook in that time, but apparently I was an expert bouquet maker now.

Janet gasped. "Sophie! It's like you knew exactly what I wanted when I didn't even know."

I had been cursing flowers all month but now I was relieved. "I'm happy you like it," I said, meaning it. Janet's expression made me smile.

"I do. I love it."

"It's really pretty, Soph," Micah said.

Janet picked up the rose bouquet and cradled it in her arms. "People still save these, right? How do I save it? Put it in the freezer or something?"

"No, that's what you do with the cake. This you can just hang upside down and let dry out."

She raised the bouquet to her nose and inhaled. Her eyes fluttered closed and she let out a happy sigh. "It smells amazing. I just love roses. Don't you?"

"Yes, they are nice." I picked up the box. "Did you need anything else?"

"I need for the rain to stay away."

"Do you want us to put the tents up?" I offered. "We brought the tents."

"The tents are so intrusive. I want to see the stars tonight."

"You'll see the stars."

She smiled her perfectly painted lips. "Will you send my mom in if you see her? She's supposed to help me put on my dress."

"She's in the kitchen," Micah said. "Talking to Jett."

"Jett Hart," Janet said. "Do you believe Jett Hart is catering my wedding?"

"Pretty unbelievable," I was able to cough out with effort.

"I hope the food is good," Janet said worriedly. "He talked me into this weird thin-cut, seasoned meat when I just wanted pulled pork on buns."

"The food is amazing," Micah said. "You'll love it. And I just had one question for you . . ."

I squeezed Micah's arm and went out into the hell. Several women in matching maroon dresses—bridesmaids, no doubt— poured out of the room across the hall and swept past me into Janet's room.

I took the stairs and poked my head into the kitchen. Jett was at the stove, and sure enough, Mrs. Eller was on the other side of the counter. She was giving him a second-by-second accounting of the day.

"Mrs. Eller," I said. "Your daughter is looking for you. She's ready to put her dress on."

"Oh! Yes, it's time! Thanks, Mr. Hart!" She whirled around and flew by me.

Jett gave me a curt nod, like I had done that for his benefit. Of course he thought the world revolved around him.

I had basically given up on climbing out of the hole I'd somehow dug with him. If we were going to have a good working relationship, if he was going to see my worth at all, it would have to happen naturally. I still hoped it might, but I wasn't counting on it. I couldn't count on it.

I took a step back and let the kitchen door swing shut. I had plans before he came and they would still be the same after he left. I didn't need him.

Minnie was right; outside felt like a sauna. The dark clouds hanging overhead had turned the air muggy. I questioned my own sanity at wearing a silk blouse. I should've gone with cotton. Understated was best for weddings, I'd learned. So I wore a pale pink top with a black skirt and black heels. I had been tempted to sew a ruffled flare to the bottom of my skirt, and my red heels had been calling my name, but I'd resisted. I hadn't resisted the line of small pearls I'd sewn along the pocket of my blouse. But they were subtle. The only person people should be looking at today was Janet.

"Hey, Soph, where can I plug this in?" Kyle stood on a makeshift stage, holding the cord to his amp. Janet was Kyle's cousin, so it shouldn't have surprised me that he and his band were playing tonight. But his music was not wedding material at all.

I pointed. "There's a power strip behind Bryce's drums there."

"Cool, thanks." Kyle exuded rocker tonight in a pair of dark jeans and a white collared shirt with a thin black tie. His blond hair was getting longer and looked a bit greasy hanging in his eyes. He plugged in his amp and then did a few test chords on his guitar, tuning it as he did.

I wasn't sure why I was lingering. Kyle and I had gone nowhere fast lately. We hadn't moved forward but we hadn't moved back, and it seemed like neither of us was willing to change that. "Do you have everything you need?" I asked.

He pushed his hair off his forehead. "Yeah, I think so."

Bryce jumped up on the stage, slapping Kyle on the back. He held up his phone. "Tell me this isn't the playlist."

"We talked about this," Kyle said. "It's a wedding."

"Did Janet give you this list? Do you have no dignity?"

"Do you want to sing about leaving the girl and living alone at a wedding?"

"Yes, yes I do," Bryce said, moving over to his stool and adjusting its height.

"Me too," Kyle said. "But it's not happening."

"Probably a good call," I said.

Jodi and Lincoln came to join their bandmates on the stage, and I said hi to them. Just then, Micah, carrying a tray of salt shakers, and Lance, carrying a tray of pepper mills, walked past us.

Micah paused next to me while Lance continued walking.

"What's so interesting over here?" She wiggled her eyebrows at me, seeming to answer her own question.

"The cover songs that have to be played tonight," I said.

"I love covers."

Bryce curled his lip at her. "Take your blasphemous tongue away from me."

"I'm going to make a couple requests tonight," I said. "Maybe some Céline Dion, some Journey."

Bryce hissed. Kyle smirked my way and I smiled back.

"So adorable," Micah whispered. She was wrong. The weird standstill Kyle and I shared was not adorable.

"I need my other half!" Lance yelled from a table across the reception area. He held up a pepper mill.

"Where is *he* on your spreadsheet?" I asked. I knew the answer to that question. Micah and Lance had dated freshman year and had both decided to move on. She probably had a big red X through Lance's name, even though I felt like they had both changed since then. But Micah was Micah; once she'd made up her mind and moved on, that was that.

"Funny," Micah said, then left to join Lance.

I needed to go too. I had boutonnieres to pin before the ceremony started. "Good luck, guys," I told Kyle and the band.

"We're not taking requests tonight," Bryce called out after me. I laughed.

I walked around the outside of the Stanton Estate and toward the gravel parking lot where the flower van waited. I collected the box with the boutonnieres and turned to head back when I saw someone standing by a black car. He was facing away from me, talking on his phone, but I could tell who he was by his posture alone. My gaze drifted to Andrew's tuxedo and right away I knew we had a problem.

Chapter 14

I marched up to Andrew and tapped his shoulder.

He turned, saw me, and held up his finger. He gave a few affirmative hums into the phone. There was a tense set to his jaw that I had never seen before. "Okay," he said. "Talk to you later." Then he hung up and stared at me expectantly.

Every curious bone in my body wanted to ask him who he'd been talking to, who had turned his normal smug expression serious, but I resisted. "What are you wearing?" I asked.

"Hi to you too."

I hadn't seen him since Mother's Day. On purpose. He and Micah had invited me along to an in-depth tour of our tiny town a couple of weeks ago, and I had politely (probably not politely) declined. Micah had been serious when she told him that he now had a friend, and she was always good at following through on her declarations.

"Andrew, you can't wear that," I said.

He held his hands out to the sides. "It's a tux. Have you seen one before? You wear them to events like weddings and galas and fund-raisers." His tux was beyond fancy: obviously designer and tailored to fit him perfectly.

"Have you met the groom?" I said. "He's from a middle-class working family. His dad is a construction worker and his mom is a schoolteacher. Are you *trying* to upstage him? He probably rented his tux in the next town over at the local mall. It would not surprise me if some guests come in jeans." I paused for a breath. "And you're not even a guest!"

Andrew looked down at his shoes, which I hadn't noticed before but were black and white and, if possible, even nicer than his tux. "Oh."

"I thought you said you'd spent time in a small town before this," I hissed. Then I took his arm and dragged him into the house and down the hall to a room that wasn't being used. I pulled us both inside, set the box of boutonnieres on an end table, and crossed my arms.

"You need to change," I said.

"What?"

"Your clothes. You need to change."

He raised his eyebrows and unbuttoned the top button of his jacket. "Like right now?"

"What? No!" I hated that my face got hot. "Just . . . wait. You can't go out there in that tux."

"I think you're overreacting. Not that I'm surprised."

"I promise you I'm not."

He pointed to the window. "You're worried about what I'm wearing when you should be worried about the rain."

"Shh. Do not say that anywhere in the vicinity of the bride."

He took in the room. "Is she in here somewhere?"

"I'm going to go and do some reconnaissance. See what the other guys in the wedding party are wearing. I'll come back and let you know if you will feel like the biggest jerk if you keep that on . . . or only the second biggest."

He sat on the arm of an overstuffed chair like he had all the time in the world. "Can't wait to hear your report."

"Are those cuff links?" I asked. "For the love of all that is holy . . ." I muttered as I picked up the box of flowers and let myself out of the room.

Down the hall, I reached the door that had been labeled *Groom*. I knocked. "Flower delivery."

The door squeaked open and Mr. Johnson Sr. smiled at me. "Sophie Evans. Good to see you."

"I have some pinning to do."

He opened the door wider and I stepped inside.

"Son, come give this lovely lady your lapel to pin."

The groom, Chad Johnson, stepped away from the window and turned to face me. He was glowing with happiness. "You think it's fixin' to rain, Sophie?"

"I don't," I said, praying I was right.

Chad stepped up to me. He looked nice in a basic black tux with a starched white shirt. But of course his tux was nowhere near as nice as Andrew's. I pinned the rose onto his lapel and did the same for his father, who wore a simple black suit and red tie.

"Where are all the groomsmen?" I asked casually.

"I imagine they're scattered about," Chad said, straightening his bow tie.

"Okay, I guess I have my work cut out for me." I turned to go. "And Chad, congratulations. I'm so happy for you."

"Thanks," Chad said with a grin. "I'm a lucky guy."

It took me longer than I'd hoped to find the four groomsmen—some were in the garden, taking selfies—but their basic suits confirmed what I already knew was true: Andrew was going to outshine the entire wedding party.

I quickly ran back inside, but instead of going to Andrew's room, I went to the kitchen. "Micah, can I speak to you?" I asked my best friend when I found her.

She turned to me. "What's up?"

"Does your dad still keep extra cater waiter pants and jackets in his trunk?"

"I think he has a few. Why?"

"Because golden boy wore an Armani today."

"He did not!" she said. I was glad I wasn't the only one who was appalled by this. "An Armani?"

"Well, I don't know which designer exactly. But definitely *a* designer."

"I'll get you the keys."

There was no way Mr. Williams was going to have

Andrew's exact size, but I hoped for something close. In the catering van, I dug through the box of uniforms, found my best guess, and went back to the room.

Andrew had actually waited for me. He was still in his tux, looking at pictures on his phone. I thrust the cater waiter jacket and pants out to him. "The ceremony starts in less than thirty minutes. You don't have time to go home and change. So here is my solution."

He held up the jacket like it had committed a crime. "What is your solution?"

"Don't play dumb."

"Oh, you want me to wear this?" He laughed.

"At the very least, lose your jacket and tie, roll up your sleeves, and call it a day." I gave him a tight smile and left to go make sure all the flowers had been tied to the chairs along the aisle.

The sky looked ominous. Dark clouds hung overhead like they were dying to ruin the day. I made my way to the ceremony area, where most of the seats were full, and adjusted a few flowers along the aisle that had jostled loose when guests had sat down. There was the low buzz of chattering all around. I heard the word *rain* several times.

A little girl of about six or seven with a basketful of rose petals came running up to me. "Flower lady, how do I drop these?" She held up the basket.

I looked around for potential parents but didn't see anyone concerned that the flower girl was missing from her post. I smiled and led her back toward the house. "You come out right before the bride, and you just take a few petals at a time and drop them on that white aisle back there."

"That's what my mom said too, but I wanted to check."

We made it to the back porch and she took off into the house, leaving me behind.

I was about to head to the reception area when I saw Chad walk out the door and straight toward the pergola. The first thing I noticed was that his boutonniere was crooked. The second thing I noticed was that he was wearing Andrew's tux and he looked amazing. I couldn't believe the suit fit him. I couldn't believe any of it.

Chad swept past me, then walked down the aisle to stand under the rose-draped arch. It took me another second to shake off my shock and rush over to him.

"Let me fix your flower," I whispered. "It's crooked."

"Thanks."

"You changed," I said, unpinning the rose.

"Yeah, Jett Hart's kid delivered this up to my room. He said it was a gift." He tugged on the bottom of the jacket. "I had no idea Jett was so generous. The tag said Burberry. I've never heard of this Burberry guy before but he makes a good suit."

I straightened the flower and pinned it in place. "Yes, it's amazing." I gave his arm a pat then snuck off to the side and around the guests. I went back into the house and the room where I'd left Andrew, but he wasn't there. Wherever he was, he was either wearing Chad's rented tux or the cater waiter attire I'd brought him.

I really didn't have time to keep looking. The ceremony was about to start, and while Chad and Janet were getting married, I had to put finishing touches on the reception area.

Chapter 15

The ceremony went off without a hitch, I was told. And more importantly, without rain.

The guests were now filing to the tables as the sun crept lower in the sky. Fairy lights were strung up between the poles that had been installed for that very purpose, and despite the muggy heat, it looked magical. I, on the other hand, did not feel magical. My hair was sticking to my face, and sweat made my shirt cling to my back.

I lit the last citronella candle (our attempt to repel any and all winged critters) and plucked a dangling petal from a rose.

"Finally, a client with taste," a voice next to me said. "*These* are centerpieces."

"You like roses. How original." I turned to face Andrew. He had obviously gone home, because he was wearing neither the rented tux nor the cater waiter outfit. Instead, he was in a tailored navy-blue suit that was less showy than the Burberry but still expensive.

"I figured if I wanted to look nice, I needed to make the groom look nicer," he said, obviously noticing my gaze.

"And here I thought you'd done it out of the goodness of your heart."

"I did it out of the goodness of *your* heart, right?"

I bit back an angry response and instead said, "I guess taking pictures isn't the most important thing at events. The way *you* look is?"

"There is zero food at a wedding ceremony. I come for the reception." He raised his phone and took a picture of Micah, who had just come out with the appetizer course.

"That better not go on the website," she said as she passed us.

"It's going front and center," Andrew said back, and she shot him narrowed eyes over her shoulder.

Their friendly relationship seemed to be extra annoying tonight. I blamed the heat. I pushed a lock of my damp hair off my cheek just as the sky lit up with a crack of lighting.

"Am I allowed to say that it looks like it's going to rain *now*?" Andrew whispered.

"Andrew, you are allowed to do whatever you want," I said, then whirled around and headed for the house. I needed the air-conditioning, at least for a moment.

When I'd seen Chad in that tux, I thought I owed Andrew an apology, or at least a thank-you. I had offered him neither because, like always, his personality got in the way.

I found the closest AC vent and stood under it, pulling my shirt away from my skin and aggressively flapping it. I had been standing like that for some time when I figured I'd better check on things.

I headed back down the hall. Lance nearly knocked me over with a trayful of food on his way out.

"Sorry," I said, knowing about the huge blind spot a full food tray created.

"No worries," he said, and kept walking.

Micah came in as Lance went out, and when she saw me, standing flat against the wall, she said, "Um . . . what are you doing?"

"Staying out of the way."

She smiled. "Good strategy." Then she said, "Close your eyes."

"Um . . . what?"

"Do you trust me?"

And of course I did, so I closed my eyes.

"Now open your mouth."

I opened my mouth and she stuck some sort of food inside. I chewed it hesitantly at first, but as my entire mouth watered with the savory taste, I opened my eyes. "Was that shrimp?"

"Yes, the shrimp appetizer. Amazing, right?"

"So good," I said. Then my eyes drifted to the tray of dirty dishes. "Wait, was that from one of those plates?"

"What?" she asked innocently. "I couldn't let an excellent piece of shrimp go to waste."

I elbowed her with a laugh. "I'm never trusting you again."

She considered this. "So you wouldn't have eaten it if you'd seen it on a used plate?"

"Fine, I probably would've if you'd told me it was good."

"Exactly. I know you." She nodded over her shoulder. "I better get to the next course."

I went back outside, where I immediately couldn't breathe again. One reason was the air; the other was my mother. She was standing next to a full table talking to one of the ladies sitting there. My mom wore a skin-tight, short purple dress that I had never seen before in my life.

I made my way to her. "Hi, Mom."

"Oh, there you are. I have no idea where I'm supposed to sit."

"Over here." There weren't assigned seats so I took her by the arm and led her to a table in the corner that had open spots.

"Also, my invitation said *plus one*, but I didn't know if that meant Gunnar, so I left him in the car."

"You left Gunnar in the car?"

"The windows are rolled down and it's unlocked. He's ten, Soph, why are you looking at me like that?"

"I'm just surprised. You didn't mention bringing him . . . or coming at all. I thought you had to work."

Mom shrugged. "I got done early. I see other kids here. Go tell Gunnar it's fine."

She was right, there were other kids at the wedding, but they were related to the bride or groom. "I'll go talk to him."

122

I walked to the gravel parking area and found Mom's car. Gunnar sat in the passenger seat, his feet on the dash, playing a game on his iPad. His jeans were dirty but he wore a clean green polo shirt and his hair was combed.

I leaned my arms on the open window. "Hey, kid. What are you doing?"

"Playing motocross."

"Are you winning?"

"I keep getting flipped."

"Did you want to come in and watch people eat and dance, or do you want to stay out here and play your game? I can bring you food."

"You'll bring me food?"

"Yes."

"Then I want to stay out here."

"Probably a good choice. I'll be right back."

I returned to the reception area and found Micah on her way back inside the house. "My brother is in the car. Think you can steal me a plate of food for him?"

"You know he can come in," Micah said. She looked around and gestured at the flower girl racing across the grass. "There are tons of kids here. This is a country wedding, Soph."

"I know. But Caroline had that talk with me, and I'm just trying to show her that I'm professional."

"Yes, I'll sneak you some food. Give me a sec."

"Is this the secret meeting for party workers?" Andrew asked, joining us.

"I'm sorry, are you working this event?" I said. "Or do you own the place?"

"Sophie doesn't like my suit, Micah. Tell me I look nice before I get a complex."

Micah laughed. "You look so handsome."

I gave an exaggerated eye roll.

"Stop distracting me, you two," Micah said. "I'm supposed to be working here." She tapped my shoulder with her empty tray, then flitted off.

Andrew and I stood there for a moment in silence. The sound of Kyle's voice singing a slow song filled the air between us. Kyle had a nice voice. The songs the band was forced to play tonight made that more apparent. At the head table, Chad stood, pulling Janet up with him, and they danced right next to their seats, him holding her close.

"What are the odds?" I said, more to myself than anything.

"Of what?" Andrew asked.

"Of two people who can be compatible for the rest of their lives actually finding each other."

"Not sure I know the exact numbers on that," he said.

"The odds are low. Very low," I said.

"A cynic about love," Andrew said dryly. "How original."

Maybe I *was* a cynic about love. My gaze drifted to Kyle. Was I the one not letting us move forward? I wasn't exactly surrounded by good relationship examples. If my dad could up and leave, no looking back, after fifteen years with a person, what guarantees were there?

I started to walk away when several loud screams sounded from somewhere in the middle of the tables. My first thought was that it had finally started raining. But people weren't looking at the sky, they were looking at the ground. One guest was up on her chair. Chad and Janet had stopped dancing and were leaning over their table in an attempt to see what was happening.

"What do you think that's about?" Andrew asked, but I was already moving toward the commotion.

A group of men stood around a very large opossum. Its razor-sharp teeth were bared and its black eyes were glowing. Several of the guys had their cell phones out and were snapping pictures or videos. One guy had his jacket off and was swatting at the animal, supposedly in an attempt to get it to move along. The poor opossum was frozen in fear, seconds away from playing dead, I was sure.

"That is terrifying," Andrew said from where he stood at my shoulder.

I whirled around and ran back to the house in search of a trapping device. The closest room was the kitchen, and the first thing I found was a large box on the ground. I swiped it up and went running, vaguely hearing the sound of Jett shouting something after me.

When I reached the group again, I turned the box upside

down and lowered it over the opossum. There were a few cheers and a couple of boos as well, as if I had taken away a fun toy. The guests scattered back to their tables or to the dance floor.

Janet shouted out a "Thank you!" to me, and I waved to her and Chad.

"What now?" Andrew asked, nodding to the box. I still had my hand on top of it.

I took a breath. "Now we slowly slide this box through the tables and let the wedding crasher loose past the trees over there."

"We?"

"Yep. Welcome to country life, sir."

I thought he might object, but Andrew, nice suit and all, moved to the other side of the box and said, "Ready?"

I nodded. We slid the box and immediately felt the pressure of resistance. We kept pushing and moved it a couple of inches at a time around the tables.

"Does this happen often?" he asked.

"Never at a wedding. At least not one I've been to."

"But at other events?"

"I once found an opossum in the shed behind the flower shop. And at Grandma Harris's ninetieth birthday, a raccoon tried to eat her cake."

"What a rude raccoon."

"She thought so too." We made it past the reception area to the grass, but my heels kept sinking into the earth. "Hold on a second." I kicked them off.

Andrew stood straight and stretched, then slid off his jacket. "It's hot." He started to put his jacket on the ground next to my shoes but I stopped him.

"What are you doing? It'll get dirty."

"I'll get it dry-cleaned."

I held out my hand. He looked confused but gave me his jacket. About thirty feet to the left of us, the chairs from the ceremony were still set up. I could see their white silhouettes in the darkness. I jogged over and tucked my shoes under a chair and laid his jacket over the back. Then I returned and placed my hands back on the box. "Ready?"

He pointed. "All the way to the trees?"

"Yes, then it won't come back."

"Okay, let's go."

It took us another ten minutes to inch the box to the trees. When we arrived we both stared at the overturned box.

"It's not going to attack us or anything, is it?" he asked.

"No, he just wants to get away."

"Okay. Here goes nothing." Andrew lifted his foot, placed it on the side of the box closest to us, and tipped it back. We waited for the creature to go scurrying, but nothing happened.

"Did we lose it somewhere along the way?" Andrew asked, looking behind us.

"No, I felt it." I moved around the box slowly. There was nothing on the ground. I crouched down to look inside.

A loud hiss sounded before the creature scurried out of the box.

I screamed and fell back onto my butt. Andrew laughed, and the opossum ran into the trees.

I scowled at Andrew and he stepped in front of me and held out his hand. I thought about rejecting it, but that seemed worse than just taking it. So I did. He pulled me to my feet too quickly, causing me to trip forward. My free hand used his chest for support. He kept hold of my other hand until I was steady.

"You good?" he asked.

I met his eyes to say yes, but couldn't quite get my words out—his stare seemed so intense. I pushed off his chest, taking a step back. "Yes, fine."

He turned and bent down. "Wait, is this . . ." He flipped the box, open side up. "Where did you get this?"

"I grabbed the first one I could find in the kitchen."

"This is the box my dad stores his mixer in." Andrew pointed to the picture of a red mixer on the outside and bit his lip. "He's going to be ticked."

"Oh."

He held out the box for me to take. "Good luck."

I groaned. "Thanks a lot."

Chapter 16

I'd seen a lot of scowls on Jett Hart's face over the last several months, but this was the worst one yet.

"It's filthy," he said, his scowl now directed at the open flaps of the box. He was right. They were damp and streaked with dirt and grass.

"I'm sorry," I said, wishing I had thought to grab my shoes before returning the box. I already felt stupid enough, and being barefoot wasn't helping my case. "Speed was necessary, and this was the first box I could find big enough to trap the opossum."

"There was a rodent in my box?"

"Not really *in* it. Sort of *under* it." I looked around for Mr. Williams. He would put in a good word for me, or at least be the witness that kept Jett from annihilating me. Mr. Williams was nowhere in sight. He must've gone outside with the wedding cake. He often did.

"Haven't I asked you before not to be anywhere near my things?" Jett was barking. "Can you not follow simple directions?"

"I really am sorry," I said. "I can probably find you another box similar in size that would work for your mixer." We received boxes all the time with flower deliveries.

"I don't want another box! I want you to grow a brain so that you have at least a drop more common sense."

I took a step back. Had he really just said that? *"What?"*

"Out! Now!"

I squared my shoulders and was about to say something— I wasn't quite sure what—when someone pulled me out of the kitchen by my arm. In the hall, Micah turned me to face her.

"I know you're mad," she said quietly. "Cool off before you do something you'll regret."

"Like tell off that monster?"

"Yes."

"Why shouldn't I, though?" I shook my head, still in shock over Jett's behavior. "I can't believe I ever wanted his help for anything. There is no way he has any contacts because nobody could possibly like him."

Micah's eyes turned pleading. "Soph. Come on. For me and my dad?"

Finally, I gritted my teeth and nodded once.

She let go of my arms. "Thank you."

"Does he talk to *you* like that?"

"He yells sometimes, but usually isn't quite so insulting. It's his artistic temperament."

"Is that the excuse he goes with?"

She led me toward the exit, as if she didn't trust me not to dart back into the kitchen the second she left me.

"By the way," she said, "when you were taking care of the oversized rat problem, I took a plate of food out to Gunnar."

"Oh! Gunnar!" Now I felt even worse. "I got caught up in other stuff. Thank you."

"Of course."

"And he was okay?"

"Yes, just playing on his iPod."

"And my mom?" I asked as we stepped outside. "How is she?"

"She's mingling. You know how social she is."

I searched the crowd until I saw Mom's purple dress over by Kyle and the band. There was no music playing, and she was standing on her tiptoes saying something to Kyle. He didn't seem irritated or embarrassed by whatever it was she was doing there. Kyle nodded a few times.

The band started playing some upbeat song and my mom cheered, "To Janet and Chad!" She grabbed the arm of the nearest guest and attempted to start some sort of conga line. Several people joined but most just looked on and laughed.

"I am not my mother's keeper," I said, just as a drip of moisture hit my face. One at first, followed by several more.

Oh no.

"Looks like this party is ending early," Micah said. "At least they cut the cake."

It was like her words gave the sky permission to open up. Screams and shouts could barely be heard over the noise of the sudden storm. Raindrops pounded down, and I ran straight for my mom, weaving in and out of bodies that were heading for the house or the parking lot.

Kyle had his guitar wrapped up in his arms, trying to keep it dry. Bryce had his suit jacket spread out over his drums. "My precious kit!" he wailed. "We needed to put a tent clause in the contract!"

"We had no contract!" Kyle yelled back.

My hair and clothes were drenched by the time I reached my mom.

She laughed. "That storm blew in quick!"

"Does Gunnar have the car keys?" I yelled. "All the windows were open."

She cussed loudly, then took off.

The reception area cleared fast. I turned my face skyward. The stifling heat of the day made way for cool relief. It seemed to wash away all the tension I had been feeling moments ago about Jett Hart. And my mother. And everything. I smiled at the sky. "Is that the best you can do?"

"Don't challenge the sky, Sophie," Bryce said. "Please." He, Jodi, Kyle, and Lincoln were carefully disassembling all the band equipment and carrying it offstage.

I took in the rain-soaked reception area and saw Janet's bouquet sitting on the head table. It wouldn't survive this storm. I picked my way around toppled chairs and over dropped silverware. This cleanup was going to be more work than normal.

One of the centerpieces tipped over right in front of me. Clear marbles from the vase rolled off the table and onto the ground, rain making them shine. I suddenly pictured diamond-studded shoes and embellished skirts, their wearers twirling across rain-soaked pavements, water and diamonds making the shoes sparkle.

The sound of a crashing cymbal pulled me out of my thoughts.

"Be careful with that!" Bryce yelled. I looked over to see the band disappearing around the corner with the last of the equipment.

I redirected my attention to the path in front of me. Too late, I noticed the amber-colored glass of a broken beer bottle and stepped right on it with my still-bare foot.

Ouch.

I sucked air in between my teeth. I looked around but there was nobody.

There was no way he could hear me but I tried anyway. "Kyle!"

The rain had let up a little and I heard cars starting in the gravel parking lot. My skirt didn't have pockets so I'd left my cell phone in my purse in the coat closet when I'd arrived. Now I cursed myself for that.

Carefully, I made my way around the rest of the glass on my tiptoes until I reached the bouquet. It still looked good. I picked it up then hopped on one foot to the first tree I could find for a bit of cover. Still holding my bouquet, I leaned against the tree, hiked up my skirt a little, and lifted my foot to assess the damage.

A large piece of glass protruded from the center of my foot. Blood slowly trickled around it. My stomach flipped. I had only eaten that one piece of shrimp all day and the sight of blood was making me light-headed. Out of the corner of my eye, I saw movement through the rain.

I lowered my foot. "Over here!" I called out.

The person changed direction and soon stood in front of me, water dripping off his hair and down his face.

"Sophie?" Andrew was holding my shoes in one hand and his jacket in the other. "What are you doing?"

I held up Janet's bouquet. "Saving this."

"And trying to get hit by lightning?" He nodded to the tree.

"There hasn't been lightning since before the rain," I said, pushing my bangs off my forehead so they would stop dripping in my eyes.

"I was saving these." He held out my shoes for me.

"Thanks. Wish I would've had them ten minutes ago."

That's when he seemed to realize I was favoring one foot. And that's when I realized my skirt was still halfway up my thighs.

I tugged it down, my cheeks going pink. "I stepped on glass."

It took him a second to process those words, and then his eyes shot down to my foot. "That sucks." He took two steps back. "Well, see you later."

I narrowed my eyes at him.

He laughed. "Okay, so here are your choices. Fireman's carry or piggyback ride."

"I don't need you to carry me. Just lend me your shoulder and carry this bouquet."

"Really?" he asked. "You're going to be stubborn about this? Why am I surprised?"

"I'm wearing a skirt, Andrew. I am not jumping on your back." I gestured for him to come closer and he stepped up next to me, offering his shoulder.

I handed him the bouquet and grabbed hold of him.

"Do you want to put on at least one shoe?" he asked.

"I'll probably twist my ankle if I try to hop in one heel."

"True." He took a step and I jumped forward, my toes squishing in the muddy grass.

We moved like this all the way back to the Stanton Estate. Andrew was bent as far forward as he could go, and held the bouquet under the shelter made by his chest. After navigating the walkway and many misplaced items—a shawl here, a glass there—we finally made it inside.

I thought there would be a loud mess of guests clogging the halls, but it was like a ghost town. Micah, who must've heard the door open, poked her head out of the kitchen.

When she saw who it was, she smiled and joined us. "Where have you two been? You look like a couple of drowned rats."

I took the bouquet from Andrew and held it up. "Is Janet still here?"

"She was on her way out a minute ago."

"Will you check? Or find her mom or someone?"

"Of course. What's wrong with you, though?"

"Stepped on glass."

"That's why we wear shoes at weddings, darlin'," Micah said, laying on a thick Southern accent.

"Yeah, yeah," I said. "You just sounded eerily like my grandma."

She took the flowers. "I'll take care of this."

"I think I got it from here," I said to Andrew when she was gone. "The bathroom is literally ten steps away."

He hung his wet jacket on the coat rack by the door and dropped my shoes beneath it. "I think I can handle ten more steps. I made it this far."

We did our awkward dance to the bathroom, where he opened the door and led me in. There was a long counter and I leaned back up against it.

"Here," he said, "just let me." He put his hands on my waist, and I wasn't sure what he was trying to do until he lifted me onto the counter. I let out a little gasp. He offered me a wide smile, then shook his head, sending water spraying. I held up my hands with a squeal I hadn't meant to release.

He laughed and then squatted down, his hand brushing along my calf until it reached my ankle.

Tingles spread up my leg all the way to my stomach. My cheeks went hot, and I leaned my head back against the mirror to try to keep that fact to myself. He wasn't allowed to have this kind of effect on me.

"Wow," he said.

"What?" I asked. Was he really going to call me out on the fact that I was blushing? He so *would*.

"This is a decent-sized piece of glass."

I wiped at some water that was still dripping from my hair down my temple. "Oh. Yeah. Micah has Band-Aids in her *just-in-case* if you . . ."

I trailed off because he was giving me a stare of disbelief. "You think a *Band-Aid* will work on this?"

"Probably not."

He started opening the lower cupboards. "Maybe they keep a first aid kit in here."

"Actually, they do," I said, remembering. I leaned over to the far side of the counter and opened the mirror cabinet. A white box with a red cross sat sideways on the first shelf. I plucked out the box and opened it. Inside I found some gauze pads and a roll of white tape along with little packets of ointment. I pulled out the supplies. "If you want to go get Micah, she can help me. You might get blood all over your nice pants."

He reached behind him, pulled a fancy towel off the rack, and draped it over his knee. "Would you stop trying to talk me out of helping you? I can be a nice person every now and again."

"Fine." I unwrapped the gauze and squeezed some ointment onto it. "Just do it fast. Once you pull that glass out, it's going to gush."

He smirked at me from his crouched position. "This might hurt."

"Why do you look like you're going to enjoy that?"

He let out a single laugh, yanked out the glass, and dropped it in the trash by the toilet.

I swallowed down my scream of pain and Andrew quickly applied pressure with the towel, both his hands wrapped tightly around my foot.

"Mr. Stanton is not going to be happy about his ruined towel," I said.

"I'll buy him another one."

Everything was as easy as that for Andrew, I sensed. I leaned my head back against the mirror again, the light-headed sensation returning.

"You okay?" he asked.

"Fine. Let's just get this over with."

"Yes, ma'am."

He removed the towel and pressed the gauze to my foot. Then he wrapped my entire foot three times with the tape and tore it with his teeth. He stood, brushing against my knees. He didn't move, just remained standing there with his hands on either side of my thighs, and met my eyes.

I stared back, no words coming to me no matter how hard I searched for them. I willed my hands to move, to push him away from me, but they wouldn't. They stayed there, braced on the counter, inches from his.

"Not even a thank-you?" he asked.

"Right . . . yes . . . thanks," I said, not sure why I had such a hard time saying that to him, even when he deserved it.

"You're welcome," he said, still not moving. He was studying my face and I wasn't exactly sure what he was looking for there. His expression was unreadable. I tried to make mine equally so.

"You should go," I was finally able to say. "Your dad informed me he doesn't want me anywhere near his things."

Andrew frowned. "What?"

"I think he mainly meant you."

"He didn't say that," Andrew said.

"No, he did."

"I think, *Soph*, that you hear only what you want to hear."

"I think, *Drew*, that you see only what you want to see. Especially when it comes to your father."

He clenched and unclenched his jaw, then handed me the bloody towel and left the bathroom.

Chapter 17

ay that again," Micah said, popping open her trunk. "You need my organizational skills to save you?"

I let out a heavy sigh. "I'm not sure you keeping a pair of *my* shoes in your trunk can be considered organized. Maybe just obsessive. How long have you had them in here anyway? What shoes are they?"

There was no way I could navigate cleaning up the reception area barefoot or in heels, not with all the glass still littering the pavement. But Micah was coming through for me once again.

She reached around her *just-in-case* to a shoebox toward the back. "No, they aren't your shoes. They're shoes I bought for myself but they ended up being too big on me, so I figured I'd save them for you for a moment like this."

"Because moments like this happen often?"

"It's happening, isn't it? How about just praising me for my foresight."

I hugged her. "Thank you, Micah, for being my overly prepared best friend in the whole world."

She smiled and handed me the box. "You're welcome." She picked up a folded T-shirt. "And put this on too."

My clothes were still wet and it would be nice to feel dry. We were going to be here at least another hour, if not longer, with the disaster that awaited us. I took the T-shirt and opened the shoebox. "Cowboy boots? So *this* is why you didn't just gift them to me in the first place. You knew I'd never wear these."

She smiled. "Beggars can't be choosers. Now swallow that pride of yours and go change so that we can actually go home at some point tonight."

She always knew the exact words to say. *Pride.* That word got to me every time. I limped my way to the passenger seat of her car, changed my shirt, and pulled on the boots. The rearview mirror proved I'd seen better days. I finger combed my hair and worked off the smudged mascara beneath my eyes. Then I joined everyone back at the slate-paved reception area. At least it had stopped raining.

"Cute!" Micah said from where she was collecting abandoned dishes from the tables.

I pointed one finger at Andrew, who had looked up with Micah's declaration. "Don't," I said.

"What?" he returned. "I didn't say a word."

"Your face said it." My foot still hurt, but at least it was protected. I limped around for the next hour, mostly collecting marbles and vowing to never use them in vases again if I could help it.

My back hurt from bending over. I stood and stretched, taking in what we had left to do.

Micah was standing by what remained of the destroyed wedding cake. "Your dad didn't make this, did he, Andrew?"

Andrew dropped a tablecloth onto the pile we'd created. "No. He doesn't do wedding cakes. I think this was made by a local bakery."

Micah nodded. Andrew picked up a chunk of cake and popped it in his mouth only to make a disgusted face.

"What?" I said. "Rainwater isn't a good additive?"

"Why didn't you guys use tents today?" Andrew asked. "There was a thirty percent chance of rain." His tone made it sound like he thought we were idiots, which was surely what he did think.

"Because the bride wanted to avoid tents at all costs. She hates the way they look," I said.

"Oh right, I forgot. The client always knows best."

"It mostly worked out," Micah said. "It was a beautiful wedding."

"It was a five out of ten," Andrew said. "I've been to a lot of weddings. This was average."

Micah picked up a big chunk of cake and threw it at him. It hit him right on the side of the face, then slid off and landed with a wet splat on the ground.

I sucked my lips in, trying not to laugh.

Andrew slowly turned to face her, his expression a mix between anger and humor. "What was that for?"

"Being a snob," she said.

He picked up a handful of cake himself. Micah shrieked

and ran toward Lance, who had just come out of the house. Micah ducked behind him. Lance looked confused until Andrew came barreling around him and smashed his handful of cake right in Micah's face to her squeals of laughter.

"I am not in this fight," Lance proclaimed.

Micah blew air between her lips and wiped her face along the back of Lance's shirt.

"Micah!" Lance tried to shake her off but she continued.

"This cake is nasty," she said.

I laughed this time; I couldn't help it. Andrew, Micah, and Lance all looked my way, and I knew I was in trouble.

"No!" I yelled. "I didn't do anything! And I'm injured. I can't run!" I limped toward the parking lot.

Andrew caught up with me first, grabbing me around the waist from behind, my feet lifting off the ground. Then Micah and Lance were in front of me and I received an entire face full of cake.

"Not cool!" I wiped my face with my hand. Lance and Micah were now in a mini cake fight, chasing each other around some tables.

"Put me down," I said.

"Put your feet down," Andrew said next to my ear.

"Oh. Right." I lowered my feet and he released me.

I heard the sound of a buzzing phone. Andrew pulled it out of his pocket and swiped on the screen. I watched his jaw tighten again, like it had earlier.

"Who's texting you?" Micah said, sliding up beside

us. She must not have noticed he wasn't happy about this text.

He put on a smile. "Just my mom," he said.

His mom. I vaguely remembered him saying that his mom had left when his dad's career had ended or something along those lines. I had thought he was implying she wasn't in his life at all, but maybe I was wrong.

"Tell her we say hi," Micah responded happily.

My eyes went between Micah and Andrew. Micah knew him better than I did. Maybe he and his mom had reconciled or had never had a falling out to begin with. Maybe I was imagining the tense jaw and anger in his eyes. He was smiling, after all.

Andrew met my eyes, as if silently asking if I had anything to add, as if wanting me to say something that gave him permission to drop the fake smile. My mind went back to that day in the van when he admitted that it was hard for him to make friends, to let people in, to bare his soul. He feared getting close to anyone because he always moved. He always left. That was his deal. And I wasn't the right person to change how he normally dealt with it.

"Yep," I said. "Say hi to your mom."

With his smile more firmly in place, he looked back at his phone and started typing.

It was official. I was still a jerk. What was it about Andrew that brought out the worst in me?

Fourth of July Town Barbecue

CARNATION

A flower with a potent fragrance and distinct shape, mostly known for being the choice of cheapskates. Bring someone a carnation and you may as well have plucked a dandelion out of a crack in the sidewalk. But carnations don't mind their reputation. They are both hardy and long-lasting. Stubborn little flowers. Long live the carnation!

Chapter 18

My fingertips were various shades of blue and red. I'd spent the night before dyeing white carnations with food coloring. It wasn't hard: Trim the stems under water, then add the dyes. The flowers soak the color right up to produce the cool effect of color-streaked tips. Bundle some red, white, and blue flowers together and you have instant all-American patriotism.

"This is what passes for a lake around here?" Andrew asked, joining me at the picnic table where I had set up shop. "Are there any gators in there?" he added in a horrible attempt at a Southern accent.

"Andrew." I nodded at him in greeting. "A month away from you almost made me forget how charming you are."

"My charm is unforgettable," he said with a grin.

"No gators," I said, arranging the red, white, and blue carnations in a vase. "They like southern Alabama better." I gave him a sideways glance. He was wearing a blue polo shirt, its collar turned up, and some plaid shorts that no guy around here would've been seen dead in, because they hit him above the knee.

"How cute!" Micah said as she walked up. "You two look like you could take a couple's picture together." She set a large glass beverage dispenser on the table.

I glared at her, then looked down at my outfit. I wore a sundress, but she was right; it was almost the same exact plaid as his shorts. "Nice," I said.

"How's your foot?" Andrew asked me.

It took me a minute to remember that the last time he'd seen me, I'd cut open my foot at the wedding.

It was summer, so not much had happened since then aside from working at Every Occasion and going to drive-in movies with Micah and on diner runs and lake trips with Gunnar, but it felt like forever ago.

"Fine," I said. "Healed." With a killer scar. "How's . . . whatever you do when you disappear?"

"Good. I got to get out of this town for several weeks and actually see things and people."

I rolled my eyes.

Micah gestured toward the lake in front of us. "And now you get to enjoy the real life. Simple and uncluttered."

The lake (at least what we called the lake) barely qualified as such. It was more like a watering hole. People could fish in it and swim in it. Right now, in fact, it boasted a couple of colorful inner tubes and their owners, lingering from the hot day. As the sun went down, the lake would empty and the park around it would fill up with people ready to watch the fireworks that happened every year, right here. Hank was bringing the barbecue and Mr. Williams (and Jett Hart this year) always provided the side dishes. Every Occasion, of course, provided the flowers.

"Is that what real life consists of?" Andrew asked, eyeing the lake. "Or is that what you say because you have nothing to compare it to?"

Micah's brows shot down. "Going out of town was not good for you. Maybe I need to go baptize you in that lake and hope it cleanses the grump out of you."

He closed his eyes, took a deep breath, then opened them again. "You're right. I'm sorry. Bad day."

"What's your excuse for all the other days?" I asked.

"Mostly you," he said.

I laughed a little. I could appreciate a good comeback.

"Well," Micah said, rolling her shoulders back, "I'm going to have a great day. Do you know why?"

Andrew and I waited for her to finish.

"Ask me why," she demanded.

"Why?" Andrew said.

"Because look at me. I'm wearing real clothes." She wore a pair of jean shorts and a red T-shirt instead of her usual cater waiter uniform. "And I don't have to work today. People will get their own food. I just have to refill empty dishes when necessary. And Sophie doesn't really do anything either. Just puts flowers at each table and waits to be bossed around by Caroline. It is my favorite event of the year!"

"Well," Andrew said, "I still have just as many pictures to take, so try not to rub it in too much."

"Oh please," Micah said. "You take entirely too many pictures. You only use like ten on the website. Stop being such an overachiever."

"My dad looks at every single one."

"He does?" I asked. "But you were putting them online before we'd even left the Valentine's Day event."

Andrew ran a hand through his thick, dark hair. "He reviews them and sometimes has me trade them out."

"That's when you say, 'Dad, you stick to cooking, I got this picture thing down,'" Micah said.

I let out a single laugh. "Have you met his dad?"

"He's just a perfectionist," Andrew said, defending him, like always.

"Is that the word they use instead of *jerk* in the city?" I shrugged. "I'm just a sheltered country girl so I don't know these things."

"You're impossible," he said. With that, he turned and walked away.

Micah was quiet.

"What?" I asked. "He said it himself. He's grumpy today."

"You didn't help."

"It's not my fault he lets his dad walk all over him and doesn't seem to recognize he's being trampled."

"Sophie! Just play nice."

"I make no promises."

The party was in full swing. People were eating and laughing, throwing Frisbees and footballs, or standing around Hank's huge barbecue. It was so big that it had its own wheels and was hauled in behind a truck. Ribs and steak were sizzling on the grill, smoke rising into the sky. And Micah was right, we had nothing to do. She and I were sitting on lawn chairs watching my brother throw rocks into the lake. I had my phone out and was reading a sample application on one of the New York City design school websites.

"Unique," I said.

"What?" Micah asked, understandably confused.

"This is the third time I've read the word *unique* when they are referring to the portfolio we're supposed to submit."

"Yeah . . . so . . ."

I swatted at some gnats buzzing by my ear. "My pieces aren't unique, I've decided."

Micah shook her head. "Your pieces are absolutely unique. They're originals! How can they not be?"

I narrowed my eyes and pulled up a photo on my phone. "What do you think about this sketch?" I asked, showing her the sketch of a skirt I had designed a couple of weeks ago.

Micah looked at it. "It's gorgeous. You should use that one."

"What about this one?" I scrolled to the next picture.

She narrowed her eyes, studying it. "It looks very similar to the last one, but it's pretty too."

"This one isn't mine," I said, the same sick feeling I had felt the week before settling in my chest. "I saw this on a design site I like to visit. And that's when I started to notice the word *unique* in almost every application I read. Did they just add that word like yesterday?"

Micah didn't know what to say. I could tell from her expression that she was searching her brain and coming up empty. "Those are two different skirts" is what she settled on.

"Not different enough," I muttered. "I need something that makes me stand out. Something that makes my designs one hundred percent . . . me." Which was exactly what Andrew had told me a couple of months ago. I hated that he was probably right.

"You'll figure it out," Micah said. "I have faith in you."

I was glad one of us did. "I don't want to think about it anymore." I stuck my phone in my pocket. "Let's talk about anything else."

Micah lifted her hair off her neck and leaned back in her chair. "Is Kyle coming today?"

"I don't know." Kyle. Another thing in my life that I felt unsure about these days. And he wasn't doing anything to help in that area. We hadn't texted in weeks.

She read my mind, like she often seemed to, and said, "Just ask him out again. I'm sure that's what he's waiting for."

"I'd rather let him reach out first."

"Why?"

"Because I have massive amounts of self-control. Kind of like when Walker puts that biscuit on his dog's nose."

I nodded my head toward Walker, a guy from our school who was playing Frisbee with Lance. Walker's dog wasn't here today, but that didn't matter; my point worked without the dog.

"You know that eventually Walker lets his dog eat the biscuit, right?"

Maybe she was right. Maybe Kyle and I were too alike, and we'd both wait until the cows came home if one of us didn't swallow our pride. "I guess tonight I'll eat the biscuit then."

"Wait, what?" she asked, obviously not following my metaphor.

"Kyle will be here and I'll ask him out."

"Yay!" she said, then scrunched her lips to the side. "That biscuit analogy didn't work, by the way. Don't use it again."

I laughed.

Gunnar came running over with a huge rock. "Do you think I can make this one skip?" he asked.

"No. Skipping rocks need to be flat and smaller."

"I bet I can make it skip," Andrew said, appearing beside us.

He seemed to always show up out of nowhere. Well, not nowhere. He had obviously been at the event, and it was a small event and . . . fine, he always seemed to butt in.

"How much you want to bet?" I asked.

"Five bucks?" Andrew said. The rock was the size of his palm.

"Have you ever skipped a rock before?" I challenged him.

He lowered his chin. "Is that a real question?"

"If you think *that* rock can be skipped, then yes, it is a very real question."

"Five bucks?"

"Five bucks."

Gunnar handed Andrew the rock. It didn't look quite as big with Andrew holding it but still. He and his preppy shorts walked toward the water.

Andrew rubbed the rock between his palms a couple of times. Then he wound up his arm and threw. With a *plop* I could hear from where we sat ten feet away, it sank to the bottom. Gunnar thought this was the funniest thing in the world and he doubled over with laughter.

Andrew turned to face me.

I raised my eyebrows at him. "You owe me five bucks, Hart. I'll add it to the list of things you owe me."

"What else do I owe you?" he asked, walking back.

"I believe you still owe me flowers, bought by you, arranged by me."

Andrew smirked. "Oh, that's right. Our first meeting. How could I forget? You obviously haven't."

"You make it impossible. You just keep showing up."

He held up his phone. "Get closer to Micah. You guys look like America right now."

He had a point; I took in Micah's red T-shirt and my multi-colored plaid dress. Micah leaned close to me and Andrew took a picture.

"Soph!"

I turned to see my mom walking up, holding a plate of food.

"Oh, hey, Andrew," Mom said, stopping in front of us like she hadn't come over here just because of him. "I didn't realize that was you."

Micah pinched my arm. Had I scoffed out loud?

"Hi, Ms. Evans."

"Larissa," she corrected. "How are you? Jett said you two were in New York for a couple weeks. That sounds like fun. We've never been to New York."

"You've never been to New York?" he asked my mom, and then glanced at me.

"No," she said. "Sophie wants to go there for school but she's always been a bit of a dreamer. Life has a way of turning us all into realists eventually."

Great. As if Andrew needed more ammunition for his insults.

Micah put her arm around me. "If anyone from Rockside could make it in New York, it's Sophie."

I noticed Andrew didn't chime in to agree with that statement . . . and neither did I.

"Oh, Micah," Mom said. "Don't encourage her." She laughed like this was a fun little conversation we were all having about somebody else's future. "Anyway, speaking of reality, I'm off to work."

"Isn't the entire town here today, Ms. Evans?" Andrew asked. "I didn't think the diner was even open."

"It will be a slow night, but we'll have some customers."

"I didn't know you were going to work," I said. "What about Gunnar?"

"Gunnar can stay here, of course. It's not like you're actually working."

"Mom, Caroline said . . ."

"What about Caroline? Is she going to fire you? Really? Ask her who else she's gonna get who she can order around like she does you."

I sighed. "She doesn't—"

"Don't get your feathers ruffled. I'll talk with her," Mom said.

"No, don't do that."

"We'll watch Gunnar, Ms. Evans. It's fine," Micah said, always the peacemaker.

"Thanks, Micah, sweetie. Maybe this daughter of mine could be a little more loyal occasionally." Mom patted my cheek, and then left.

Chapter 19

W ho wants food?" Micah asked as soon as my mom was gone. "I do."

"I want food," Gunnar said. "I love Hank's."

"Yes, let's go get food," I said, a bit numb from humiliation.

"I want to see what the big deal about Hank's Barbecue is," Andrew said, for once not using this opportunity to say something rude. He walked alongside Micah and me toward the grill.

"It's the best," Gunnar said, skipping ahead of us in excitement.

"Oh, look," Micah said under her breath, trying but failing to contain a smile.

"What?" I asked, but then saw what she was looking at. Kyle was in line for food, straight ahead of us.

"Time to eat your biscuit," Micah said.

"What?" Andrew asked. "Is that some kind of Southern saying?"

"That's what I call a Sophie saying," Micah said.

"Don't ask," I said.

We joined the line.

I took a deep breath in through my nose. Did I even want to go out with Kyle still? I stared at the back of his head for a moment. He was cute in his cool *I don't care* way, and he made me laugh. Yes, I was going to do this. I'd been wanting to do this and I didn't give up on things I wanted.

"Hi, Kyle."

He turned. "Oh, hey, Soph."

"How come he gets to call you Soph?" Andrew asked from next to me, and I ignored him.

"How's your summer going so far?" I asked Kyle.

"Uneventful. Yours?"

"Pretty good," I returned.

Micah nudged me in the ribs, encouraging me to say more.

"Anything fun going on?" I asked.

"Not that I know of," Kyle said with a lazy shrug.

Now or never.

"Maybe . . . we should do something, then," I said.

"Well, I got that new job so I'm pretty busy, but . . . uh . . . okay." Then he gave another shrug and turned back around to talk to Lincoln, who was standing by him.

I blinked once. That wasn't the reaction I had anticipated. I'd thought I was the one holding up the progression of the relationship, not him. The rebuff stung. I tried to play it off like it was nothing.

"That was fun," I said quietly to Micah. "You satisfied now?"

"No, I'm very unsatisfied," she said. "I have a right mind to box him in the ears."

I glanced at Andrew, who was silent. I was sure he understood what had just happened, but he had the decency to pretend he didn't.

The line went fast and soon we each had a plateful of meat and a few sides. We found an open picnic table and sat. Gunnar watched Andrew intently as he took the first bite of ribs. I wasn't sure if Andrew knew he had an audience or if he was being sincere in his reaction, but he said, "Mmmm. Wow. That's good."

"See," Gunnar said. "I told you."

"You know your food."

Micah gave my arm a squeeze that let me know she felt bad about what had just happened with Kyle.

"I'm fine," I said under my breath. And I was. Embarrassed, but fine, I assured myself.

"Are you going to be a cook when you grow up like your dad?" Gunnar continued the conversation with Andrew.

Andrew laughed. "No."

"Why not?"

"Because I have no idea how to cook."

"Your dad didn't teach you?" Gunnar asked.

"My dad was a television chef. They provided him with top-of-the-line sous-chefs." He paused, then added, "That means other chefs who help out the big chef. And then when my dad was finished with his show, he was helping other people with their food businesses."

"Oh," Gunnar said, nodding along.

"Sometimes these people really don't know what they're doing even though it's their job, and he has to teach them from scratch." Andrew circled his fork at Micah. "Not your dad. He's good."

"Aw, shucks. You probably say that to all the girls," Micah said.

"I do," he returned with a wink. And then to me he said, "I'm sure your dad's a great chef too."

"My dad is a two-bit loser," Gunnar said, sounding exactly like our mother.

"Gunnar," I said. "Not cool."

Andrew began coughing, probably choking on his food. Micah patted his back until he stopped.

"You okay?" she asked.

"Yes." He coughed a few more times then took a drink of water. "I'm good."

"It's okay," Gunnar said. "Everyone knows it."

Andrew smiled a little, then looked at me like I should say something more. I probably should've, but I wasn't in the mood to defend anyone tonight, especially not my dad. It went back to my mixed feelings about him. I may have understood why he wanted to leave, and most of the time I liked him, but he could've done a better job at keeping in touch. Especially with Gunnar. He could've come back to visit. He could've at least acted like he wanted to. He didn't. He was never big on pretending. Which is probably where I'd gotten that from.

"Well, my mom's a loser," Andrew said. "Maybe they're friends."

Gunnar thought that Andrew was serious. "Does your mom live in California? That's where my dad lives."

"I'm not sure where my mom is living at the moment. Last I checked she was in Oregon."

So I'd been right. He and his mom *didn't* get along. Micah seemed surprised and concerned by this exchange. "Really?"

"Really. Why is your dad in California?" Andrew asked Gunnar.

"Because he thinks he's twenty and wants to surf all the time," Gunnar said, again sounding like our mother. Mom usually added the part about Dad feeling like he needed to regain his youth after marrying too young. She said too much in front of Gunnar.

"Okay, Gunnar," I said, finally stepping in. "Let's not be gossips."

"It's not gossip if it's true."

"It's gossip if you're telling people who have no business knowing."

Gunnar shrugged and took a bite of his ribs.

I saw Caroline coming from fifty feet away. Her movements were big and purposeful. When she reached the table she said, "Sophie, can you show Bryce how to connect his phone to the speakers? I thought all you kids understood that wireless thing, but apparently not. The fireworks are starting in about twenty minutes."

"Sure," I said.

She walked away, not even glancing at Gunnar. I wondered if my mom really had talked to her. I stood and pointed to Gunnar. "Stay here. I'll be right back."

He nodded.

"We'll watch him," Micah said.

"Thanks."

Bryce was cursing at his phone when I reached the parking lot. The trunk of his car was open and a pair of large speakers pointed toward the park.

"You've given us all a bad name with Caroline because you don't have technology skills," I said.

Bryce's parents were in charge of the fireworks, and Bryce was in charge of the music that went along with the fireworks. When night fell, fireworks would go off over the lake.

"Sophie, it's these stupid speakers Caroline lent me," Bryce groaned. "Will you tell your boss to come into this decade?"

I held out my hand for his phone. "Let me try?"

"Jodi and Kyle couldn't figure it out either."

My stomach tightened at the mention of Kyle's name but I continued holding my hand out. Finally, Bryce relinquished his phone.

I went into his settings and tried to find the name of the speakers. It took me a while to realize the speakers weren't turned on. When we finally powered them on, music blasted at both of us. I quickly turned down the volume, my ears ringing.

"You did it!" Bryce yelled loudly even though the music was low. His ears must've been ringing too. "Thanks."

I had taken one step back, ready to walk away, when I stopped myself. "Is Kyle seeing someone? Are he and Jodi a thing?" I'd wondered this before. Jodi had been in their band for at least a year. She was cute, with dyed-pink hair and a nose ring.

"They better not be," Bryce said with a half smile. "Since me and her are talking."

"Oh." I realized how much I wanted Kyle to have a good excuse when I was disappointed by that answer. I shook it off and left Bryce probably thinking I was pathetic.

Back by the tables, Micah was refilling the bowl of fancy potato salad that Jett had made. I wasn't sure, but it had tasted like it had grapes in it.

"Hey," I said. "Where's my brother?" I scanned the area but didn't see him.

"He's sitting right there." Micah turned toward the picnic table where we'd all been sitting. But it was empty. "He was just there a second ago." She turned a full circle, taking in the surrounding area.

My eyes went straight to the large grill, thinking Gunnar had gone to refill his plate, but he wasn't there. Then my head whipped to the water. Gunnar knew how to swim, but that didn't mean I didn't panic for a moment. It wasn't completely dark, but I pulled out my phone so I could shine my flashlight over the surface of the lake.

"You don't think he's out there, do you?" Micah asked, sounding nervous.

"No." I really didn't, but better safe than sorry. When my scan of the lake produced nothing, I calmed down a bit. He had to be here somewhere.

"Wait, where's Andrew?" Micah asked.

My phone buzzed with a text. It was from an unknown number. *Your brother dragged me to the boathouse.*

I held up the phone for Micah to see.

"That's Andrew's number," she said.

"Speaking of someone who has no self-control. He couldn't have waited until I got back?"

"Are you talking about Gunnar or Andrew?"

"Both."

Chapter 20

The boathouse was on the far side of the small lake. It was a decrepit building that used to store paddle boats and canoes but now mostly stored garbage. I wasn't sure how Andrew felt about being dragged around by my little brother, but Gunnar was my responsibility. I picked up my pace, jogging along the well-worn path that bordered the lake.

I could hear Gunnar's voice as I approached the building.

"And this is a kayak, or it used to be a kayak but now it has a hole in it."

"I think it's still a kayak," Andrew said.

I pushed open the wooden door that was only connected by one hinge. Andrew's phone flashlight was on, illuminating the scene with a soft glow.

"Sophie!" Gunnar said. "I was showing Andrew the boathouse. This is a paddle boat. Have you ever seen a paddle boat?"

"Yes, I have," Andrew said. "But I've never been on one."

"You've never been on a paddle boat?" Gunnar asked with a laugh.

"Gunnar," I said. "We better head back. The fireworks are about to start."

"Let's watch them from here." Gunnar pointed to the ceiling and I looked up to see a large jagged hole.

Andrew tilted the flashlight a little so it shone on his face, and he mouthed, *"He's scared of fireworks."*

I shook my head. I knew Gunnar wasn't scared, regardless of how self-assured in all opinions Andrew pretended to be. "We won't be able to see them that well from out here."

"They won't be as loud," Gunnar said.

"They'll probably be just as loud," I said.

"But maybe not," Andrew said back.

"Yeah," Gunnar said. "Maybe not."

Was Andrew right? Was Gunnar afraid? The first firework shot into the sky, and a big explosion of red lit the inside of the boathouse.

Gunnar jumped. "Let's just sit over there." He pointed to the far wall.

"Okay," I said, taking his hand. It was cold and clammy. We walked to the wall and sat down, Andrew on one side of Gunnar, me on the other.

As the next firework exploded in the sky, Gunnar buried his face in Andrew's shoulder.

"Told you," Andrew mouthed.

Of course he'd rub it in. I put my hand on Gunnar's arm. "Hey, kid. They're just fireworks. There's nothing to be afraid of."

Gunnar didn't budge and another loud boom went off. I looked up at the partial view we had through the decaying roof. I leaned against the wall, sure the entire back of my dress would be covered in dirt when we left, and watched the sky.

"When I was a kid, I was scared of thunder," I said.

"I thought you still were," Andrew said dryly.

"No, now I'm scared of rich boys who take over local businesses."

"Understandably."

A blue explosion lit the sky.

"I used to think that thunder sounded like the whole sky was fixin' to fall. I'd sit up in bed at night, unable to move. And Mom tried to tell me it was just a bunch of lightning bugs up there that were mad at each other. I knew that wasn't true, and I thought that if she had to tell me a lie then whatever was making that awful noise must've been something pretty bad."

"What did you do?" Gunnar asked, peeking up at me.

"Yes, what did you do?" Andrew asked, his twinkling eyes looking my way.

I glared at him and he smiled.

"I went on the computer and learned all about thunder. What caused it. Why it happened. And then I forced myself to sit on the porch one day during a lightning storm and watch it."

"But I know what fireworks are," Gunnar said.

"I know. But maybe you should watch a few. They're really pretty. You don't even have to move, just look up. Nothing bad is going to happen. The more you see that, the less scared you'll become."

Gunnar turned his head and watched several explode. "I know you think I'm being a baby," he said. "But I can't help it."

"I don't think you're being a baby," I said, surprised by his accusation. "There's not always a rhyme or a reason for fear."

"There's a reason for mine," he said.

"Oh yeah?"

"Last New Year's Eve when you were working, Momma had a party in the backyard and I was supposed to be asleep."

"What happened?" I asked, already dreading the answer.

"Some guys started shooting their guns into the sky and my window got broke and a piece of glass hit my arm and I thought I was shot. And nobody came to help me. And now loud noises just make me remember that." I could tell he was trying not to cry. He had his brave face on, the one that consisted of a quivering chin.

"What?" I said. "That's how your window was broken?" Anger coursed through my veins.

He nodded.

"Gunnar, I had no idea. I'm sorry. Why didn't you tell me?"

"Because I knew you'd get mad at Momma. You always get mad at her."

I swallowed hard. "I'm sorry. You can tell me things. Anything you need to. I'll try harder not to get mad."

Gunnar sat up and leaned against me instead of Andrew. I put my arm around him, and we all watched the fireworks together in silence for a while. We were quiet for so long that Gunnar's head drooped onto my shoulder and got heavier and heavier. His nerves had obviously made him exhausted.

"You know," Andrew said, "your Southern accent gets thicker when you tell stories."

"Yeah?"

"Yes."

"Probably because I was talking about my mom. She's Southern through and through."

"Speaking of. What's *too big for your britches* mean?"

"I didn't say that."

"I know, someone at the party said it."

"Let's see, how can I explain it? I guess it means you take yourself too seriously or think you're more important than you are."

"Oh," he said, sounding disappointed.

I smiled to myself. "Don't worry about it. People are a little prejudiced against city folk around here."

"They weren't talking about me," he said.

"Oh." Then it occurred to me. "Wait, were they talking about *me?*"

He shrugged. "It doesn't matter."

"Thanks," I said, feeling a bit defeated.

"I thought it was a good thing."

"Who said it?"

"Your mom."

I probably should've been more offended about that, but I actually felt the opposite. Maybe because I already knew my mom felt that way about me.

"If she doesn't like your plans for your future," Andrew asked after a minute, "what does she want you to do instead?"

"She wants me to be something more practical. Like a schoolteacher. Or a dentist."

"Your mom wants you to be a dentist?"

"They have job security. People will always have teeth."

Andrew laughed. "True. But you want to move to New York and be a designer?"

"I mean, first I want to go to design school there, but yes, eventually I want to be a designer." I heard my voice as I said it, and it didn't sound as convincing as it normally did.

"A fashion designer?"

"Yes."

"Says the girl who couldn't stand my designer suit."

"Says the girl who knows when designer suits are appropriate."

A smile touched his lips. He looked down at his phone and pushed a button on the screen. His flashlight went off. Now we could see the fireworks even clearer.

"What about you?" I asked. "What do you want to do?"

"I honestly have no idea. My dad wants me to be a web

designer. I guess I already know how to do that and it feels like people will always need that kind of service."

"But you don't want to do that?"

He shrugged one shoulder. "It works for now."

"What about pictures?"

"What about them?"

"You seem to enjoy that aspect. Maybe you could do photography."

Andrew shrugged again. "My dad is like your mom in that way. He's told me all the reasons that photography is not a very stable career choice."

"Your dad is a chef! That is a dream-fulfillment career if I've ever heard of one."

"I think that's part of the problem." Andrew fiddled with his phone. "He knows how hard it was to break in, to stay in. He doesn't think it was worth the stress."

The firework finale began, one explosion on top of another, and we fell silent to watch what we could through the opening. Then everything was still, and I swore I felt the fireworks still rumbling in my chest.

"Do you have an actual camera or just your phone?" I asked.

"My phone *is* an actual camera," he said.

"I know but . . ."

"No, I don't have a fancy camera. Website pictures don't need to be blown up or anything, so a really nice phone camera works perfectly well." He leaned his head back on the wall.

"One time I saw this camera. It was one of those older ones where you had to hand wind the film. I wanted it so bad, but my dad pretty much controls my bank account."

"So you didn't get it."

"No."

I wasn't sure what to say in response to that. I'd already said many times what I thought about his dad. I didn't think that would help right now.

Andrew nodded toward the hole in the ceiling. "That's kind of like a picture. We only get to see a part of the whole."

"Except in this case the part is picked for us." I tilted my head to try to see more of the sky. "How do you ever decide which part of the whole you're going to include in an actual picture?"

He turned his phone light back on and held up his hands, creating a square with his fingers. He gestured for me to do the same. I did, then he moved my arms until my hands were pointing at a section of the paddle boat. "You just find the part that stands out the most or makes the most interesting shapes or tells the best story."

Through the square made by my fingers, I could see the pedals of the boat. One was barely attached, dangling as if about to fall, the other in perfect working order.

"And if you don't find it with your first shot, you have all the chances you want." Andrew moved the frame of my hands to the corner where an intricate spider web spanned the space between two walls. I stared at it, a wisp of inspiration winding its way through my mind. The skirt, I could make it different. Unique. Webbing. I could add a lining and trim the bottom with my own design of lace. It could work.

I dropped my hands back into my lap, realizing I'd been quiet for too long.

"You're good at that," I told Andrew at last. "You should get a camera and make art."

He laughed a little, as if to say it wasn't that easy.

"Well, my mom doesn't get to dictate my future," I said. "I'm going to New York." There, that sounded more convincing.

"New York is . . ."

"Amazing?" I asked.

"It's pretty great. It's a hard place to make it. It can eat you alive."

My lips tightened. Great. The only person I'd ever talked to who had actually been to New York agreed with my mom. He didn't think I'd survive there either.

"I better get back outside," I said. "Those flowers aren't going to clean themselves up." I shook Gunnar's shoulder until he opened his eyes and then I helped him to his feet.

Chapter 21

Gunnar, Andrew, and I headed back toward the picnic area. The park lights were on and I watched people packing up and clearing out.

"Where've y'all been?" Micah asked as we approached.

"Hide-and-seek," Andrew said, which obviously only confused Micah even more.

Gunnar thought it was funny, though. "I think I won."

"I don't know," Andrew said. "Sophie found us, so I think she won."

Micah's gaze shifted between Andrew and me and she gave me questioning eyes. I mouthed, *I'll tell you later.*

She nodded. "Caroline already left. She said she had a pounding migraine and that you'd have to clean up without her."

I laughed. "I always clean up without her."

"I know. I had to bite my tongue to keep from saying that very thing."

Andrew nodded toward his dad, who was packing away dishes. "Speaking of cleaning up, I better go help."

"See you later," Micah said.

"Is the next big event really not until October?" Andrew asked.

"Are you going to miss us?" I asked.

"Not you, Evans, but Micah for sure."

I smiled, but the jab didn't bother me as much as it normally would have.

"You don't have to miss me," Micah said. "I'll text you. Let's do something."

Andrew's eyes flitted to me, like he thought I suddenly wanted to hang out with him outside of work. I just held up my hands. "Have fun, you two."

He joined up with his dad, and Micah said, "What was that about? You two looked as thick as thieves walking out of the dark night together."

"With my little brother," I reminded her.

"Little brother or not, I know a happy glow when I see one."

I made a face. "Give me a break. More like an angry glow. Andrew had just gotten through telling me that he didn't think I'd make it in New York."

"He said that?"

"Yes."

Micah pursed her lips. "That was not very nice."

"It doesn't matter what he thinks. It doesn't matter what anybody thinks." At least that's what I told myself.

"Atta girl."

I picked up half a grape off the table and held it up. "Who puts grapes in potato salad?"

"Apparently Jett Hart," Micah said.

"And now your dad. Is he happy that he's doing this yet? Is it going to work?"

"He's decided to see it through. He got a call to cater a fancy benefit dinner in Birmingham in August."

"Birmingham? That's almost two hours away!"

"I know."

"I thought you guys were going to try to expand to closer areas."

"We are. But two hours isn't bad and people in the city are willing to pay more money."

"Really? That's good news."

Micah nodded. "My parents were having a heated debate last night about whether or not Jett himself had convinced the party host to hire my dad. But either way, it's a job, right?"

"Which side of the debate were you on?" I asked.

"I was Switzerland." She gathered some used plastic forks off the table and put them in the trash. "Which side would you have been on?"

"Do you want me to be honest or encouraging?"

"Honest."

"I think Jett had some pull. This town has been averse to the changes Jett's made. So I can't imagine that word of mouth has caused some fancy benefit host to call in."

"You would've been on my dad's side." Micah held up a

finger. "But we've gotten some good reviews online, like my mom pointed out. Mostly from her friends, but out-of-towners don't know that. And my dad is hoping that because the people won't have any preconceived notions of what the food *normally* is, that they won't have already formed an opinion about it."

"He makes a good point. The food *is* pretty amazing." I flicked another grape off the table. "That said, I don't know if *our* town is ready for this change. Jett might be a little out of touch with his client base."

"I've heard my dad say that to Jett so often that I'm surprised Jett hasn't commanded it never to be said in his kitchen again." Micah was quiet for a moment, then said, "I'm sorry Jett didn't turn out to be an in for you."

I poured the water from a vase onto the grass and tucked the empty vase away in a box. I shrugged. "I don't need an in. I'll get there. I'm just glad he seems to be working out for you guys. Maybe the Birmingham event will lead to more referrals."

"That's what my dad hopes."

"Well, I'm sure Andrew will feel much closer to home in Birmingham."

A shadowy figure walked up behind Micah and into the ring of light from the overhead park lamp. It was Kyle.

"Hey, Soph, you want to go grab dessert?" he asked.

My stomach jumped in surprise. "Right *now*?" I looked at my phone. It was after ten o'clock.

"Yes, you should go," Micah said too quickly. "I'll take Gunnar home in the flower van for you." She had arranged this, I was sure of it. She widened her eyes at me.

If I hadn't wanted to go out with Kyle, I wouldn't have gotten so upset about his rejection earlier. This *was* what I wanted, right? "Right. I mean, sure, okay, sounds good."

"Cool." Kyle walked toward his Mustang. Apparently I was supposed to follow.

"Cool," Micah echoed.

"Can't decide if I'm mad at you," I said.

"Have fun," she said with an innocent smile.

I caught up to Kyle just as we passed Andrew and his dad loading the last of their things into their car. Andrew lifted his hand in a wave and I moved to do the same when Kyle reached back and slid his fingers between mine. By the time I got over the shock of Kyle holding my hand, Andrew and his dad had climbed into their car and driven away.

John Farnsworth Funeral

LILY

With a large, trumpetlike shape, the lily seems to want
to announce its presence from rooftops. And yet it is
said that a lily symbolizes the soul departing from life
and being restored to innocence. Not really sure who sat
around once upon a time deciding which flower
symbolized what, but the lily drew the short end of
the stick on that one. Instead of trumpeting away at
parties, it has to attend a lot of funerals.

Chapter 22

I brought in the last arrangement and set it on a side table in the chapel, beside the three other flower arrangements. Lilies. They reminded me of the town gas station, which seemed random, but the owner there kept a jar full of pens at the register. And on the ends of those pens were colorful fake lilies, their stems attached with green floral tape.

For the last two weeks, though, that gas station had reminded me of Kyle. When he and I had left the park to get dessert on the Fourth of July, nothing in town was open. So Kyle drove us to the gas station, and we sat in his Mustang with the top down, eating Hostess cupcakes and watching bottle rockets light the sky. It should've been romantic, but then Kyle said, "I could spend every Fourth of July for the rest of my life right here," and I knew. I knew that the quiz I had taken with Micah was wrong. Kyle and I weren't compatible. At least that's what I'd thought that night. Then I'd spent the next two weeks wondering if I was just sabotaging myself. If I was trying too hard or not trying hard enough. If I was reading into things or not reading into things enough. After all, if

I'd been thinking about this, about Kyle, for the last two weeks, didn't that say something?

"That's it?" Caroline asked, bringing me out of my memory. I looked up to see my boss pointing to the lily arrangement I'd just set down. I had already brought in the large standing spray that Caroline had spent the entire morning on. The family had ordered it and it would stand by the casket at the front of the church. "Four arrangements?" Caroline added, frowning. "Nobody else ordered one?"

Funerals were different from most events we did. The flowers for funerals depended solely on attendees' orders. And John was . . . well, John. Not exactly the winner of any popularity contests. "Yep, just four." I wasn't about to tell her that I had bought one myself when I saw how few orders we had. I liked John. I liked him even more after our interaction at the Valentine's Day Dinner. It was the best fake money I'd ever spent. Remembering that brought a lump to my throat.

Caroline looked at her watch. "We have time. Will you run back to the shop and grab two or three more arrangements from our half-off fridge?" The half-off fridge was full of flowers that hadn't sold in their prime. Caroline shook her head. "Poor old bugger. He was grouchy in life so people are trying to prove a point with his death."

"I think he was misunderstood," I said.

She waved her hand at the flowers. "There's no misunderstanding here."

"I'll run to the store." I walked down the aisle between the pews and to the outer foyer. A side room was open and the Farnsworth family was gathered there for the viewing. It was very quiet. The open casket sat on one end of the room and John's family sat in chairs lined up on the other. I was sure they'd already said their goodbyes and now had no idea what to do with the lifeless form in the room.

When I got the first call at the shop three days ago, from one of John's sons, he had said it was a heart attack. That it happened in the night and he passed on peacefully. I swallowed the lump in my throat.

I kept walking and stepped outside. "Sorry about the lack of flowers, John," I said to the sky.

"Are you talking to dead people?" Micah was leaning against the flower van.

"Yes, actually," I said. "Nobody but family, well, and me, bought him flowers." It wasn't until the words were out of my mouth that I noticed Andrew coming over to join Micah. "What are you two doing here?" I added. "This event isn't catered." Much like the flowers, in this town the food was brought to an open house, potluck-style, after the graveside service.

Andrew cleared his throat. "My dad made a dish to bring to the family later, but Micah said it would be strange to show up at the house without having attended the funeral. So here I am. And this feels stranger to me—going to the funeral of a man I've never met."

"You met him." I walked around to the driver's side and climbed into the flower van.

"Are you going somewhere?" Micah asked.

"Yes, I have to run back to the shop."

Micah slid open a side door and gestured for Andrew to get in. He did, and Micah climbed in after him and shut the door.

"I've met him?" Andrew asked as I started the van.

"At the Valentine's Dinner. He was my dessert date."

"The guy who gave me a hard time when you were the one abusing me?"

I looked both ways and pulled out onto the street. "I disagree with your memory but yes, that guy."

"See," Micah said, "you have met him. Now you can stop whining about having to come to this. Besides, weren't you just saying at the Fourth of July thing that you were bummed there wasn't another event until October? Your wish has been granted."

"I wasn't wishing death upon someone!" Andrew said.

"It's the silver lining," Micah said. Then she leaned forward and tugged on the layered sleeve of my black blouse. "You look cute."

"Thanks."

"What about me?" Andrew asked. "Do I look cute?"

"No," I said at the same time Micah said, "Always."

"Why do you encourage him?" I asked.

Micah pinched his chin. "Because look at this face. It's so adorable."

Andrew smirked, eating up the praise.

Micah turned her attention to the road in front of us. "Where are we going again?" she asked me.

I made a left onto Main Street. "Like I said, we only have four flower arrangements. I'm getting a few more from the shop."

"We get to see headquarters?" Andrew asked.

"Yes, you get to see where Sophie gets her powers," Micah replied with a laugh.

"Ugh," I said. "You get to see what drains all my energy in a huge fragrant time suck."

In the rearview mirror, Micah gave me a big eye roll. On the right, we passed Everything, and then I pulled into the parking lot of Every Occasion.

I shut off the engine, and we climbed out of the van. The sign on the door of the shop announced we were closed for the John Farnsworth funeral, basically shaming anyone who wasn't doing the same. I unlocked the door and held it open for Micah and Andrew. The scent in the shop was powerful. Roses, mainly, with a hint of decay. The door shut behind me with a bell ring.

Two walls of the shop were glass-doored fridges to keep the already-arranged flowers fresh. The display table at the center of the shop was full of various types of fresh-cut flowers. We also had a wall with cards and small stuffed animals.

"We won't be here long," I said, making my way to the half-off fridge on the back wall. I examined the selection in there. Most were completely inappropriate for a funeral—a pink-and-red rose display, a cheery yellow-daisy-and-orange-chrysanthemum arrangement—but I found some more neutral options. One that was all white roses, one that was various shades of hydrangeas. I remembered we had some leftover lilies in the back, so I decided I would quickly grab those as well.

Andrew laughed from somewhere behind me, and I turned to see him examining the large standing chalkboard in the corner. We usually displayed it right outside the door during business hours. Caroline used it to make store announcements. I used it to highlight different flowers. This morning, before we closed, I had added a paragraph about lilies. At first Caroline hadn't liked my snarky, seemingly negative assessments of flowers, but the customers liked them so much that she'd eventually come around. Now I'd even found her chuckling at a few.

I went to the back, grabbed the bucket of lilies, and brought them to the front counter.

"So many lilies." Micah picked a large white one out of the bucket and tucked it in her tight curls, which she wore natural today.

"Didn't you say lilies were your favorite?" Andrew asked, walking over to the counter.

He remembered what I said my favorite flower was? "No, I said calla lilies were my favorite."

"Um . . ."

"They're not the same thing," I said. "They're not even in the same genus." Okay, so I wouldn't have known this before working at the store, but that didn't mean I wasn't going to use it against him.

"They just have similar names," Micah said. "Not sure why you would've confused them at all."

"Gee, thanks," Andrew said.

I looked back and forth between two vases, trying to decide which one I wanted to use. I picked the one on the right. I didn't have a lot of time so I bundled a group of lilies together in my hand, creating a symmetrical pattern.

A car pulled up outside.

"Is that Mrs. Davis?" Micah asked, peering through the store windows. "I'll go tell her the shop is closed before she has to get her three kids out of the car."

Andrew pushed himself off the counter to follow Micah but she held up her hand. "I got it. Stay here, I'll be right back."

"I think she did that on purpose," I said after Micah had left.

"What?"

"Left us alone. She wants us to be friends."

"She's delusional," he said.

I laughed. "So delusional. Hold these."

He took the flowers from me. I clipped the stems and added several more to the bundle in his hand.

"What's the secret to a good arrangement?" he asked.

"Shape," I said, and took a step back to get a better look. "Good enough." I slid the vase up the stems and Andrew released his hold.

187

"They look nice," he said.

"You can't compliment the ones I make in less than five minutes."

"It's the first one I've seen that you weren't making specifically with a client in mind."

I shook my head. "I definitely had John Farnsworth in mind."

"The dead guy? How so?"

"I used lots of lilies."

The bell rang on the door and Micah poked her head in. "My friends, we should probably go before we miss the funeral."

"We wouldn't want that." Andrew picked up the two arrangements I'd pulled out of the fridge and I carried out the third. This would be a much better showing. John deserved it.

Chapter 23

At the pulpit, Pastor Greenley was giving a sermon about death and salvation. One of John's grandsons, Joseph, in from out of town, kept looking over his shoulder to where Micah sat in the back row of the chapel, smiling at her.

"That guy is going to give himself a neck strain," Andrew said. "This is a funeral. Even I know it's not the appropriate time to flirt."

"Everyone deals with grief in different ways," Micah said, smiling at Joseph as he looked back again.

"Do you see the good in everyone?" Andrew asked.

"Pretty much," she whispered.

"She's more forgiving of the cute ones," I said.

"So untrue," she said.

The couple sitting in front of us turned around and shot us annoyed looks. We went silent.

The sermon wasn't too long and it was followed by John's son giving a eulogy. There was a large photograph of John set up by the casket and I stared at it as the words about his life were read: He'd served in the military; he was married for fifty-four years; he had two sons, one daughter, and eight grandchildren. He volunteered at the veterans' hospital; he had a problem with alcohol when he was younger that he overcame. The facts of his life were read off like a checklist and I, like I assumed most people did at funerals, started thinking about what facts would be read at mine.

She got by in school; she loved her brother; everyone loved her best friend; she longed for a life she couldn't even imagine because it was so foreign to her.

"He had a special place in his heart for the underdog," John's son said, bringing me back to the moment. "Probably because he felt like he was one. So he always stood up for them."

"I guess that makes you an underdog," Andrew whispered.

I elbowed him in the ribs and he let out a grunt.

Mr. Farnsworth finished up with a teary declaration of gratitude to his father and then sat down.

Pastor Greenley stood back up again. "We will now all proceed to the graveside. After the burial, Mrs. Lawson has opened up her home for a reception." He closed with a prayer and then everyone was leaving.

Andrew headed for the door with the rest of the congregation but stopped when neither Micah nor I followed.

"We have to bring the flowers," Micah said.

"Oh, right." He came back to stand next to us.

Joseph headed up the aisle right next to us and gave Micah a wink as he passed. I shot him a dirty look and Andrew chuckled. I scanned the rest of the people filing by. I hadn't seen Kyle during the ceremony and I didn't see him now. The last of the patrons left the room and then it was just the three of us. Micah grabbed the flowers from the pulpit while I went for the ones on the credenza next to the wall.

"Um . . ." Andrew said.

"What?" I asked.

"I think the family forgot something."

"What?" I asked again, joining him. "Oh." The casket sat unassuming on its wheels, the large picture of John and the spray of flowers on either side.

"They forgot?" Micah asked. "Isn't that what pallbearers are for? It's like their only job."

"Maybe they forgot to assign pallbearers," I said. "Or the pallbearers were just thinking they were required at the cemetery?"

"I'm sure the hearse is out front right now," Andrew said. "The hearse wouldn't leave without the casket."

"You know who drives the hearse?" Micah said.

I put a hand to my forehead. "Oh crap, you're right. Harry."

"What's wrong with Harry?" Andrew asked.

"He's a total space case," I explained. "He'd forget his own name if someone asked him."

We were all walking to the double doors that led out of the chapel. By the time we got outside, we saw the last car pulling away. Only the flower van remained.

"It's possible . . ." Andrew said, staring at the van.

"No," I said.

Andrew crossed his arms. "Why not? By the time they get to the cemetery, realize the mistake, and come back, it will be forever. It's hot out here. Hot and muggy. Do you really want to make everyone wait outside for Mr. Farnsworth?"

"We couldn't even lift that casket with just the three of us," I said.

"It's on wheels," Micah said. Why did she always take his side? Even when it was dumb. "And the cemetery is twenty-five minutes away."

"I know how far the cemetery is," I said. "They'll realize before they get there." I looked at both of them. Andrew had an *of course you're chicken* look on his face, while Micah had a *they will never realize* one on hers.

I let out a breath.

"Fine," I said. "Let's see how hard it is to move."

Andrew smirked like he'd just played me. He hadn't. Micah's logical argument—the distance to the cemetery— was what swayed me.

The casket was surprisingly easy to wheel down the aisle and out the doors. It was when we got to the back of the flower van that we realized we might be in trouble. The van was higher than the casket. I began clearing away buckets and bins so we'd have room.

"I think there's a way to raise or lower the wheels," Andrew said, bending down.

"Like an office chair?" I asked.

"Yes, something like that, smart aleck." Despite his confidence in casket knowledge, though, Andrew couldn't find this device he was sure existed.

"Well, we tried," I said.

"Is this really happening?" Micah wondered out loud.

Andrew pointed. "How about if I stand at the end, and you two lift it up front from the sides so it clears the lip, and then I shove from the back?"

"You'll be in the back?" I asked. "Okay, yeah, let's see how that plays out."

Andrew crossed his arms. "She wants me to get smashed. By a coffin."

"It was your idea," I said. "I'm just agreeing with it."

"While she's picturing you being smashed," Micah said.

"Are we going to try this or not?" I moved into position.

Andrew got into place, putting his back against the end of the casket. "Ready?" He paused for a minute. "You're actually going to try, right?"

I laughed, Micah laughing along with me.

"It's a fair question," Andrew said.

"We'll try!" she said.

For a moment I had a surge of guilt at how we were acting. There was an actual dead body in this casket. But then a realization came over me.

"John would've found this hilarious," I said. An image of him eating that tiny cup of dessert, of him telling Andrew to move along, popped into my mind. His smiling, satisfied face. His bright, shining eyes. And suddenly I was crying.

"Soph," Micah said, coming around the casket and putting her arms around me, which immediately had this way of making me feel better. "What's wrong?"

"One of her only dates in the last year is dead," Andrew said.

"Seriously," Micah said to him, "you think now is the time?"

"I was trying to lighten the mood."

I closed my eyes and took a deep breath. The finality of John's life had just hit me. Had he done everything he wanted to do? Did he feel like nobody understood him? Like nobody supported him? Was he ready to move on? "It's fine. I'm fine," I said, wiping beneath my eyes.

"Are you sure?" Micah asked. It's not that she'd never seen me cry, but it was still a pretty rare occasion.

I nodded. A car pulling up beside us had me straightening up. I wiped my eyes again and looked over. The long black hearse idled there.

Harry rolled down the window. He was twentysomething and clueless. "Yeah, we forgot that."

"You think?" Micah said.

Harry hopped out and, like it was nothing, transferred the casket into the back of the hearse. The wheels being the exact right height really did make a difference.

"Bye, Micah. Later, Sophie," he said. He climbed back into the hearse and was off.

"Am I invisible?" Andrew asked, and sat down on the back of the van.

"He just didn't know your name," I said. "So it's more polite to ignore you."

Micah rolled her eyes. "That's not true." She looked at Andrew. "You're like a celebrity around here so people are embarrassed to treat you with familiarity."

I scoffed.

"It's true!" Micah said.

I watched the hearse disappear down the street.

"You okay?" Micah asked.

I didn't have time for this weird breakdown I seemed to be in the middle of. "The flowers are supposed to be graveside too," I said.

"Then I guess we'd better get them," Micah said, and started heading back to the church.

Andrew was a little slower to comply. He lingered, as though he had something to say.

"I don't have time for you to analyze me," I told him. "Keep it to yourself."

He shrugged and walked off after Micah.

Chapter 24

The graveside service itself was surprisingly uneventful. Hot, a bit depressing, but uneventful. Now we were at Mrs. Lawson's house. I stood in the middle of the crowded living room all alone. Micah and Andrew had driven over with me, but now I couldn't find them and I was ready to go home.

"Soph." There was a tap on my arm and I turned to see Kyle.

"Hey, you're here." I swore I said those words to him more often than normal. Was it weird that I was always surprised to see him somewhere? "I mean, I didn't see you at the church."

"Yeah, I wasn't there. Had band practice." He nodded his head to Jodi, who was at the table filling up a plate with food. I didn't see Bryce or Lincoln, though. "Are you here alone?" Kyle asked me.

"No. I'm here with . . . friends," I said. It would be nice if those friends showed up now so I didn't seem so pathetic, but apparently Andrew only appeared when I didn't want him to.

"Cool," Kyle said. "I'm going to go get some food."

"Okay. Have fun." Have fun?

He gave me a slow smile and joined Jodi at the food table.

We'd been out three times. Interactions shouldn't still be so awkward. I wound my way through the crowd and out to the back patio. It was empty except for two couches and a porch swing. I opted for the porch swing.

Minutes later, Andrew walked outside with a plate of food. Of course he'd show up now.

"For one second I was wondering why everyone was packed inside and nobody was out here," Andrew said. "But then I was suffocated by the air and understood perfectly."

"Yeah, it's hot," I agreed.

He sat down next to me, the swing jostling a little.

"Where's Micah?" I asked.

"I saw her talking to Lance," he said.

"Oh, okay."

"They like each other, right?" Andrew said. "Tell me I'm not the only one who sees that."

I laughed a little, glad *I* wasn't the only one who thought that. "They already dated once. You know how stubborn Micah is. Maybe you can talk some sense into her."

"I may have mentioned it a couple of times, but you're right, she shuts me down." He looked at his food. "So, etiquette coach, what is the appropriate amount of time to stay at a funeral reception?"

"We have done our duty. We just need to get Micah."

"Maybe we should give her a minute, considering who she's talking to." He took a bite of ambrosia salad. "What is this?" he asked through his mouthful.

"Dessert pretending to be healthy."

He nodded. "What are the little chunks?"

I looked at what remained on his plate. "I don't know. Probably coconut?"

He scooped up a bite and held it out for me. "That is not coconut. Try it."

I wasn't in the mood to argue. I ate the salad off his fork, let it sit in my mouth for a moment, then said, "Cherries? Is that what you're tasting?"

"Ah. That's probably it. I'm not a maraschino cherry fan."

"That's one of those things people are either passionate about or loathe. Like cilantro."

"Or pecan pie," he said.

"Pecan pie?" I asked. "There is no debate about pecan pie. And if there is, then you haven't tried . . ." I trailed off, about to sound like a small-town girl again.

"Whose pecan pie do I need to try?"

"Never mind. You don't know her."

He nodded slowly. Then, despite his claimed hatred of maraschino cherries, he continued to eat the salad. "Do you believe in an afterlife?"

"From pecan pie to the afterlife? That's quite a jump."

"Funerals."

"Yes."

"Yes, you believe in an afterlife? Or yes, funerals?"

"Yes, I believe in an afterlife." I paused and looked up at the clouds. "I'm not sure exactly what it will consist of, but I believe we all have a soul, something that makes us who we are. When my gran died, I remember looking at her body and knowing something was missing, that she was no longer her." I gave him a sideways glance. "What about you?"

"I agree."

"Wow, something we agree on," I said.

"I know, weird." He tapped his foot a few times on a nail that was jutting out of the wooden railing around the porch. "Is that why you got upset today? Because this reminded you of your grandmother's funeral?"

"There it is," I said. "I knew you couldn't resist analyzing me."

"I just need this last little puzzle piece and then I'll have you all figured out." I could tell he was kidding but I wondered for a small moment if there was a hint of truth in there—if he really did think he'd figured me all out. Maybe he could provide me with a list because I was feeling a bit undefined lately.

"Let's find Micah so we can leave," I said.

"Something else we can agree on." Andrew took one more bite of food and we stood. He dumped his plate in a metal trash can by the back door and we went inside. The cool air-conditioning immediately brought relief, but the noise level inside was intense. We stayed together, searching the living room, the halls, the bedrooms. I even knocked on the bathroom door, but it was not Micah who responded.

"I left my phone in the van," I said to Andrew. "Do you have yours?"

"I left mine in the van too, since at the cemetery you told us that was the polite thing to do."

I sighed. "I did, didn't I? I guess I *am* your etiquette coach."

"Country-living etiquette. I'll return the favor if you ever come to New York."

I clenched my jaw and headed for the front door. I didn't need a lesson on city etiquette. I had common sense, unlike him.

I'd parked down the street so I hurried there ahead of Andrew. I noticed Kyle's car before I saw him in it. The Mustang was parked behind the flower van and I saw some movement inside. The engine was running. Was he waiting for me?

But when I approached the passenger side, it was apparent that Kyle wasn't in there alone. Jodi was in the passenger seat, and they were kissing. I gasped just as Andrew came up beside me.

Kyle must've heard or sensed something because he stopped kissing Jodi. He looked over, saw me, and gave a head nod. I didn't wait to see what came after that head nod. Jodi was already starting to turn around. With my cheeks flushed, I fled up the road, past the flower van, car keys clutched tightly in my hand.

Andrew caught up with me. "Hey, you okay?"

"What? Why wouldn't I be?" I didn't mean to snap at him, but I did.

"That was Kyle. I thought you and he . . . ?"

"What? Yeah, no, it doesn't matter. We weren't . . . I didn't even . . ." *Like him* was how I was going to finish that sentence. And I knew that was true, but it didn't mean I wasn't hurt and that was hard to explain. I didn't want to explain. "It's a funeral" was how I finished instead.

"People mourn differently?" Andrew offered, repeating Micah's sentiment.

There was a neighborhood park at the end of the street and I cut right, heading across the grass toward the big slide tower. I climbed the steps and sat at the very top, leaning my back against the blue metal bars. Andrew followed and sat opposite me, our legs stretched out alongside each other. The platform was smaller than I'd anticipated.

"I forgot to get my phone," I said.

"Me too."

I slipped off my shoes and pressed my toes into the bars next to him.

"So," Andrew said, "you're definitely moving Kyle to the undatable column of Micah's spreadsheet, right?"

I laughed a little and rolled my eyes. "You think I'm upset. You think I had something with Kyle?"

"I think you did."

"We didn't. Not really," I said. "And there is no actual spreadsheet, you know that, right?" I blew out a breath between my lips. "It honestly doesn't matter. We start school in a couple of weeks. It's senior year and then as soon as that's done, I'm leaving."

We sat in silence for a few minutes. I wiped at some flakes of blue paint that were chipping off the metal bars, trying to act like I was perfectly fine. Because I really wanted to be. I should be. I was.

"You're not going to miss it here?" Andrew finally asked.

I brushed my hands together. "I'll miss Micah. But she wants to stay, work with her dad. I'll come back and visit tons. My brother lives here."

"And your mom."

"Right . . . and her."

"You won't miss her?"

"I love my mom."

Andrew nodded. "Your mom's not so bad."

"We're just very different."

"True." He smiled at me. "So . . . senior year."

"I know. Yours too. But . . . how is that when you do independent study? Are you still as excited?"

"For school to be over? Yes."

"I guess that's true. But I don't know, there's something about being on a school campus and being the oldest and . . . I don't know."

"I get it. It's a rite of passage. One I'll miss." He was quiet for a minute, then said, "I've thought about going back to school for my senior year."

"But . . . ?"

"But then we move."

"Right."

"Right." He bumped his knee into mine and, for the second time in the conversation, changed the subject. "Do you realize I've only ever seen you wear skirts? Do you own a pair of jeans?"

"You only ever see me at events."

"There was that one time Micah and I saw you at the movies."

I nodded, remembering our brief interaction; I'd been taking Gunnar to see the latest superhero flick and had bumped into Micah and Andrew in the lobby.

"Was I wearing a skirt?" I asked.

"You were."

"Huh. Good thing I have killer legs," I said, lifting one up.

"You do." His eyes went to my foot and narrowed in on something there. "It made a pretty good scar."

"Excuse me?"

He grabbed my foot and ran a finger along the middle. "The glass."

I pulled my foot away as a zing went up my leg. "You've touched my feet entirely more than anyone should have to."

"Very true."

"Hello! Are you guys over here?" Micah yelled out. She was standing at the entrance to the parking lot, waving. "Let's go home!"

I reached forward to grab my shoes and Andrew must've leaned forward to stand up because suddenly we were shoulder to shoulder, his face inches from mine.

"Sorry," he breathed. "Go ahead."

I stood quickly. "We're up here!"

Micah ran up the stairs to the slide, then plopped down between us, pulling us both back down to sitting with her. There definitely wasn't room for all three of us.

"What have you been up to?" Andrew asked in a teasing voice.

"Oh, you know . . ." Micah said. "I ran into Joseph."

"Joseph?" I asked in surprise. "Andrew said you were talking to Lance."

"I was, but then Joseph came and we had a nice talk."

I sighed in frustration. "You just need to give Lance another chance already," I said.

Micah's brows dipped down. "What? Why would I do that? We're not . . . I'm not . . . Lance wants to go away to college," she said matter-of-factly.

"And?" I asked.

"And long-distance relationships never work." She looked between Andrew and me as if that statement was for us. She really *was* delusional if she thought that applied to us. "What have you guys been doing?" she asked.

Andrew looked at me, a challenge in his eyes. He probably wanted me to tell Micah what had just happened with Kyle and Jodi. But I didn't want to talk about it anymore than I already had. It was over.

"Sophie needs to bare her soul," Andrew said.

"I do not." I didn't appreciate his prying. I met his challenging glare, grabbed hold of the bar above the twirly slide, and sent myself sliding down.

Micah laughed and followed after me. Andrew took the stairs. Micah hooked one arm in Andrew's elbow and one in mine as we headed back toward the van.

"I didn't get to try your dad's salad today," Micah told Andrew. "It was gone by the time I went to get a plate."

"It's a good salad," Andrew responded.

"Plus, like four people brought hash-brown casserole," I said. "So there wasn't much variety."

A sleek black car that had become familiar to me by now screeched around the corner and stopped next to us on the street. Jett Hart climbed out of it and slammed the door behind him, fire in his eyes.

Chapter 25

"Where is your phone?" was the first thing Jett barked at Andrew.

Andrew pointed to the flower van. "I left it in there."

"I asked you to deliver a dish and our sympathy, not to stay and hang with the locals."

Micah and I exchanged a glance.

"I'm sorry, I thought I should attend the funeral," Andrew said in a quiet voice.

"Of a stranger?" Jett snapped.

"He wasn't exactly—" Andrew started but was interrupted by the more powerful voice of his father.

"I have been trying to get ahold of you for over an hour. This total lack of regard for anyone but yourself is wearing on me, Andrew."

"He just told you he went to a funeral. How is that selfish?" Once it was out of my mouth, I realized I should've kept it in there. This was not my battle, not anywhere close to it, but suddenly I'd just made it that.

Jett's angry eyes turned on me. "Did I ask for your opinion?"

"When I see someone in the wrong, I give my opinion without it being asked for." Great, there was no controlling my tongue now; it had a mind of its own. Micah nudged me.

"Andrew," Jett said, obviously choosing to ignore me and my unasked-for opinion. "Gather your things and be home in thirty minutes." With that, Jett got into the car and drove off.

I wasn't sure why Jett had left without Andrew. Maybe my pushback threw him off. Maybe he didn't want to ride in the same car as his now-seething son.

Silence stretched between the three of us until finally Andrew said, "Why did you do that?"

"Me?" I asked, when I realized I was the only person he could be talking to. Micah had remained silent through the whole encounter.

I looked at Andrew. I'd thought he was angry at his dad. But he was angry at me? "Because you weren't saying anything. You were just letting him walk all over you, like normal."

A muscle jumped in Andrew's cheek. "I can handle my father."

"It didn't look like it."

He faced me full-on. "You don't know everything, Sophie, even when you act like you do," he said.

"Ditto," I shot back.

Then just like his dad, Andrew stormed off.

"Seriously?" I turned toward Micah, confused. "They're both jerks."

She crossed her arms over her chest. "Soph, come on. You did kind of overstep some boundaries there."

"You heard his dad. He was treating him like dirt."

"His dad was angry because he couldn't get ahold of Andrew. You know how parents are."

"He was degrading him like he always does. Like he does everyone."

Micah sighed. "Well, you better go find Andrew and say you're sorry."

"You want me to apologize? I did nothing wrong."

"Soph, just swallow your pride and apologize so we can leave?"

I whirled around. Why was everyone being so annoying today? And why was I having to search everyone out? I just wanted to go to a flippin' funeral in peace. I had a mind to walk straight to the flower van and drive away. But I didn't. Instead I circled Mrs. Lawson's house angrily. Andrew wasn't inside. I pushed through the back door, walked the porch, then the yard, and finally found him leaning against a shed.

"I'm sorry," I spit out.

Andrew avoided my gaze. "Do you know what those words mean? Because you used them all wrong."

I put my hands on my hips. "Can we just go?"

"Go ahead. I didn't ask you to wait for me."

"We drove here together."

He was silent, his head down.

So stubborn.

208

"Am I that bad?" I asked, stepping closer to him. "I'm the only person in your life who's ever told you that your dad is a jerk? I find that really hard to believe."

He finally looked up at me. "It is none of your business. That's the point."

"Oh, but who Kyle kisses and how that relates to me is *your* business?"

"That's not even close to the same thing."

I stepped closer again and jabbed his chest with my finger. "It's exactly the same thing. And if someone—even your dad—is talking to you like that when you don't deserve it, then I'm going to call them out on it."

Andrew grabbed my wrist, pulling my hand away from his chest. "And if you're just going to pretend you're perfectly okay when it's obvious you're not, then I'm going to call *you* out on it."

"Fine!"

"Fine," he said.

My eyes shot down to his hand holding my wrist then back up to his face. His blue eyes were intense, his lips slightly parted from the sharp breaths he was taking. And suddenly my body seemed to be on autopilot. I leaned forward and pressed an angry kiss to his lips.

He froze, and then so did I, our lips pressed together. Then all at once his free hand moved to the back of my neck. His hand still gripping my wrist pulled me closer, bringing my hand around his back. He tilted his head, deepening our kiss. I took a quick breath in through my nose as a jolt of electricity surged through my body. I wrapped my arms around him, my body against his. He rotated 180 degrees and pressed me against the shed, his mouth still on mine. This wasn't allowed to feel so good. No. This couldn't feel so good.

I wedged my hands between our bodies and shoved him away. He dropped his arms to his sides and stared at me for a moment. Then he twisted until his back was against the shed next to me. I tried to even out my breaths and I could hear him doing the same.

"Why did you do that?" I asked.

"You did it," he said, and he was right. "You did it because you felt sorry for me."

My brows shot down. "Don't tell me why I did something."

"Even if it's true?"

"Especially if it's true."

He chuckled a little.

"Maybe *you* felt sorry for *me*," I said.

"I didn't."

"Good."

"Good," he repeated.

"We should go," I said, not moving.

"We should definitely go," he said, not moving.

"Are you worried?" I asked.

"About you attacking me again? Yes, very."

I smiled and a slight breeze picked up, providing some much-needed relief from the heat. The leaves in the tree across the yard rustled.

"About going home," I said.

"See, I knew you did it because you felt sorry for me."

I bit the inside of my cheek. "I did it because everybody mourns differently."

He laughed. "It's not a bad way to mourn."

"I'm beginning to see the merits," I said, wishing that I wasn't suddenly blushing.

"So you admit that I'm a good kisser?"

He was an amazing kisser. "I will never admit that," I said.

He turned, one shoulder and the side of his head pressed against the shcd. "My dad's all I have. At the end of the day, it's just me and him. I can't afford to lose that."

"He's your dad. It's not like he'll stop being your dad if you say how you feel." The second I said it, I realized that his mom had left for stupid reasons. That my dad had left, maybe not for stupid reasons but for reasons that I couldn't control. Maybe blood wasn't always the strongest bond. "I'm sorry I stood up for you . . ." I started to say. "Well, no, I'm not sorry I stood up for you. I'm sorry I upset you."

"Which time?" he asked, his eyes sparkling.

"Just this one. The other times you totally deserved it." I reached out and grabbed his hand, lacing our fingers together. "Today is all about one-time things." I met his eyes, wondering if he understood what I was saying. That I wouldn't yell at his dad again. And that regardless of how good it felt to kiss Andrew Hart, we couldn't do it again. We were far from compatible. We'd proven that time after time.

He gave me a single nod.

"What are the odds that your dad would give me a referral after I just told him off like that?" I wondered out loud.

"A referral for what?"

"I don't know. Nothing."

He narrowed his eyes. "You think my dad can somehow give you an in to the fashion industry?"

"He knows more people than I do. I thought that maybe . . ."

He raised our linked hands. "Is that why . . . ?"

I let go of his hand. "No! If I wanted to use you, wouldn't I have started a long time ago?"

He ran both hands through his hair. "I don't know, Sophie. I told you I've never had real friends before. It's hard for me to know if I do now."

"You do, Andrew." And I meant it. "We're . . . friends." How had *that* happened? It seemed even more surprising than our kiss, somehow.

Andrew nodded slowly. "Can you come to the benefit in Birmingham in a few weeks? The one Mr. Williams is catering?"

I shook my head. "Every Occasion isn't doing flowers for it. They hired someone closer."

"I know. Come be a cater waiter with Micah. It will be fun."

I let out a laugh. I wasn't sure how fun it would be, but maybe I would go. I loved Birmingham. "Okay."

"By the way, my dad can't be your in," Andrew said as we headed back to the flower van. "He's like me. He doesn't really make connections."

Birmingham Children's Hospital Benefit

PEONY

Want a bloom as big as your face? Peonies have you covered. Okay, maybe they aren't as big as a face, but peonies are known for their large gorgeous blooms and are said to bring luck. The problem? They have a short life span. Sometimes the most beautiful things don't last very long.

Chapter 26

I think it's entirely unfair," Micah said to me as we drove into downtown Birmingham, "that you can look so cute in a pair of polyester pants."

"Nobody looks cute in this outfit." I was sitting in the passenger seat, wearing the same cater waiter uniform as Micah. My hair had grown long enough to wear up in a ponytail. I reached back and pulled on the ends to tighten the holder.

"You do," Micah argued.

It probably helped that I'd made a few adjustments. I'd tailored the white button-down shirt so it wasn't some shapeless form, and I'd added cute silver rings to the belt loops on the pants.

"I wonder if you'll still think I look cute after I do horribly at this event," I said, feeling my stomach twist. "What was I thinking, trying out waitressing for the very first time at a fancy benefit?"

Micah kept her eyes on the road. "You'll do fine. There's nothing to it."

My nerves were on edge and I was trying to pretend it only had to do with the fact that I'd be carrying large trays of food around to rich people. That it had nothing to do with seeing Andrew again tonight after three weeks of silence from both of us. I'd kissed him. What had I been thinking? I obviously hadn't been thinking at all. It had been a weird day. I blamed it on that.

I looked out the window at the city passing by. "There's one of my benches," I said. It wasn't often my mom let me go into Birmingham, but when I did, one of my favorite things to do was sit on a bench in the heart of downtown, people watching.

"The most boring bench in the world," Micah said. I had dragged her there a few too many times, apparently.

"I think you mean the most interesting bench. Can't you just feel the energy?" I grabbed her shoulder and shook it.

"I can feel that there are too many cars around me right now and it's making me claustrophobic. Is that the energy you're talking about?"

I rolled down the window and car horns and sirens and scents drifted in with the wind. I smiled. "Nope. *This* energy."

"You're weird," she said.

"You made me this way."

She laughed. "Did you forget what you said to me at that kindergarten family night when we were five?"

"You make sure I never do."

"'My name is Sophie and I don't really want to talk to you but my dad said I had to.'"

I laughed. "I don't think I sounded like that."

"You did."

"I've always been kind of difficult, haven't I?"

"Yes." Micah leaned forward and looked up at the high-rise in front of us. "I think it's this building. Do you see the parking garage entrance?"

"To the right," I said.

She drove up the ramp and into the garage. We followed the directions her dad had given us and saw the catering van, its back doors open and Lance unloading.

Micah powered down her window. "Where do I park?" she called out.

Lance pointed to an open spot down the aisle.

We got out of the car and headed to the catering van. Lance was still there, holding a large plastic bin.

"We get the flower girl today?" he asked, handing me the bin. "Do we have a bet going yet on how many broken dishes there will be?"

Micah scrunched her nose at him. "Stop. She's already nervous."

"This is quite the event to learn at," he said.

I swallowed.

"Lance," Micah said.

Lance pushed a box into Micah's hands and grinned at me. "You'll do fine, newb. Top floor, ladies." He gestured toward the door.

"Maybe this was a bad idea," I said as we headed inside. "Your dad actually wants a referral from this event. I can just go wander in the park or check out the food trucks."

Micah used her elbow to hit the button for the elevator. "Trying to get out of it already? My dad wouldn't have let you do this if he didn't know you were fully capable." She gave me a steady look. "We went over this. Just follow my lead all night. You'll be fine. You act like you haven't carried huge boxes full of centerpieces. You have muscles, girl."

"I'll be fine," I repeated.

The elevator arrived. The doors opened and there was Andrew. He took a step forward before he saw us.

"Andrew!" Micah said. "Lookin' good."

He wore another one of his dark suits with a small-print floral tie. He stepped to the side and used one hand to make sure the elevator doors didn't shut on us. Micah and I tried to step into the elevator together, which resulted in me knocking into Andrew.

"Sorry," I said at the same time he said, "Excuse me."

We both laughed a little, and he said, "I'm completely in your way."

I turned sideways and so did he and we shuffled past each other. Once Micah and I were inside, Andrew let go of the elevator door and it slid shut. I shifted the bin onto my hip and pushed the button for the top floor.

The elevator whirred into motion, letting off a ding as it passed each floor. One ding, two, three.

"What was that?" Micah asked.

"That was floor number four," I said, watching the red digital numbers over the door change.

"You know very well what I'm talking about. The politeness. The blushing."

"What? I didn't blush."

"You blushed. It's like you two finally released some tension or something."

My eyes went to the bin in my arms and before I could defend myself Micah gasped.

"You did? When?" she asked.

"It was nothing."

"Define nothing."

"We kissed. Once. It was a mistake."

"You kissed!" Micah's mouth dropped open. "Sophie! When? Why didn't you tell me?"

"It was after John's funeral." I bit my lip. "I'm sorry I didn't tell you."

Micah shook her head. "The fact that you didn't say anything makes me think it was more than you're letting on."

"It wasn't," I said quickly. Too quickly.

"What were you thinking?" Micah asked. The elevator reached the top floor and the doors slid open.

I swallowed hard and stepped out into the hall. "I wasn't."

"Sophie, he's leaving in four months. You remember that, right?" she said, following me.

"I know! I told you, it was nothing. We both acknowledged that."

"Good," she said. But she sighed, as if she wasn't willing to drop it quite yet. "I thought you didn't even like him."

To our left was a set of white swinging doors that led to the kitchen. I could hear the clinking of dishes inside. I stopped and took a deep breath. "I don't like him. He's infuriating and arrogant and entitled and opinionated."

"And yet?"

"Nothing. That was the end of my speech. He has zero redeeming qualities."

Her shoulders dropped. "Crap. You're lying. If not to me, then definitely to yourself. If you can't think of one good thing about Andrew Hart, then you're trying awfully hard not to."

I shook my head firmly. "It doesn't matter. That's what I'm trying to say. Like you said, he's leaving in four months and that's how I feel about him. Plus, I know the feeling is mutual."

Micah raised her eyebrows. "How do you know that?"

"I have instincts."

"Your instincts—"

"Are spot-on. Remember Kyle? Remember how I sensed there was something off there and I forced myself to push it? Well I was right. He let me know exactly how right I was."

"How?" she asked.

"I caught him kissing Jodi."

"Sophie! When? Why didn't you tell me this? Am I not your best friend anymore?" The hurt in her eyes let me know I'd made a mistake in not talking to her, in not telling her all of this when it had happened.

"I'm sorry, I just wanted to forget about it. I still do. But I promise I'll fill you in on everything later, okay?" I held her gaze but she glanced away. "Thinking about it now is only going to stress me out more." I held up the box I was holding. "Plus, this is heavy."

"Fine . . . Yes, let's talk about this later." She pushed through the doors to the kitchen. "Or not at all if that's how you want it to be."

I squeezed my eyes shut. Micah was mad, and she had every right to be. But for now, I needed to think about work.

Chapter 27

I stepped out onto the roof of the building. It was amazing. The large expanse of space overlooking the city was lush with greenery: like a yard sitting on top of the world. There was a lawn, potted plants, trees, and flowers. I'd never seen anything like it.

Draped tables and chairs sat in the center, and all around the perimeter were drink stations. There weren't any guests yet but it was a bustle of worker activity.

Micah was talking about which tables I'd be serving and busing, but my gaze had stopped on the centerpieces. Huge pink peonies the size of my open hand were packed into golden vases. White hydrangeas and pale green succulents were in the mix as well. I'd never tried that combination before but it was stunning. I instantly imagined girls in flowy pale-pink skirts and draped white tops walking barefoot through a garden of green.

"Hello?" Micah said. "Do I need to leave you alone with the flowers?"

"They're so pretty. Can you imagine anyone in our town requesting a centerpiece like this?"

"Take a picture and maybe you can suggest them to Caroline for a future event."

"My phone is in my bag in the locker inside."

"Ask Andrew to take a picture," she said.

I looked over my shoulder, thinking she meant he was out here somewhere. He wasn't. "I'll just draw it later. I left my journal at home." I wished I hadn't, because I really wanted to sketch.

I was still struggling with what was unique and different about me as a designer. But thankfully, I had managed to eke out a couple of sketches in the last several weeks that didn't completely suck. Maybe I'd make my December deadline after all.

"You'd rather draw this than ask Andrew for a favor?" Micah was saying. She clucked her tongue. "Wow. This is worse than I thought."

"It is not." I pointed to the group of tables around me. "So these are my tables?"

"Yep. Just five. Easy peasy."

"How many do you have?"

"That doesn't matter. It's not my first night."

"Okay, I just don't want you taking on more because you think I can't pull my weight."

"It's good, Soph. We'll be fine." Something caught her eye behind me. "Oh, look, there's Andrew. He can take a picture for you. Andrew!"

I knew she was trying to get me to admit that there was something more going on with us, but I wasn't going to do it.

I put on my indifferent face. Because that's what I was. Very indifferent.

Andrew came over, his phone in hand. "These center-pieces are amazing," he said.

"That's what Sophie was just saying. Will you take a picture of one and send it to her?" Micah asked cheerfully.

Andrew held up his phone and snapped a few pictures. "You going to try to copy them?" he asked in that condescending way of his.

"What? No. I don't copy things."

"There's no shame in that. Don't they say imitation is the best form of flattery?"

"There's a difference between imitation and inspiration," I said.

"What is the difference?" he asked. "The level of guilt you feel?"

Good. He was proving to me that our kiss was a total fluke. "Don't be a tool," I said.

"But I'm so good at it."

I raised my eyebrows at Micah as if to say, *See, nothing going on here.*

She just shook her head and rolled her eyes.

"Nice pants, by the way, Sophie," Andrew added, tucking his phone back into the inside pocket of his jacket. "Good choice for your first pair ever."

"Nice suit," I said. "How does it feel to spend so much money on a dozen that look exactly the same?"

He gave a faux gasp. "I have at least two dozen."

I smirked. "I don't doubt it."

I wasn't sure if Micah and I had more to do on the roof, but I walked back toward the door like suddenly I was the one in charge. I was grateful when Micah followed me.

"You know," she said, once she'd fallen into step beside me, "you didn't have to act that way for my benefit."

"I didn't. That's who we are."

"Perpetual flirts?"

My mouth fell open. "That was not flirting!"

"You two are impossible. Let's just talk about *anything* else."

"Gladly."

We pushed our way into the kitchen. We'd already come in briefly to drop off our stuff and say hi to Micah's dad before going outside to see the roof. Now Jett Hart was standing at one of the stovetops, adding vegetables to a large skillet. My entire body went tense. Jett looked up and, much to my surprise, a smile came over his face. I tried to remember if it was the first one I'd ever seen there. It made him look much more like Andrew.

"Micah," he said. "My worker bee."

Ah. *That's* who the smile was for.

My brows went up and I looked Micah's way. "We get along," she said under her breath before she moved forward to talk to Jett. "Is there anything we can do to help?"

"Your father is bringing up some boxes. Can you see if he needs extra hands?"

"Yes." She gestured toward me. "You remember Sophie."

Jett gave a single nod, the scowl back on his face.

"Hi," I said tentatively. "It's . . ." Several adjectives about how I felt to see him again went through my head all at once—*nice, good, lovely, great*—none of which I meant, so I ended up spitting out, "A good night for a party. I mean, great weather and everything."

"Yes," he said.

Micah tugged on my arm and I followed her out of the kitchen.

"Since when did you start getting along?" I hissed.

"Since he thinks I'm excellent at my job."

"You are, but . . . you *like* him now?"

"He's not so bad. He gets a little gruff when he's stressed or under pressure, but don't we all?"

"Really?" She was going with Andrew's standard line now.

"I know, he can be a jerk. But, Sophie, I have to work with him. I'm trying to like him at least a little bit."

I held up my hands. "I get it. But *I* don't have to like him."

"Just for tonight," she said.

I groaned.

Waitressing was hard. My arms felt like Jell-O as I carried yet another tray of dirty salad plates to the kitchen.

Mr. Williams smiled at me as I moved the plates onto the counter by the other stacks. "You're doing great,

Ms. Sophie," he said. "Maybe I'll have to hire you for our next event."

"Only if I gain some arm muscle by then."

I went to the counter where entree dishes were waiting.

"You're moving at half-speed," Jett said to me. "Pick it up."

He'd been short with me all night, tougher on me than he had been on the other waiters, I felt. I wondered if he was still angry from our last interaction. I just clenched my teeth.

"Sorry, sir," I said, loading up my tray.

"I don't care about words, Ms. Evans, just actions." Well, at least he knew my name.

I lifted the heavy tray to my shoulder and left without saying those words he didn't care about.

A woman at my first table raised her finger at me. "Can I get a refill of wine?" she asked.

I nodded my head toward the closest drink station. "You have to go to a drink station, ma'am." There were at least four and none of them busy.

"You can't get it for me?"

"I'm underage. I'm not allowed."

She pushed air between her lips. "I won't tell." She held up her glass.

"I'm sorry. I can't."

She sighed and pulled out a small handbag, fished through it, and came up with a twenty-dollar bill. "How about now, sweetheart?"

"I'll get that for you," Andrew said, lifting the woman's glass and giving her a smile as well.

She tried to hand him the money but he refused it.

"What a gentleman," she said.

I had been clenching my teeth an awful lot tonight. I finished passing out the rest of the plates and moved to get another load when a man called out, "Girl, please take this dish with you."

"Of course." I picked up his half-eaten food and looked around for others. I ended up walking away with another full tray.

"Want me to carry that tray?" Andrew asked, joining me as I made my way inside again.

"No, and thanks for making me look bad with the wine lady back there."

"I was just trying to help."

"It didn't help. It just made it look like I wasn't willing to fill her drink."

"You weren't," he said.

"Because I'm not allowed to," I shot back.

He shrugged. "Well, I am. I don't work for Mr. Williams."

I laughed. "Like you'd ever work a real job."

Andrew furrowed his brows. "What's that supposed to mean? I work."

"For your dad."

"Micah works for her dad."

"How much does your dad pay you?"

"Excuse me?"

"Like, do you buy your own suits?" I shook my head. "Never mind. It's none of my business. Just go"—I nodded toward the phone I knew was in his pocket—"work."

"And you call *me* a jerk," he said before he turned and walked back outside.

I took a deep breath, stung. But he was right. I'd been a big jerk. To him. I hated who I was around him—this insecure, small version of myself. I hated that I knew, deep inside, it was because I cared what he thought about my talent, my work, my creativity . . . me.

Chapter 28

For once I had an empty tray and not an immediate need to fill it. On the roof, a chic woman in a business suit was speaking into a microphone about how grateful she was for the continued support of the hospital. Micah was standing with a tray by one of the drink stations. Out of the corner of my eye, I saw Andrew slip inside the building. Trying not to draw attention to myself, I went inside as well.

I didn't see Andrew right away, but unless he took the elevator down, there were only two places he could be—in the bathrooms at the end of one hall or the kitchen at the end of the other hall.

I hoped he wasn't in the kitchen, so I turned left and waited. Only a few minutes had passed when the door to the bathroom swung open and Andrew walked out. He startled slightly when he saw me but then put on a guarded expression.

"So," I started, feeling a pang of nerves. "I'm sorry for what I said earlier. I know you work. Your pictures are amazing and you put a lot of thought into them."

"Why?" was all he said.

"You were right." I clasped my hands together. "I was being a jerk and it's not me."

"It's not?"

"Well, it wasn't before you came around."

"Are you blaming me?"

I sighed. "No. I'm trying to be a bigger person."

"Did you mean *the* bigger person?"

I crossed my arms. "No. I didn't. I meant that I want to be better."

"Better than what?"

"Better than I've been, Andrew. Okay? Are we good?" I held out my hand.

He stared at it. "What are you doing? Are you trying to shake my hand?" He laughed.

I laughed too. "Yes." I used my left hand to reach out and lift his right arm so that I could shake his hand. "There. Now it's official."

"What's official?"

"We're friends again."

"Did we stop being friends? Or start for that matter?"

"You're not going to bother me anymore," I declared. "We shook hands. Now I'll just think your goading is adorable. Like Micah does." If I kept telling myself that, it would be true. I would be the secure, happy version of myself, even around Andrew.

"Soph, don't challenge me like this." He gave me a half smirk.

"Not a challenge. I need to get back to work." I picked up the tray that I had set on the ground and went back outside where the same woman with a microphone was still talking about the same gratitude.

Micah joined me by the wall closest to the door. "It's dessert time," she said.

"I'm ready."

Lance was in the kitchen talking to Mr. Williams as we came inside. Jett was drizzling chocolate over some slices of layered cake and Micah's dad was drizzling strawberry glaze over other slices.

"Hey, flower girl," Lance said to me. "I'm impressed. You didn't drop a single dish."

"You just jinxed me. Take it back," I said.

"Take it back? I don't think it works that way."

Micah giggled. "It does in her world, Lance."

"Okay, I take it back."

"Thank you."

We filled our trays with the dessert plates. As we walked back outside, Andrew took a picture of the three of us.

"I'm going to start charging you for those," Micah said.

"And I'll gladly pay," he answered.

Instead of rolling my eyes, I smiled. He was looking right at me and I said, "Adorable."

He laughed.

"What?" Micah said as we continued walking toward the tables.

"Nothing."

"You two are giving me whiplash."

"Yeah, I know."

We separated to our respective tables and I began placing cake in front of people.

The wine lady said, "I want a chocolate piece, not a vanilla. Or do I need to get the young man over here to do that?"

"No, I can do that." I placed a piece of chocolate down.

"No, I changed my mind," she said. "I want vanilla instead."

I picked up the chocolate and placed a vanilla down.

"Come to think of it, I don't want cake at all. I want a caffè macchiato. Do you know what that is?"

She could tell I wasn't from the city. One look and she knew. She thought I was dumb. And I kind of felt dumb because I actually didn't know what a caffè macchiato was. "I'm not sure if they offer that, but if they do, it's at—"

"The drink station?"

"Yes, ma'am."

"And do you have to be a certain age to fill that as well?"

Remain calm, Sophie. "No, I can check for you as soon as I finish serving the cake." I moved on to the next person.

"I'm sorry," the man sitting next to the wine lady mouthed. I wasn't sure if it was her husband or just someone who knew rude when he saw it.

I smiled and gave him the biggest piece of cake on my tray.

At the next table, when I set my last plate down in front of an older man, his glass caught on the lip of it and wine spilled.

At first I thought I had caused the accident, but when he picked up the glass and dropped his fork to the ground, I realized he was drunk.

I bent down to pick up the fork and felt a hand brush my leg. The man gave me a creepy smile as I stood. I pointed his own fork at him. "Please keep your hands to yourself."

"Or else what?" he slurred.

"Or else I'll get security to escort you out."

The man put on a faux-serious face and deliberately folded his hands in his lap. I really didn't care if he was joking around or not, as long as he didn't touch me.

I left, without looking back. Once inside, I pressed my back against the closest wall and used my empty tray to fan myself. It had been a long, tiring night.

I knew I should go back outside but I didn't feel like moving. But then I saw Jett Hart and Mr. Williams coming out of the kitchen. And they clearly saw me, leaning against the wall on an unscheduled break. Jett gave me his standard look but thankfully kept talking.

"You'd fit in well here," he was saying to Micah's dad. "City life looks good on you. I've already gotten three business cards from guests tonight. If you get three referrals from every event, you'll be booked for . . ." His voice trailed off as they went outside to the roof to visit with the guests.

I tried to take in what I'd just heard. Mr. Williams would never leave Rockside. It didn't matter what Jett Hart said. Right?

I followed them out to see if I could hear Mr. Williams's response, but they had already disappeared into the crowd. The crowd that was now mostly out of their seats, mingling, dancing, drinking.

I saw Micah standing at the railing, looking out over the city lights. I started toward her when the wine lady approached me. Great. I hadn't gotten her caffè macchiato and now I was going to hear about it.

But instead of her normal haughty expression, she wore a curious one. "Was that Jett Hart?" she asked.

"Yes," I said warily.

"So does that mean this catering company is part of his program?"

"Yes," I said.

She smiled wide and began digging through her purse. She came up with a small card that she held out for me. "Give this to him, will you? My sister owns a catering company about thirty minutes west of here that could use someone like him. She applied for his program but hasn't heard back."

I gestured to where Jett had disappeared into the throng. "He's here. You should find him."

"I'll try, but in case he's too busy, you'll be my backup." She pressed the card into my hand. "Thank you!"

I nodded.

With that, she flashed me a smile and went on her way, probably to look for Jett.

I furrowed my brow and continued toward Micah by the railing.

"Who was that?" Micah asked.

I held up the business card. "Some lady who wants Jett to work with her sister. She was rude to me all night but apparently didn't realize it at all. She thought it was perfectly normal to ask me for a favor without saying anything about her behavior."

"Welcome to the world of waitressing."

I tucked the card into my pocket and watched lines of headlights and taillights move along the highway in the distance like a string of Christmas lights.

"Oh, by the way," I said, "you're never going to guess what I overheard Jett Hart saying to your dad."

"What?" Micah asked.

"He said he thought the city was where he belonged, or something to that effect."

Micah nodded. "Yeah, he said the same to me."

"He did?" I frowned. "Is this the way he works? How he helps you grow your business? He just takes you out of the small town and plops you into the city and voilà, instant growth?"

She rubbed her arms as though she were cold. Suddenly, I also felt a slight cooling in the air, a reminder that summer was coming to an end. "Maybe," Micah said.

"I mean, you'd either be constantly driving to and from events or have to move here. And living here would cost at least thirty percent more than Rockside, which would just be a wash," I pointed out. "And besides, could you imagine living here?"

I looked back toward the crowd on the rooftop and, for the first time tonight, realized just how diverse it was. Very different from our little town. "Maybe . . ." I began.

"Maybe what?" Micah asked when I didn't continue.

"Maybe Jett's right. Maybe this place would be better for your business. You wouldn't have to deal with the Hobbs or the Smiths." Both those families had refused to hire Mr. Williams for events and everyone knew why.

"There are racist people everywhere," Micah said.

"I know, but you'd have more options here."

Before she could respond, Andrew came over and leaned on the rail on the opposite side of her. "What's so interesting over here?" he asked us.

"Nothing," Micah said. "Just taking a little break before cleanup."

Andrew nodded my way. "You handled that drunk guy well earlier."

I lifted my chin. "You think big-city parties hold a monopoly on drunk guys? I would argue that country drunk guys are even drunker and more handsy. So yes, I know how to hold my own."

"Because everything about the country is worse than everything about the city," Micah said.

"What?" I asked.

Micah turned to me, her mouth tight. "You're already checked out, aren't you?" she said. "You have stars in your eyes and a fire at your back. Is that why you stopped telling me things?"

My stomach clenched. What was she saying? "No—no, I'm not checked out," I stammered. "I've just been a bad friend, I'm sorry. We'll talk, let's talk. Just not . . ." I looked at Andrew. "Now."

She shook her head. "Whatever. I'm tired. I'm going to get started on the cleanup." With that, she walked away.

I stared after her, tempted to follow, but I knew my best friend needed some time. I'd give her that.

"What was that about?" Andrew asked.

"Me. It was about me." I owed Micah a major apology and a best-friend talking session. It would all work out. I'd make sure of that.

"So was she right?" Andrew asked. "Is everything about the city better than everything about the country?"

I turned my attention back to the lights in the distance, thinking about his question. "No. The stars are way better in the country. City stars are pretty lame."

He looked up as if he needed proof of this. "I'd agree with you on that."

I watched him take in the dark sky for a moment. Then I retrieved the business card from my pocket. "Here."

"What's this?"

"That wine lady has a sister." The card spoke for itself. It read *Country Catering* with a picture of a chef hat on it. "For your dad. She applied for the program, I guess."

"Oh." He seemed to read every word on the card twice.

"It would probably be too close to this year's mentee, though, yeah?"

"Maybe. But we once did two years in nearly the same place."

"Well then you'll have to put in a good word for wine lady's sister." Maybe Andrew Hart would be closer than I thought in four months.

He smiled and finally put the card in his pocket.

I grabbed hold of the railing, then leaned back and looked up at the sky once more. I felt it again: the slight cool tinge in the air that meant fall was coming soon. "Oh!" I said, pulling myself upright. "You know what else is better in the country than in the city? Our Fall Festival. It's the best."

"Let me guess," Andrew said. "You work the Fall Festival. Are there actually flowers there?"

"There are. And a huge corn maze. And a band," I added. "Usually a decent one even." That was to say: not Kyle's band. "And so much food."

"I guess that's our next date, then." Andrew looked at me when he said it but his eyes quickly moved back to the view.

"I better"—I pointed over my shoulder—"find Micah."

"Good luck."

When I found Micah, she was in the kitchen laughing with Jett and her dad. I stood for a while, waiting for my chance to talk to her, but instead Jett assigned cleanup chores and we went our separate ways. By the time we were done cleaning up, Micah was back to her bubbly self and I asked her to sleep over at my house the following weekend. She agreed that we needed a sleepover. Hopefully that would fix everything.

Fall Festival

WILDFLOWER

A flower that grows in the wild or is exactly as it would
appear if found growing in nature, unaided. In some
places, it is illegal to pluck a wildflower in nature, but
even wildflowers can be grown
in captivity. Tamed.

Chapter 29

There was something about the Fall Festival that I loved more than all the other events. Maybe it was the weather: the leaves bright with color, the stifling heat of summer finally gone. Maybe it was that the festival took place on Mr. Hancock's farm—twenty acres of animals and apple trees and cornfields. Maybe it was the smell of a million foods being fried at once, or that I got to wear a sweater. Whatever it was, it was perfect.

I carried a tin of wildflowers in one arm and a small bale of hay in the other. I headed toward the food court section of the event, which consisted of a semicircle of food booths bordering thirty picnic tables.

"You actually do own a pair of jeans," Andrew said. He stepped away from a food booth, lifting his phone and snapping my picture. "This one is for proof."

"And you own a pair of cowboy boots." I stared in shock at his footwear. "When did that happen?"

"Micah took me shopping last week and insisted."

"She's hard to say no to."

Micah and I were in a good place. After the Birmingham benefit, we'd had our slumber party. I'd apologized for being so checked out and for not telling her about what had happened with Andrew and with Kyle. She'd helped me discover, with an extensive list of pros and cons, that Andrew and I could absolutely not work, at least not beyond friends. And everything was all right.

"She is." He put his hands in his pockets and his eyes went to the tin as I placed it on a table. "Nice flowers."

"See, here's the problem. I'm never going to believe that compliment now. You've shot yourself in the foot too many times with that one."

He smiled. "Fair enough. But for the record, I meant it." He looked around. "So this is your favorite event, huh?"

"How did you know that?"

"You said something like that at the benefit in August."

"Oh, right. Yes, it's my favorite."

Jett Hart was at his booth examining the knobs on a deep fryer alongside Mr. Williams. "Is your dad actually going to fry something tonight?" I asked in disbelief.

"I guess Mr. Williams is making his famous mac-and-cheese balls. He's teaching my dad."

I raised my eyebrows. "Really?"

"Stranger things have happened."

"Well, you'll have to try them," I said. "They're pretty much the best."

Micah came over in a pair of cowboy boots exactly the same as Andrew's. She draped her arm over his shoulder and said, "Friends, what are we talking about?"

"Fried mac and cheese," I said.

"My dad makes the best," she said.

"That's what I've been told," Andrew responded.

I glanced around at the sprawling grounds. "We should all attempt the maze later," I said.

Micah looked at the entrance to the maze in the distance. "Hopefully I'll have time. I have to work more than you do tonight."

"That's true," I said.

She patted Andrew's cheek. "And Andrew has lots of pictures to take." She looked over her shoulder. "I better go. My dad needs help."

"See you later," I said.

She joined her dad and Jett at their booth, where I watched her unpack gallon-sized bags of bread crumbs.

"Is everything okay with you two?" Andrew asked, catching me off guard.

"Yes . . . isn't it?" I turned to him. "Did she say something to you?"

"No, she didn't. It's just at the benefit, you guys . . ."

"Oh, yeah." I kept forgetting he'd witnessed that. "We made up."

"Good."

"Yoo-hoo!" I heard from behind me. "Sophie!"

I took a deep breath and turned around. My mom was waving at me from across the way.

Gunnar raced ahead of her and then around me and Andrew once and then twice before he stopped in front of us and said, "Hi, y'all. Momma said I could do four things tonight so I'm gonna bob for apples, do the pie-eating contest, the ropin' contest, and of course the maze. Momma said, seein' as how I just turned eleven, I should do it by myself this year."

The maze was huge. It covered five acres of the land. "You said that?" I asked my mom when she reached us.

"What did I say?" she asked, picking up her foot and shaking a clod of dirt off one heel and then the other. I wasn't sure why she'd worn heels to the Fall Festival. She'd never done that before.

"You said Gunnar should do the maze by himself?"

"He's eleven," Mom replied. "Of course I said that."

"The recommended solo age is fourteen."

"Recommended age?" She stuck out her tongue. "Since when? Everyone is so worried about liability these days that they have to post stuff like that. He'll be fine."

I realized that my mom, in all her high-heeled glory, probably just didn't want to have to walk a five-acre maze with Gunnar this year. "I can go with him," I said.

"Yeah, you can come with me," Gunnar said, which let me know that my mom had probably told him that if he wanted to do the maze this year, he had to do it by himself.

248

"You can't always baby him," Mom told me.

"I was going to do the maze anyway," I said.

"Will you come with us too?" Gunnar asked Andrew.

"Absolutely," Andrew said.

"Yay!" Gunnar jumped up and down several times.

"You don't have to," I told Andrew. I remembered Micah saying something about him needing to take pictures.

"I want to."

"Sophie," my mom said. "I have news."

I turned back to her. "Okay . . . what is it?"

She threw back her shoulders and pulled an envelope with a jagged edge out of the back pocket of her jeans. "You got the scholarship!"

I blinked, confused. "What? What scholarship?"

"Mr. Washington's." She thrust the envelope into my hands.

I still wasn't following. "I didn't apply for this."

"I did," she said with a beaming smile. "Congratulations!"

"But—but I'm not going to school in Alabama." I stared down at the envelope. "This is only for Alabama schools."

She blew air between her lips. "Now you have *options*." My mom pointed over to Mr. Williams's booth. "Oh look, there's Micah. I'm going to go say hi."

I watched her walk away. My eyes went back down to the envelope that was addressed to me but that had already been opened. My chest felt tight. No. Someone else wasn't going to force a future on me that I didn't want. I folded the envelope once and stuffed it in the back pocket of my jeans. I looked up to realize Andrew was still there as a witness to another embarrassing interaction.

"I have like five more centerpieces to grab," I said quickly. "I'll see you later."

He nodded, brought out his phone, and joined the crowd that was beginning to form.

When I got back to the flower van, swallowing down the frustration in my throat, Caroline was there. "You did a good job with these," she told me, assessing the flowers in the back. "I'm glad we went with your suggestion."

I smiled, momentarily forgetting Mom and the scholarship. This event marked the first time ever that I'd spoken up. The first time I'd come to a pre-event meeting with a plan. Wildflowers.

I'd come up with the idea after a Saturday I'd spent hiking with my brother in the foothills. Wildflowers made me think of nymphs and moss-carpeted forests and woodland creatures. I'd wanted to create *some* sort of design with those images. I was relieved Caroline had gone with my idea.

"Well," Caroline said. She handed me two centerpieces. "Have fun tonight."

The weight of the envelope in my pocket seemed to mock that suggestion. I gritted my teeth, pulled the envelope out, and threw it onto the front seat of the van. It wasn't going to ruin my night.

The sound of a guitar being tuned rang out over the speakers. I looked over to see Kyle on the stage in the food court area with his band. What? They were playing tonight? Usually a local country band was chosen for this event. I waited for annoyance to take over my emotions, but I felt next to nothing when looking at him.

"I will have fun," I said to Caroline. "I will."

Chapter 30

What are the rules?" Andrew asked.

"You've never bobbed for apples?" I asked. "Like ever?"

"You act like this is a normal, everyday activity."

"It's as American as baseball."

"I don't think that's true," he said. "I think you're confusing bobbing for apples with apple pie. Is that being served somewhere?"

"Maybe it's just a country thing," I said.

Micah, who had wandered over to the barrels when she saw me and Andrew there, snorted. "It's not."

Micah gestured to someone over my shoulder, and I turned to see Lance heading toward us.

"What's everyone doing?" he asked.

"We're teaching Andrew how to bob for apples," Micah said.

"This is a game where there are no winners," Lance said.

Micah laughed. "That's not true."

"Either way you end up wet," he said.

"Pay no attention to the distractions," I said. "So the rules." I pointed to Gunnar, who was on his knees assessing the barrel. "You can't use your hands."

"The only thing you can use is your teeth," Micah amended.

"Right," I said. "And you'll be timed. They'll add your name to that super-cool whiteboard there. And at the end of the night, the fastest person to retrieve an apple with their teeth will be crowned apple-bobbing champion."

"Such an honor," Lance said sarcastically.

"You're just bitter because I always beat you," Micah said.

"What?" Lance pretended to gasp. "I think your memory is off."

Micah pushed his shoulder and chuckled.

Andrew raised his eyebrows at me but then nodded to the barrel. "Sounds easy enough."

"It's so not," I said.

"Bobbers ready," Mr. Pitman called out.

"You going to do it?" I asked Andrew, who was rolling up his sleeves in preparation.

"Next round. I'm going to watch technique first."

"Good call," I said.

"Go!" Mr. Pitman said as he pushed a button on his stopwatch.

Gunnar put his whole head in the barrel, water splashing everywhere.

I took a step back.

"See what I mean?" Lance said.

"It's a perfectly good method," Micah said.

We all watched Gunnar's head circle the barrel. Andrew laughed. Finally, Gunnar came up with an apple clutched in his teeth, flinging his head back and spraying water over the watching crowd.

Gunnar took a big bite of his apple and smiled. "That's how you do it!" he proclaimed.

"Got it," Andrew said, taking a small step forward.

"Just don't think about all the slobber that's in that barrel," I said. "Nobody else around here seems to."

"Is that why you don't participate, Sophie?" Micah asked.

"No, I'm just vain and don't want to mess up my makeup."

Micah smiled then raised her hand. "I'll challenge you, Andrew."

He pointed at her. "You're on."

"Be careful, she cheats," Lance said.

"I do not!"

Mr. Pitman called out the ready signal. Micah and Andrew knelt down and put their hands behind their backs.

"And go!" Mr. Pitman yelled.

Andrew was hilarious to watch. He had no idea what he was doing. The apples kept bobbing up and down because he didn't realize he somehow had to find the resistance—the barrel's side, the barrel's bottom, something. So, of course, Micah came up first with an apple in her mouth. Then she reached over and dunked Andrew's head under. He came up laughing, flinging water from his hair all over her.

"That was fun," he said when they were done.

"That's because we know how to have fun around here," Micah replied, smiling. "That said, we need to get back to work."

She pushed my shoulder a little, which made me laugh, and left with Lance.

Andrew turned a full circle. "What's next?"

"You expect me to entertain you all night?"

"This is your favorite event. So yes, I figured I'd stay by your side all night."

I wasn't sure why, but my stomach flipped with that statement. I tried to ignore it but then I didn't know what to say. I fumbled with the handle on the barrel next to me, then noticed a roll of paper towels on the table. I handed the roll to Andrew. "For your dripping hair."

He ripped off a strip and mopped his forehead.

Behind him, the lights strung around the food booths lit up. "You ready for a sampling of true Southern food?" I asked, my stomach growling. "I'm guessing you haven't had any since you've been here. You've been filled full of eggs Benedict and broccoli salad and chocolate mousse."

"I did have that barbecue in July. You can't forget about that."

"And neither can you, obviously. Because that's what amazing food does. It changes you."

He laughed. "Have you been watching old episodes of *Cooking with Hart?*"

"I have actually. I've been trying to uncover the secrets of getting on your father's good side."

"Let me know if you find any."

I sighed. "If your seventeen years of in-depth study haven't uncovered anything, I have no hope."

"I wouldn't say that I *study* my dad in depth." He nodded his head to the side. "Which booth do we start at?"

"The okra, of course."

He wrinkled his nose. "I've had okra before and it's not an experience I want to repeat."

"It's fried, Andrew, and covered in cheese. Believe me, you have not had it like this." I took him by the hand and dragged him toward the food.

"If I have another bite of food, I will die," Andrew groaned, pushing his plate with a half-eaten fried pickle on it to the middle of the table.

"Weak," I said. "We haven't even had any of the desserts."

"Are those fried too?"

"Some of them."

"How are you not full?" he asked.

"I only took a few bites of each item. You are obviously an amateur."

"Of course you didn't tell me that secret."

"I did! I said, 'Pace yourself, Andrew, we still have half the food booths left.'"

"Oh, right." He laid his forehead on his arms on the table. "Just give me thirty minutes or so. I'll get my second wind."

Gunnar appeared at our table. "Are y'all ready to do the maze?" he asked impatiently. "Mom said we have to leave in one hour. That might not even be enough time to get through it. Is it enough time, Soph?"

"If we start now." I stood up and Gunnar whirled around and took off in a dead sprint.

Andrew groaned again.

"You don't have to come," I told him.

"No, I'm coming. Very slowly, but I'm coming."

"Micah!" I called out to where she was standing across the way, busing a table. When she looked, I pointed at the maze. "Maze time!"

She held up her finger.

Gunnar zoomed back over to me and took hold of my hand, giving it a tug. "I thought we were going."

"Almost. We're waiting for Micah."

Andrew climbed to his feet only to lean a hand on the table. A big group of guys from school walked by. One of them threw a container full of fries at the trash nearby, but it missed and landed on the ground right next to me, spraying ketchup all over my jeans.

"Thanks, Brady," I called out.

He waved. "No problem, darlin'."

"Ugh," I said as they kept walking. "Losers." I grabbed some napkins and mopped up my jeans.

"Who are losers?" Micah asked, coming over. Her eyes locked on the group, obviously figuring out who I was referring to. She didn't say anything.

I noticed my mom walking in the distance. With every step she took, she had to shake dirt off her heels.

"What was she thinking?" I asked.

"She wanted to look her best." Micah always took my side when it came to my mom so this surprised me.

"She's ridiculous," I said. "She wore heels to a farm."

"There's not a set dress code for every event," Micah persisted. "Even though I'm sure you'd like there to be."

"I know," I said. "But some things are common sense."

"Kind of like leaving this town?" Micah asked, turning to face me. "Is that common sense? Should everyone want to do it?" Suddenly, she was speaking quickly, her words running together. "Should everyone here live every day of their lives as though they're already gone? Some people can actually appreciate where they are at the moment, even if it's a small town in the middle of nowhere. But maybe only the little people who belong here can do that. The losers."

My mouth dropped open and I snapped it shut. Then I managed to speak again. "Wh-what?" I stuttered out. "Why would you say that? I thought we talked about this. I've been distracted with my portfolio and my future, but that doesn't mean I think people who want to stay here are losers."

"Then why don't you give anyone around here a chance?" She shot a pointed look at Andrew, as if the only reason I was hanging out with him at all was because he wasn't a local. "It's like you think the fewer connections you have here, the easier it will be to leave it all behind."

"What?" I didn't know what else to say. I shook my head, searching for the right words. "I—of course I wouldn't leave it behind. My mom and my brother are here. You're here."

"Your dad didn't seem to have a problem leaving everything. He left without looking back."

"My dad?"

"Yes, that man who never visits. Not once since he left."

I felt shock bubbling up in me. "And *you* have an issue with this?" I demanded, staring Micah down. "You, with your perfect family life, are not allowed to have issues because of *my* dad. Those aren't yours to claim."

"Well, I've claimed them because I sense that you are exactly like him," Micah said defiantly. And just like that, she turned on her heel and was gone.

I moved to follow her, hurt and anger competing to take hold of my emotions, when Andrew grabbed my arm.

"Just give it a minute," he said. "That's the kind of speech that needs a little thinking space."

I yanked my arm out of his grip. "You know my best friend better than me now?"

"I meant space for you."

Tears stung my eyes. I put my palm to my forehead. He was right. I didn't want him to be but he was. I needed to think before I reacted. What had just happened?

"My dad can have dreams," I said. "He shouldn't have to give up everything."

He didn't say a word.

"And I don't hate Rockside," I went on. "I mean, there are things I hate about this place, but there are things everyone hates about the town they live in, right?"

"Yes," he said.

"And I definitely don't hate Micah. She's everything." I walked three steps one way and then back three steps. "Sure, sometimes I'm judgmental. And maybe occasionally I've been condescending and . . ." I gasped. "Oh no." I looked at Andrew. "I've been *you*."

"Thanks," he said.

"Oh, you know what I mean."

He gave a half smile. "Yes, I do."

"But what she said—"

A loud crashing sound to my left rang out, followed by Jett Hart yelling a string of curses. My head whipped over. The first thing I saw was the deep fryer on the ground, steam rising from the hot oil that was now all over the dirt. The second thing I saw was my brother, standing there with his head down and his hands to his chest. I turned and ran to him.

Chapter 31

By the time I reached my brother, Jett was on another round of yelling.

"You are an irresponsible, hyperactive child who needs to be watched at all times! Where is your mother?"

I reached Gunnar's side and knelt down, looking him over. "Are you hurt?" I asked. "Did you get burned?"

He shook his head no, his eyes watering.

"Of course he didn't get hurt," Jett growled. "But he destroyed the entire booth!"

I looked around for Mr. Williams, but he was busy asking Lance to bring over a trash can.

I stood and faced Jett. "He's just a child and it was an accident."

"Ah. Your brother." He raised one eyebrow. "How could I have forgotten? You will pay for this damage, Ms. Evans! It's about time you had to face some consequences. People seem to handle you with kid gloves around here."

"Dad." Andrew's voice cut in low but hard. I hadn't even seen him come up beside me. "Stop."

"Son, this is none of your business. Help Mr. Williams clean up and take that delinquent to his mother."

I balled my hands into fists and was about to say something, but then Andrew spoke again.

"It *is* my business," he said, "because these are my friends, and how you're acting is not okay. You have a temper problem."

Jett's expression hardened. "Walk away, boy, before you say something you regret."

"Pretty sure I've lived my whole life regretting the things I didn't say."

"Andrew," I said. I didn't want me or my brother to be the reason that he and his dad had a falling out.

Andrew held up his hand but continued to stare his dad in the eyes. "He's just a kid. A young kid who has no way to defend himself against you. You can't expect him to be a mini adult who has all the answers and does everything exactly the way you would do it."

I was beginning to wonder if Andrew was still talking about Gunnar.

"I can certainly expect a kid not to run through a cooking site and trip over all the cords," Jett snapped.

"If he tripped over the cords, that's on you," Andrew said.

His dad's face was getting redder by the second. Was he going to blow a fuse?

"Andrew, you will shut your mouth right this instant," he thundered.

I reached out for Gunnar's hand but my hand only met air. I looked over to see that he was gone. "Where did Gunnar go?" I asked, looking all around.

"Actually, I won't," Andrew responded to his dad.

"My brother," I said louder. "Did anyone see where he went?" A good crowd had formed around the spectacle, but everyone just shook their heads. My eyes met Micah's. She was standing on the outskirts of the group, and she pointed to the maze.

"My brother went into the maze," I said to Andrew.

"What?" His attention finally turned to me.

"My brother ran off to the maze. I need to go find him."

"I'm coming with you," Andrew said.

"You are doing nothing of the sort," Jett said from behind us, but both of us were already running toward the maze entrance.

"You okay?" I asked Andrew as we ran.

"Not really," Andrew responded, voice tight.

I heard footsteps behind us and turned to see Micah. "I'll help," she said.

I nodded at her. Neither of us mentioned the fight we'd had minutes before. It was obviously going to take more than a talk to fix the gulf that had opened up between us.

We reached the entrance to the maze and all barreled inside. We came to the end of the first stretch and the path split two ways.

"I'll go right," Micah said. "I'll text you if I find him."

Andrew and I turned left.

"Does this maze have any of those platform things that you can climb and try to orient yourself?" he asked, glancing around.

I pointed. In the middle of the maze, far from where we stood, was a wooden deck.

"Okay, we'll try to make it there," he said.

I nodded. My throat was too tight to speak.

"You know he's going to be fine, right?" Andrew said. "He's somewhere in here. And there are other people in here too. He'll eventually find his way out."

I nodded again, a million emotions swirling through me. We came to another split in the path.

"I'll go left," I said, and started to move.

Andrew grabbed me by the hand and pulled me into a hug. "I'm sorry, Sophie," he said. "For how my dad treated you, and for what Micah said, and about what happened with your mom earlier. And that your little brother is probably really upset right now. I'm so sorry."

It had been quite a night, I realized, when he spelled it all out like that. "It's not your fault." I felt suddenly numb. "I need to go find my brother." I pushed him away. "I just need to go find my brother." I stumbled away down the left path. Andrew didn't follow, which I was happy about.

There was something about walking through a dark maze, surrounded by tall stalks of corn, all alone, that had my brain turning over everything I had ever said or done for the last . . .

seventeen years. Was Micah right? Had I been prejudiced against everyone and everything in this town? Had it colored my relationship with my mother? Was wanting change, wanting a bigger life so wrong? My mom had applied for a scholarship for me and I'd gotten it. Would it be dumb not to at least consider it?

"It's because she doesn't believe you can succeed, Sophie," I muttered to myself. I was sure I hadn't colored that fact anything but the right shade.

I'd admit to one thing: I never really gave the guys around here a real chance. And Micah was right; it was because I knew I wanted to move on. As for the rest of the town, what little there was of it, I thought I always gave it a pretty fair shake. I'd been participating in every tradition and event for as long as I could remember. Sure, I was now being paid to do it, but that hadn't always been the case.

I heard a noise around a corner up ahead.

"Gunnar?" I called out. The Carter boys rounded the bend and went running by me laughing. "Have y'all seen Gunnar?" I yelled after them. They didn't answer.

I sighed and kept walking.

My brain wouldn't shut off. Micah wasn't perfect either. She'd obviously kept these feelings about me all bottled up for years without sharing them. She couldn't hold my dad's decisions against me. She couldn't hold on to that so tight, as though it was hers to hold on to. She couldn't feel worse about my dad than I did. I swiped at a tear that escaped from my eye.

Micah and I were fighting. Fighting for real. And I wasn't sure how to fix it.

I came to another fork and went left again. If I kept going left, would that take me in a big circle or just on a different path than Andrew?

"Gunnar!" I shouted again.

Silence.

My phone buzzed with a call and I picked it up without looking at the screen. "Did you find him?"

"What happened?" It was my mom.

"Gunnar ran into the maze alone because Jett yelled at him for knocking over the fryer."

There was silence on the other end for so long that I pulled my phone away from my ear to check and see if we had been disconnected. She was still there.

"It was an accident, Mom. No need to get mad at him. I'll find him and you can take him home."

"Jett Hart yelled at Gunnar?" Her voice was ice.

"Yes," I responded quietly.

"Oh, I'm gonna give him what for," she said.

"You are?" She was going to yell at Jett Hart?

"Why wouldn't I? Kind of like I defend you when people down at the market call you a weirdo."

Wait, what? "What?" I asked.

"My point is, I stand up for my kids. And I'm going to give Jett Hart a piece of my mind."

"Momma, no. It's fine. Andrew talked to him and so did I and . . . Hello?" I looked at my phone again. She was gone. I bit my lip, staring at the black screen.

I stood on my tiptoes to try to locate the platform in the middle of the maze but couldn't see anything but cornstalks.

Another group of laughing kids came from around a corner.

"Anyone seen Gunnar?" I asked them.

"No," one of them replied, and kept walking. I continued on, weaving my way toward the middle of the maze, hoping to find the lookout point.

"Soph!" a voice called out.

I turned in a circle but nobody was around.

"Up here!"

I looked up. Andrew stood above the maze, obviously on the platform that I couldn't see. The wooden structure was right below the tops of the stalks.

"Can you see Gunnar from up there?" I called back to Andrew.

He shook his head no. I wanted to get up and see for myself, but he was at least two rows over from me.

"How do I get over there?" I shouted.

He scanned the area around me. "Follow your path straight. About halfway down your row, turn to the right. Then stay right at the fork and it will lead you to the stairs. I'll meet you halfway."

"No, just stay there in case I get turned around," I said, but it was too late; he'd already disappeared from above me.

I followed his directions. Or so I thought. But I couldn't find the corridor on the right he'd been talking about. The path only led to one veering left. Maybe he hadn't realized which row I was in. I kept going, then turned right as soon as I possibly could. But I knew after ten minutes of not discovering stairs that I'd taken the wrong path.

I texted him: *Go back to the platform. I got turned around.*

How could you possibly have gotten turned around? There were literally three steps.

Maybe you give bad directions.

I don't.

You obviously do.

My phone buzzed with a call, making me jump. It was my mom again.

"Hello?"

"He made it out."

"What?"

"Gunnar's out."

"Is he okay?" I asked, relief pouring through me.

She must've handed the phone to Gunnar because he got on and was talking a mile a minute. "I did the whole maze by myself. I was good at it too on account of I'm so fast. Momma was right, I am old enough to do it. I didn't even have to use the lookout. I just remembered all the turns like a map in my head and it was so fun. I should race you next time. The

268

Carter boys were racing and I think I could beat both of them—"

"I'm glad you're okay," I said, cutting him off. "And good job on the maze."

"Thanks. Here's Mom."

"Hey," she said. "So we're takin' off then."

"Okay . . . How's Jett? Was he . . . mean to you?"

"That man is all hat, no cattle."

So my mom could hold her own against Jett Hart. I was impressed. "Did you take it easy on *him*?" I asked.

"I said what needed to be said."

"Thank you, Mom."

"What? I actually get a thank-you? I bring you a letter that says you get free money, nothing. I yell at some grown man, and 'thank you, Mom.'"

The angry feelings that I feared were never going to leave surged in my chest. "Mom . . ."

"What?"

"That scholarship. You know I didn't want it. I've been perfectly clear on what I want to do with my life. To me it only represents the fact that you don't believe in me." There, I'd said it. Sure, I'd said it on the phone so I didn't have to look her in the eye when I did, but still.

Mom didn't respond right away. I held my breath. Apparently I was going to fight with everyone tonight.

"Sophie, I live in the real world," Mom said at last. "And in the real world, this is the money you need to go to college."

"I've been saving and Dad's been saving."

"Dad? You mean that man I loaned a hundred bucks to last week because he's never been able to save a penny in his life? That Dad? Or did you adopt a different one who doesn't have money issues?"

I blinked. "That's not true. He's been matching me."

She just laughed.

My dad hadn't been saving money for me? A pit formed in my stomach and seemed to want to swallow me whole.

"That's not the point!" I protested, feeling desperate. "It doesn't matter. I can apply for grants and aid and . . ."

"Scholarships?" she said.

I couldn't respond. I could hardly breathe.

"I'll see you at home, Sophie," Mom said in a voice that was slightly more sympathetic. "And hey, bring me some of Miss Angel's cookies on your way out. She said another batch was on its way." The line went silent. She'd hung up.

I closed my eyes. Then, with that rage still burning inside me, I sent off a text to my dad.

Is it true? Have you not saved any money for me for college? I never asked you to so why did you need to lie about it?

I pushed Send.

Seconds later he responded back with only two words: *I'm sorry.*

And then my screen went black. I hadn't noticed my battery running low, but that must've been the case because I couldn't power it back on.

I stared at that black screen, a shadowy image of my angry eyes staring back at me. Great. Mom was right. My dad hadn't saved a dime for me. I was screwed.

I tucked my phone in my back pocket. I needed to find a way out of here, even though I really just wished I could melt to the ground and become one with the corn. But I did know *some* wishes weren't realistic. Maybe more than some.

Chapter 32

My kid brother could get out of this maze, but I couldn't? And why did it seem like nobody was left in here but me? I hadn't seen another soul for at least fifteen minutes.

"Hello?" I yelled out. "I give up! Send in the rescuers!"

I pulled my phone back out and tried to power it on again. The battery hadn't magically been charged by my jeans. I shook the phone in frustration. I was shoving it back into my pocket just as I rounded a corner and slammed, full body, into someone. I tripped backward, barely keeping myself from falling.

"Andrew," I said in relief.

He smiled down at me. "This place is like a . . ."

"Maze?" I finished for him.

"Like a really hard one."

"One that apparently an eleven-year-old can accomplish." I brushed my hair out of my face.

"Are you saying Gunnar found his way out?"

"Yes."

Andrew smiled again, letting out a breath. "Good."

"Can I borrow your phone?" I asked. "Mine ran out of battery."

"Ah. Is that why you stopped answering my texts?" He handed me his phone. "I thought maybe you got tired of me mocking your sense of direction."

"That too."

I pulled up his contacts, found Micah, then pushed Call.

She picked up after one ring. "Did you find him?"

"Yes," I said.

"Oh, it's you. You and Andrew never split up?"

"No, we did. We just now found each other again and my phone ran out of battery. Anyway, do you need to be rescued?"

She let out a single laugh. "No, I'll find my way out. I actually circled the entrance twice now. My dad is going to kill me."

"Yeah . . ." I shifted from one foot to the other. "Thanks for helping."

"Yep," she said, then she hung up.

I sighed, trying to decide whether to call her back or not, when Andrew said, "It's probably not a conversation to have over the phone."

"You think you can read my mind?" I asked, handing him back his phone.

"I already told you that I can. I have you figured out, Sophie Evans."

I shook my head, feeling tired. "Maybe you can clue me in."

"What?"

"Nothing. Why don't you figure us out of here, Mr. Know-It-All?"

He jerked his head back the way he'd come from. "I think I can at least get us to the platform. That will help."

"If not, I have a match in my pocket. We can burn this mother down."

He laughed. "Maybe I don't have you all the way figured out."

We walked in silence for several moments before I said, "You see what I mean about the stars?"

He looked up and so did I. "They are pretty incredible out here." His voice sounded as heavy as mine.

"You okay?" I asked. He'd stood up to his dad and I knew that hadn't been easy for him.

"Walking in a maze all alone has a way of making one analyze oneself," he said.

"I agree. We should all be required to do it once a week. A therapy maze or something."

"How has nobody thought of this before?" he asked.

I let out a small laugh and we kept walking.

"So what did you figure out?" I asked.

"That's maze-client privilege."

"You're right. I hope the maze is good with secrets." Because I didn't feel like telling anyone what I'd been dealing with in this maze tonight either. I just wanted to put it all out of my mind, let the maze hold on to it for a while.

Andrew met my eyes, his expression teasing again. "Should we give it some more secrets to keep?"

I shoved his shoulder. "You're funny."

Andrew reached out and batted at a leaf as we walked. "Here's the thing: My dad is a jerk. You've always known that, I've always known that, the world knows that. But I just wanted to . . . I don't know, give him the benefit of the doubt. Try to understand why he is the way he is. And since you know how good I am at figuring people out, obviously—"

"Obviously."

"I thought I understood why he does what he does. Stress, pressure. Trying to climb out of some failure hole he feels he's fallen into."

"Failure hole?"

"Yes. His show failed, his marriage failed, his restaurant—the one he tried to open after the show—failed. So he takes on these failing businesses and helps make them successful. I think it keeps his demons at bay. But just barely, apparently. Because the demons that make him think it's okay to yell at a little kid are still thriving in there."

"For what it's worth," I said, "my brother is going to be fine. It's not like he's never been yelled at. Plus, he got through the maze on his own and was super proud of that."

"As he should be. This thing is no joke."

"Right?"

Andrew sighed. "There's no excuse for what my dad did and since I doubt he'll say sorry, I apologize for him."

"You don't need to do that. By the way, my mom told him off. Your dad, I mean."

Andrew's eyebrows shot up. "Your mom?"

"Yep. My normally selfish, usually apathetic, often oblivious mom stood up to the man she's been flirting with for the last five months. It's been a strange night."

"For the record, I don't think your mom should've worn heels to a farm either," Andrew said. "I'm not sure why that particular comment set Micah off."

"Thanks," I said quietly, but I wasn't sure I believed him. "I'm sure it wasn't that comment. This has obviously been stewing in her." A stalk of corn brushed my elbow, and I shook it off. "But I do have a bias when it comes to my mom. She pretty much can do no right. She has this habit of embarrassing me."

"*What?*" Andrew asked in faux shock.

"I know. I'd lost my patience for her and stopped seeing *her*, I think." I shrugged. "I don't know. The maze didn't really tell me exactly what my deep-seated issues with my mother are. We were working on that before I ran into you. But maybe I've been wrong . . . about a lot of things."

We turned a corner, and in front of us were the wooden stairs leading to the platform.

"I knew I could find it," he said. We took the stairs, climbing to the top. When we were there, we gazed out at the whole cornfield in silence.

What *were* my issues with my mother? Aside from her embarrassing me at every turn. There had to be more than that, didn't there? Because that would be a really dumb reason to be so angry with her all the time.

276

"Maybe I blamed her . . . for my father leaving," I said at last. "If she wasn't so . . . *her* . . . then he'd have wanted to stay. My dad would still be here." I put my hands on the railing of the platform and lowered my head. "That's so wrong of me. He left. I should've been mad at him, but it's like I thought I understood why he wanted to. I mean, look at me, I can't wait to get out of here. Micah is right about me. I'm a judgmental, self-righteous, horrible person." And Micah had finally figured that out. Had finally had enough of me. She'd called me out and was done.

"Sophie," Andrew said, putting his hand on my shoulder.

I turned into him, letting him wrap his arms around me.

"You aren't horrible," he said.

"I am. I'm not mad at my dad. I mean, I wasn't until tonight. He's been lying to me and he's irresponsible and flighty and selfish and what if I'm exactly like him?" Tears streaked down my face, the ones I'd been holding in all night. I couldn't hold them back now.

Andrew rubbed my back softly. "It was easier to be mad at your mom because you see her every day."

"I'm tired of being angry."

"My mom left and I only blamed her, never saw that my dad would be hard to live with. We're opposites."

"We are," I said. "In so many ways."

"Is that why we have a hard time getting along?" he asked, his breath on my temple.

"Probably. Or you're just impossible."

He chuckled a little and I could feel it rumble against my chest.

I started to smile but then the night weighed on my shoulders.

"The maze will keep this a secret, right?" I asked, looking up at Andrew. "We can't have people getting the wrong idea about us."

I couldn't make out the expression in his eyes, but he nodded. "I have complete faith in the maze."

When we finally made it out, we both let out a shout of victory.

"Remind me never to enter us into any sort of puzzle race," Andrew said.

"If this was a puzzle, I would've figured it out a lot faster," I argued.

"Oh really?"

"Yes."

He started to respond but then he looked around. "Um . . . the whole town was just going to leave us in there?"

I looked around too. How long had we been in that black hole? All the booths were broken down and trucked away. All the tables were stacked and waiting to be moved. And nearly every car in the dirt parking area was gone. All except the flower van. The tins of flowers were lined up beside it. Caroline had left. Micah had left. Everyone had left.

"You think you can give me a ride home?" Andrew asked.

"Of course."

Our jovial mood from before subsided as we walked to the van. "Your dad will get over it," I said after a few minutes of silence.

"So will Micah," he responded.

I could tell that neither of us completely believed the words we'd just uttered. Because if I knew one thing about Micah it was this: Once she'd moved on from someone, she moved on for good.

Thanksgiving Dinner at the Williamses' House

ORANGE CALLA LILY

According to Greek legend, Zeus brought his love child to his wife, Hera, to drink her milk while she was asleep. When she awoke in anger and pushed the child away, milk flew across the sky. The drops that landed on the earth grew into calla lilies. This is about the strangest origin story ever for a flower. But sometimes strange is beautiful.

Chapter 33

Tradition was that every year on Thanksgiving, we went to the Williamses' house. Mr. Williams cooked most of the meal, and my mom and I brought a side dish, pretending our contribution was needed. And we ate and laughed and were grateful. But this year was different. Micah and I hadn't talked to each other in a month. One month. I had tried to apologize, she'd tried to apologize, but then we had immediately rehashed the same argument again, unable to agree.

So I'd spent the last month pretty much alone with my design journal. Applications were due basically now, and I hadn't turned in a single one. Micah, of course, who had lots of connections in this town, had spent the last month busy with friends. Which had only driven home her point.

Despite our fight, our clueless parents were keeping tradition alive, which was why I found myself sitting in the car in front of Micah's house, my brother holding a pan of corn pudding in the back seat and my mom wearing the dress I'd gotten her for Mother's Day.

I suddenly understood why she'd never worn it before. I had prided myself on always doing what was best for a client, and yet I had picked her out a dress that was utterly and completely not her. It had an empire waistline and hit her below the knee. It was loose fitting and had vertical stripes, and she may as well have been going to Sunday school with how proper she looked in it. What had I been thinking? I had been trying to change her, that's what I'd been thinking.

"Y'all ready?" my mom said, turning off the car.

"I'll be up in a minute," I said. My design notebook was open in my lap. "I want to finish this sketch."

"Sophie," my mom started, but I just gave her a look. "Okay, okay. See you in a minute."

She and Gunnar climbed out of the car. I watched them walk to the door and be welcomed in by Mrs. Williams. I watched as Mrs. Williams waved to me. I waved back. Then I stared down at my journal.

"Ugh." I drew an X through the sketch of a dress I'd been half-heartedly working on. Maybe everyone was right. Maybe New York was out of my reach. I'd been thinking about that a lot in the last few weeks too. I had a scholarship and could apply to a school here in Alabama. It was time to admit defeat. I tucked my journal into my bag and climbed out of the car, dreading today.

I knocked on the door and Mrs. Williams opened it with a big smile. "Sophie Evans! Where have you been the last few weeks? Get your cute butt in here." She grabbed me by the face and kissed my cheek.

"Hi, Mrs. Williams. Happy Thanksgiving."

My mom and Gunnar were still lingering in the entryway, talking with Mr. Williams.

"I hope y'all don't mind our additional guests this year." Mrs. Williams looked directly at my brother. "I know Mr. Hart wasn't kind to you a few weeks ago but he promised to be on his best behavior."

I hadn't realized the Harts were coming. My mom didn't seem surprised, though, so she must've been warned.

"It's okay," Gunnar said. "Andrew brought me a milk shake from his dad last week, so that means he's real sorry."

I was sure the milk shake hadn't been from his dad, but it had worked on Gunnar perfectly.

"Is that for me?" Mrs. Williams asked Gunnar, gesturing to the pan he held.

"It's corn pudding." Gunnar extended it out to her.

"Perfect!" Mrs. Williams said. "That's exactly what we were missing." She said this every year, no matter what we brought. We could bring a bag of air and she'd probably say, *That's exactly what we were missing.*

Gunnar looked very pleased with this pronouncement.

"Micah!" Mrs. Williams called out. "Sophie is here!" When Micah didn't come, her mom gestured down the hall. "I think she's in her room. You can go on back."

"Okay, thanks."

"Point me to the wine," Mom said. Mrs. Williams laughed and walked with my mom farther into the house, my brother trailing after them.

I clutched the strap on my backpack and stared at the long, dark hall in front of me. In the past month, Micah might not have noticed my absence, being surrounded by all her friends, but to me it felt like a piece of my soul was missing. We needed to work this out. The first step forward was the hardest. After that my feet easily found their way to her door.

I knocked quietly.

"Come in," she said.

I opened the door and stood in the doorway. She sat in front of her mirror, applying a shimmery gold eye shadow. Her eyes met mine in her mirror.

"Hi," I said.

"Hi," she said back. She put her eye shadow into its makeup bag, then burst into tears.

I let my backpack slide off my shoulder and onto the floor. I rushed to her side, tears pouring down my face as well.

"I'm sorry, Soph," she said. I knelt down and hugged her tight, and was so relieved when she hugged me back.

"Me too," I said. "Really sorry."

"I've missed you. I can't live like this, without you."

"Me neither." Just her saying those words seemed to put back together something inside of me. "You were right. I have been a snob. And I have dreamed of nothing but leaving this town and I was rude and judgmental and hard to be around."

"No." Micah sniffled and pulled back from our hug. "I mean, yes, you kind of were, but I've just been scared to lose you. You're right. I've taken something that happened to you, your dad leaving, and acted like it was some sort of omen of the future." She shook her head. "I know you're not him. I know you would never forget about me."

"Never."

"And I've kept you away from your one true love."

I started to nod but then her words sank in. "Wait, what?"

"Andrew."

I laughed a little, drying my eyes. "What are you talking about?"

"I wanted you to be with someone from Rockside, someone like Kyle. I hoped it would keep you here. So from day one I've tried to get you to ignore this connection you have with Andrew."

I covered my face with my hands. "That wasn't your fault at all. Andrew and I don't need any help being at odds."

"Believe me, a little push was all you needed from the beginning," Micah said. "Instead I've been pulling you both away from each other. Please don't be even more mad at me."

I chuckled. "I'm not. He's not my one true love."

She groaned. "See, I've talked you out of him. You hate him because of me."

"Andrew's fine. I mean, I can see why people like him. I definitely don't hate him. We get along now . . ." I trailed off. "Oh no."

"See! You love him."

Fear gripped my chest. Holy crap. She was right.

Well, okay. I didn't know about the *love* part but . . . I couldn't deny it anymore. I had feelings for Andrew Hart. I had feelings for someone who was not only leaving in less than two months, but who was so far out of my league that we technically should've never met in the first place.

"He's leaving in like six weeks," I said. "It's too late to figure this out."

"I know. That's my fault!"

I squeezed her hand. "Stop. It's not your fault. Has he said anything to you about where they're going next? Has his dad picked yet?"

"I don't think so. Why?"

"I just . . . There was this lady who applied who lives nearby. I met her sister at that benefit. I thought maybe . . ."

"Oh!" Micah brightened. "I hadn't thought of that. That could work. We have to make that work. It will be my penance."

"What's my penance, then?" I asked.

"Just stop being a snob," she said with a smile. "And come back and visit me on every major holiday. You can do the flowers."

I laughed. "No flowers, but I'll be here." I swiped beneath my eyes. "Look at us. We're both a mess."

She turned toward the mirror. "I just did my makeup too!" She pulled a makeup wipe from her *just-in-case* and handed it to me. "Guess we get to start over."

As we worked on our makeup, side by side, I couldn't help but smile. When my eyeliner was fixed, I reached for the small bowl of assorted candy Micah always kept on the dresser next to her mirror. I plucked a Hershey's Kiss from it, unwrapped the candy, and put it in my mouth.

"Why did you bring a backpack?" Micah asked, nodding toward where my bag had dropped in the corner. "Planning on doing homework today?"

"Ugh, my design journal is in there. But, also . . ." I scooted over to my bag then dragged it back to Micah. "I was in Everything the other day and I found something." I undid the zippers and pulled out a tall rectangular box with two lenses on the front and several knobs on either side.

Micah peered at the object. "What is it?"

"A vintage camera. Someone must've cleaned out their attic and didn't realize what they had. Tell me this isn't cool?"

"It's cool . . . but I didn't know you liked cameras."

"Not me. It was cheap." Sort of. "I thought Andrew might like it. We could give it to him for Christmas."

She took the camera from me and turned it over a few times in her hands. "Are you seriously trying to tell me that you didn't know you liked Andrew before today?"

"I . . . apparently don't know myself very well at all. I've learned that lately."

A knock sounded at the door, followed by the sound of Andrew's voice. "It's me. Can I come in?"

Chapter 34

I quickly shoved the camera back in my backpack and zipped it up. "Don't tell him."

"Which part am I not telling him about?" Micah asked with an innocent smile. "That?" She pointed to the bag. "Or that?" She pointed to my face, and I could feel my blush.

"Please," I said, and grabbed a mascara tube from Micah's makeup stash and turned toward the mirror.

"Come in," Micah sang out.

Andrew poked his head around the door. "I was told this was where the party was."

I laughed, even though his statement wasn't funny at all. Crap. Micah wouldn't have to say a word about anything—I was going to give myself away all on my own.

He couldn't know I liked him yet. Not with him leaving in six weeks and me having no idea at all how he felt about me.

His eyes flickered to me. "Sophie Evans," he said. "My maze partner. Nice shirt."

I looked down at my long-sleeved tee, which was navy blue with little bumblebees all over it. Then I said, "I can get you one."

He stepped all the way into the room. "Does it come in turtleneck form? I only wear my tight shirts in that style." He sat on the edge of the bed.

"Don't tempt me," I said.

He shrugged. "You're the one who offered."

I studied him from where I sat. Andrew Hart was handsome. It wasn't like I hadn't noticed that before. I mean, I had noticed it the first day I met him. But personality always played a bigger role for me, and the more I got to know him, the more his looks had faded. But somewhere in the last couple of months—maybe it was sitting watching fireworks through a hole in the roof during July Fourth, or eating ambrosia salad off his fork at a funeral, or finding our way through a corn maze together—he had turned a corner and I could now objectively say he was very, *very* handsome. It was a combination of a lot of things—the way he carried himself with ease and confidence, his thick brown hair, his playful blue eyes, his contagious smile.

"What?" he asked.

He'd caught me staring. I tried to play it off and started applying mascara.

"So is this what you've been doing for the past however many Thanksgivings?" I asked, facing the mirror with Micah.

"Coming to Micah's house? No, we just met at the beginning of the year."

Micah laughed and swatted at his leg.

I rolled my eyes. "I meant spending it with the family of the business your dad is mentoring or whatever."

"Actually, we usually cater on Thanksgiving," Andrew said.

"What?" I asked, meeting his eyes in the mirror. "Really?"

"Really."

"You poor, overworked white boy," Micah said.

"I know. It's a true sob story," he said.

Micah held her hand out for the mascara and I placed it in her upturned palm. "It *is* kind of sad, actually," she said.

"Sad, pathetic? Or sad, you now want to take care of me?"

"A little of both," Micah said.

"I'll take care of you," I said, then my ears went hot. It was supposed to come out as a joke but it sounded extra flirty.

Andrew's brow furrowed in confusion.

"Well, that's the best offer you're getting all day," Micah said. "Although my mother might make a similar offer."

"Um . . ." he said.

"That sounded inappropriate," Micah said. "It wasn't meant to. I just meant, she really likes to mother people. All of us will be taken care of by my mother today. I'm going to shut up now."

I laughed, grateful she had hijacked the awkwardness because I had been on a one-way street to There's No Turning Back From Here.

Micah capped her mascara and threw it into her makeup bag. "There. I am now even more beautiful."

I smiled at her. She already had naturally long lashes and didn't even need mascara at all. "Should we join the others?" I asked.

"Well, unless someone else wanted to borrow any makeup." Micah winked at Andrew.

"I have always wondered what I'd look like with eyeliner."

"You'd look amazing," Micah said, then stood and pointed to the carpet where she'd been sitting. "Come. It is time for your wondering to be over."

"I was joking," he said.

"Joking has consequences, my friend. And this is yours." She dug through her makeup bag for her eyeliner. "Andrew. Now."

He rolled his eyes and sat on the carpet next to me.

"Sophie is better at applying eyeliner than I am. It's her steady artist hand," Micah said. She extended the eyeliner that she'd freed from her bag to me.

I held her gaze. She raised her eyebrows in a challenge, as if asking me what I was going to do about my newly discovered feelings.

"I *am* pretty good at applying eyeliner." I swiped the pencil from her hand and turned to face Andrew. I uncapped the pencil, then examined the point.

"These are dire consequences for a joke," Andrew said. "Letting you near my eyes with such a sharp object."

"You don't trust me?" I asked.

He raised one side of his mouth into a half smile and said, "No." But he also lowered himself off his knees and turned to face me. My heart was racing and I tried to ignore it.

"Do you want the *I'm a lead singer in a rock band* look or the *I'm Captain Jack Sparrow* look?" I asked.

"I want the minimalist look, whatever that is."

"He wants the *just make these baby blues look even bluer* look," Micah said. "Seriously, I don't know why more guys don't wear makeup."

I leaned closer to him and his eyes were intent on me. "You need to look down," I said.

He followed my direction. Never before had I analyzed how I put eyeliner on someone until that moment. The edge of the palm holding the liner had to rest on his cheek and my free hand went to his chin to hold him steady and control his movement.

"I'll be right back," Micah said. "I need to make sure Dad doesn't need help."

I gave her wide eyes as she left but she just shot me an innocent smile, then closed the door behind her. My breathing went shallow, but I tried to steady it. I continued lining his right eye.

"You smell like chocolate," he said.

"Yes, I ate a . . ." I trailed off.

"A what?" he asked.

My cheeks went hot and I knew I couldn't say the word *kiss* without completely giving myself away. "Some chocolate," I said. "Look up."

His whole head went up.

"No, just your eyes."

"Oh." He readjusted, and I lined the bottom of his right eye. Then I dropped my hand and leaned back to assess.

"How does it look?" he asked.

This very handsome boy in front of you is leaving. He always leaves, I reminded myself. "Um . . . yeah, so blue. Let me do the other side."

He looked down without me having to ask and I now had to rest my palm across his nose.

"Sorry," I said.

"The lengths we go to for beauty." His hand brushed my knee and I nearly smeared liner across his temple.

I managed to steady my grip on the pencil. "Look up." He did, and I finished off the last of it. "There." My hand that was still on his chin moved his face one way, and then the other, so I could make sure I got it even. "You're a babe." I didn't know why I said that—it just flew out. I pretended like it was a completely normal thing to say. It actually probably was. It was something Micah would say to a friend. He would think nothing of it unless I acted weird. Which I kind of was. I dropped my hand and scooted away from him. "Have a look." I pointed to the mirror.

He turned to look at his reflection. "How much do you want to bet nobody out there even notices I'm wearing it?"

"You already owe me so many things, sir, but I will take that bet." I held out my hand.

"You with your shaking of hands." He took my hand and gripped it tight, meeting my eyes. That eyeliner really did make his eyes pop. They were gorgeous. He shook my hand several times, then hopped up from his sitting position and pulled me up with him.

"How are things with Micah?" he asked, not letting go of my hand.

"Getting better. And you? How are things with your dad?"

"Getting better as well. He actually apologized if you can believe that. Said he's been under a lot of pressure." He finally dropped my hand.

"You were right about that, then."

He shrugged. "It's not a good excuse, but maybe he needed to blow up at a little kid to see how bad he's gotten. He seems to be trying."

"Good." We stood staring at each other. My stomach was fluttering with a million winged insects that seemed to want to escape. And I wanted to escape with them.

So I did.

"We better go help in the kitchen." I turned on my heel and left the room too fast to pull off casual.

Chapter 35

The kitchen was a bustle of activity and I dove right into it, needing the distraction. Mr. Williams was stirring some gravy at the stove and I sidled up next to him.

"I'm a really good stirrer," I offered.

He handed off the chore and moved to slicing up some butter to add to the mashed potatoes. Micah was getting plates from the cupboard and taking them to the dining room next door. Jett was standing in the middle of all the action, but he looked more lost than I'd ever seen him look in a kitchen.

"Jett," Mr. Williams said, obviously not for the first time. "You are my guest today. You can join the others in the living room."

Jett probably didn't want to be in there with my mother, and I wasn't sure if it was because he was worried she might yell at him or flirt with him.

He didn't listen. He moved to a bowl on the counter and tossed the salad, which looked like it had already been tossed. "I still don't understand why you aren't catering today," he said to Mr. Williams. "People pay triple the amount on Thanksgiving."

"It's a family day, Jett. That's why," Mr. Williams said. "Sometimes it's not about the money."

Jett harrumphed.

"I also won't be catering on Christmas."

"Your loss," Jett said.

"I'd like to think of it as my gain," Mr. Williams said. "You're welcome to join our family for Christmas Day if you'd like to as well."

"Since you're not catering, I think we'll go home for Christmas," Jett replied.

"To Manhattan?" I asked.

"Yes," he said.

"Sophie wants to go to college in Manhattan," Mr. Williams said.

"Maybe," I responded. Lately, I'd realized something in all my realizing—the city wasn't going to turn me into this sophisticated person that I had always thought would emerge once I was there. Who I was, who I was going to be, depended on me, not where I lived. "I'm going to apply to a lot of places."

Micah's head whipped toward me as she headed for the door, carrying four glasses. "What?" she said. "No New York for you? Since when?"

"Since . . . I don't know. One day. I still want to be there one day." Maybe I needed to be surer of myself first, so I didn't completely lose what bits of myself I was finding in all the chaos.

For the first time . . . ever . . . Jett looked at me with a hint of interest.

Micah pushed through the door with her hands full of glasses.

I stopped stirring. "I think the gravy is done," I said.

"Good, good," Mr. Williams said. "Pour it into the boat over there and let's start putting food on the table."

I carried the single boat of gravy into the dining room. The first thing I saw was the flower arrangement I had made the day before sitting in the center of the long table. It was mostly calla lilies, framed by some palm leaves. The note Caroline had left for me from the call-in request had said: *An orange calla lily arrangement, your discretion. Will be picked up on Wednesday evening.*

I'd gotten off work at four yesterday, so I had no idea who'd come to pick it up. Had Mrs. Williams ordered it? I looked around, but I was the only one in the dining room. I could hear laughter coming from the living room.

"I have paid off one of my debts," a voice said from behind me. "A flower arrangement, bought by me and arranged by you. Orange calla lilies."

I turned around to look at Andrew, a bit of gravy sloshing onto my hand. It was hot and I sucked some air between my teeth, then set the gravy on the table and wiped off my hand.

"They're pretty," he said when I still didn't speak.

"They're my favorite."

"Because they're pretty, or do you have a history with them?"

I did have a history with calla lilies. There'd been a daddy-daughter dance at school and my dad had brought me a single calla lily. My mom had threaded it into my ponytail. It had been a good night. We used to be a pretty solid family. My dad had thrown that all away. He was continuing to throw it away. After his *I'm sorry* text, I'd called him and he'd confirmed all his lies. He hadn't saved a dime of money for me. He said that he was planning to do it. He kept hoping he'd catch up. He just wasn't there yet.

"I'm sensing history," Andrew said.

I realized I was staring at the arrangement. Probably not kindly. I turned to answer him when a train of people came into the dining room, carrying food dishes.

"Thank you," I said to him quietly.

"I haven't stolen a flower since February, by the way. I'm reformed."

I smiled.

"Let's eat!" Mr. Williams said.

My plate was empty for the second time and my stomach was beyond full. I groaned and leaned back in my chair. Mr. Williams had made fried turkey, mac and cheese, fresh dinner rolls, green beans, and more, and I'd sampled almost everything.

"You didn't pace yourself," Andrew said from beside me.

My brother was on my other side, shoveling mashed potatoes into his mouth.

"I know," I said. "Rookie mistake."

Andrew picked up the bowl of ambrosia salad and held it out for me. "You didn't even get any of this," he said.

I had been purposely avoiding that salad. It would remind me of a certain hot day by a certain shed kissing a certain boy whose mouth tasted like cherries. I didn't need to think about kissing Andrew right now. I was trying to remind myself that he was leaving, not that I wanted him to stay.

"No thanks," I said.

Micah sat on Andrew's other side, and she leaned forward and looked at me. She hadn't said anything about my New York declaration in the kitchen earlier, so I waited for what she was going to say now. But all she said was, "I hope you saved room for dessert."

"Ugh," I said, rubbing my stomach. "Hey, Micah. Do you still have that karaoke machine?" I hadn't seen it in a couple of years.

"Yes," she said warily. "Why?"

"Because my mom would rock at karaoke."

"You think I haven't done karaoke before?" Mom, who sat across from me, said.

I shrugged. "I've never seen it."

"Well, you're right. I am fairly amazing at it. We could have a sing-off."

I smiled and Micah gave me another confused look. It wasn't what we normally did on Thanksgiving. Normally, after dinner, Micah and I walked the neighborhood or threw a football around the backyard while the adults chatted inside, but new traditions could be fun too.

Micah looked at her mom, who gave a smile and a nod. Then Micah said, "Okay, I'll set it up after we clear dinner."

Andrew took a small bite of the corn pudding on his plate.

"Not a fan?" I asked.

"It's interesting." He set down his fork. "By the way, what do I win?"

"For what?" I asked.

"For nobody noticing my beautiful eyes."

"What do you want?" I asked.

A playful glimmer came into his eyes.

"I owe you five dollars," I said, before he gave voice to whatever was causing that glimmer. "Which really just wipes out the five dollars you owed me before. So it's a wash."

"You're no fun."

"This is true." I smiled and stood.

My mom was having fun singing her heart out to Carrie Underwood. I tried not to think about what was going through Jett Hart's mind as he sat on the armchair in the corner, with not even the hint of a smile on his face. That was what had gotten me into trouble in the first place, caring too much about how other people felt. I needed to care more how I felt. And I enjoyed seeing my mom so happy. My mom was right, she had a good voice. Probably better than Gloria and her daughter.

"*You* should've sung the national anthem in high school!" I called out to Mom over the music.

"Right?" she said into the microphone. "Some people are national anthem hogs! Jesus take the wheel!" she added, rejoining the song.

Andrew laughed. "Your mom is hilarious."

"She really is," I said.

My phone buzzed in my pocket. Since everyone I usually talked to was in this room, I was curious. I pulled it out and looked at the screen.

Dad.

I stood and let myself out the sliding glass door and onto the back patio.

"Hello?"

"Soph!" my dad said. We'd only exchanged a couple of texts since our last painful conversation, and I was surprised at the anger that coursed through me at the sound of his voice.

"Hi," I said tightly.

"Happy Thanksgiving, kid. Are y'all at Micah's house?"

"Yes."

"I miss the Williams family Thanksgivings."

"Do you?"

"Of course I do."

The back patio wrapped around both sides of the house,

and I followed it past several large potted plants to a porch swing tucked in an alcove. I sat down.

"You still there?" Dad asked.

"Is that all you miss?" I knew I was fishing, needing to hear him defend himself without coming out and saying what I wanted. But these feelings were very new to me. The chats with my dad were normally surface level and light. I hadn't really realized that until now either.

"I miss a lot of things," he said. "But mostly you and your brother."

I nodded even though he couldn't see me. "But you're happy?" I asked.

"What's going on, Sophie? Is everything okay?"

"Things are actually going really well. I think maybe I picked the wrong side all these years."

"I don't understand what you mean," he said.

"Between you and mom."

"There aren't sides," he said. "We both love you."

"I get that. But one of you is showing it more than the other."

"Is this still about the money?"

"No," I said, meaning it. "It was never about money, Dad. It was about the lie. It was about me, thinking all these years that Mom was embarrassing and hard on me and selfish. But she's a single mom trying to support us. Of course she's always late. Of course she needs help with Gunnar. She has to do everything. And you just have to call occasionally and say a few nice things."

"Where is all this coming from, Sophie?" Dad asked. "Let me talk to Larissa."

"It didn't come from her. It came from me. Way too late, but I got there eventually." I pushed myself on the swing and took a big breath. "I love you. I always will. You're my dad. But you need to step up. It's not too late. Come out here and visit, or fly Gunnar out to see you. *Do* something."

"Unbelievable," Dad said, then he hung up. It surprised me so much that I thought maybe I had imagined it. But my phone showed the call was over. I closed my eyes for a second. He was a runner, I reminded myself. When things got hard, he bailed. I pulled my knees up to my chest and rested my chin on them.

That's when I heard two people around the corner, talking. They obviously didn't know I could hear every word they said. The voices belonged to Micah and Andrew, and they were talking about me.

Chapter 36

"Was it me who got in her head or you?" Micah asked. She must've batted at the leaves on the potted plant that blocked their view of me; I heard the smack and watched the over-grown bush shake.

"What are you talking about?" Andrew asked. His voice was quieter but I could still hear it clearly.

"Was it you with all your talk about how she wouldn't fit in in New York? Or me with the whole *you hate our town and people* speech?"

"I never told her she wouldn't fit in in New York."

"Yes, you did."

I strained forward on the porch swing, holding my breath.

"I may have said something about it being a hard place to live or that it eats people alive, but I wasn't talking about her. I was mostly talking about me."

"She thought you were talking about her."

"She probably *wouldn't* fit in there," Andrew said. "But New York is the kind of place you should want to stand out in. And she would definitely stand out."

"You need to tell her that."

"She thinks I was telling her not to move to New York? No wonder she hates me."

"She doesn't hate you," Micah said. "You just broke her, that's all."

"What happened to the idea that you broke her with all the *you're a snob* talk?"

"You're right. I broke her too." Micah sighed. "We both broke her and now she doesn't want to go to New York anymore. This is her lifelong dream and she's just giving up. She's quitting. She's settling or something."

"I'm not settling!" I called out.

Micah screamed, then poked her head around the bush to the alcove where I sat, pushing the swing ever so gently with my foot.

"Soph, you are such an eavesdropper," she said.

"Maybe you shouldn't be talking about me behind my back."

"I always talk about you behind your back. Mostly good things. Or in this case getting advice on how to fix you."

"I'm not broken."

Micah walked over and lowered herself onto the swing beside me. "Then why? Does this have to do with what I said at the Fall Festival?"

My eyes flickered to Andrew, who hung in the background, as though unsure if he should leave or not. My thoughts about New York versus Alabama had nothing to do with what Micah had said. It had to do with the fact that I had been feeling unworthy ever since the city, in the form of Andrew Hart, walked into my life, seeming to say my designs, me, weren't good enough. But that was my perception. My own lack of confidence that I was projecting onto him.

"It's me," Andrew spoke up. "If I made it seem like you wouldn't survive in New York, I didn't mean to. New York would be happy to have you." He lowered his eyes to the ground before they met mine again.

"No, it's neither of you," I said, looking from Andrew to Micah. "I promise. It's me. It's my stupid design journal full of nothing that is unique enough to do anything with right now. I just need to figure myself out a while and I don't need New York to do that."

Micah rested her head on my shoulder. "You know yourself. More than you realize, I think."

I laughed. "Those two sentences contradict each other and are exactly my point."

"So you're going to take that scholarship?" Micah asked. A month ago she would've been happy about this, but she didn't seem to be now.

"I think so."

"I'll be right back." Micah stood and rushed away around the corner.

My mom's voice, singing away to a completely new song, sounded and then was cut off again as Micah opened then closed the sliding door.

Andrew stood there in silence, then pointed to the seat

next to me that Micah had abandoned. I nodded and he sat down. "Was that your dad on the phone earlier?" he asked.

My dad. I'd almost forgotten how badly that conversation had ended. "Yes."

"Everything okay?"

"I don't know. A lot of things have become clear to me lately and some of them are hard to accept."

"I guess that means we're growing up." He said it like a joke but he was right. I imagined that was part of growing up—seeing things for how they really were and not just how you wanted them to be. *Like you, Andrew*, I wanted to say. There was what I wanted and then there was reality—a future that would take us our separate ways.

"You look so sad," he said, placing his hand on mine. "What can I do?"

"I'm not sad," I said, looking at him. His blue eyes seemed very intense. "Just being more realistic lately . . . I just need to . . . Your eyes are very distracting. You need to take that eyeliner off stat."

He smiled. I turned my hand palm up, letting our fingers slide together.

He curled his fingers around mine. "I'm sorry I was a jerk to you most of the year."

I smiled. "Ditto. I'm glad we're friends now."

He looked down at our hands. "Me too."

Friends, I said to myself firmly. *We have to be just friends.*

Micah's feet on the wooden porch preceded her arrival. I

let go of Andrew's hand and turned toward her as she rounded the corner. She held my design journal and wore a nervous expression.

"Don't be mad!" she said. "I know you don't like anyone touching this. But can we help you? Let us help you."

I frowned. "How can you help me?"

"Maybe we can look through it." She nodded at Andrew. "Tell you what stands out to us, what feels unique."

My automatic instinct was to throw my guard up, to bury my journal in her backyard under the willow tree. But that seemed a little dramatic. It was the wrong instinct. That was my pride talking. What was wrong with letting people help me?

"Okay," I said quietly.

"Yes?" she asked, excited.

I nodded.

She came to the other side of the swing. "Okay, scoot, scoot." She gestured for me to slide closer to Andrew. The swing wasn't built for three, but Andrew inched as far as he could to the right and made more room by draping his arm along the back of the seat. I slid over against his side. He smelled good, like fresh linen and musky cologne. Micah sat on my left and placed my journal in my lap. Then both she and Andrew leaned toward me in anticipation.

"So, it's kind of messy, and whatever inspiration catches my eye just gets added to it with no rhyme or reason," I said, clutching the journal.

"Stop stalling," Andrew said.

"Yes, we want to see what lives in that messy brain of yours," Micah said.

"Not helping," I said.

She bumped her shoulder against mine and I opened the book.

I turned to the first page: a sketch I'd drawn over two years ago. It was a basic pencil skirt with a billowy blouse. Nothing special, but it was well drawn. I remembered taking my time on each and every line. I turned the page to where I'd stored a magazine clipping of a pink dress I liked. I didn't even remember why I liked the dress. It was cute, but it didn't feel like my style at all. Micah and Andrew were exceptionally quiet and I wondered if they were waiting for me to ask their opinions. I was too nervous to do that.

I kept flipping. It was much of the same. Page after page of sketches and snippets from magazines or scraps of cloth. Micah started humming a little when I turned to something she found cute.

"How is this going to help me exactly?" I asked. I wondered if looking at these was actually lowering my confidence in my ability to become anything but just a really good drawer.

"They're good, Soph," Micah said. "I was hoping you'd see that."

I flipped to another page and was about to flip it again when I stopped myself. The sketch here wasn't exceptionally detailed. In fact, my lines were shaky and it wasn't complete, but it felt different from the others. The skirt was fitted along the hips and flared out at the bottom, the front of the skirt higher, the back coming to a soft point. It almost looked like a lily. An upside-down lily. I looked at the date I'd scribbled in the corner. I'd drawn it the week I'd started working at the flower shop.

Andrew must've noticed something different about the sketch too. He asked, "What changed?"

"I got my job this week," I said. I flipped to another page. This one was a sketch of a dress, its buttons roses, its skirt layers and layers like rose petals.

"Flowers," Micah whispered. "*That's* your spin."

I turned more pages. Not all my designs were flower themed. Not even every third one. But the ones that incorporated flowers seemed to pop off the page, seemed to come alive. I thought of all the images that had popped into my head this past year when I'd been around flowers—the girls in dresses marching through a field of tulips, the ballerinas dancing over sunflowers. Maybe my inspiration had been in front of me all along.

"Is that the flower I gave you?" Andrew asked. He kept me from turning a page again by placing his hand on the book. A pink tulip was pressed flat. The page behind it featured a sketch of a scalloped-sleeved blouse. That was the day I'd met Andrew. I'd thought the design wasn't going anywhere, but it was. Now that I looked at it, I knew I needed to add layers to the sleeve instead of just the scallops.

"That is not the flower you gave me," I protested. "I'd put this in before we even met."

"Sure . . ."

"This one was a throwaway. The stem wasn't long enough."

"Just keep talking," he said in that teasing voice of his.

I pinched his side and he laughed. I closed the journal.

"Wait, what are you doing?" Micah asked. "We're not done."

"We are," I said. "You're right. Flowers are my thing. I'm going to perfect all my flower designs and that will be my portfolio for design school applications." I felt a rush of certainty that warmed me.

"For *New York* design school applications," Micah said.

I hugged my book to my chest and nodded.

Micah threw her arms around me.

"Thank you for pushing me." I glanced over at Andrew, hoping he knew that statement was for him too. His smile said he did.

Mr. Williams appeared around the corner. "There you are," he said. "It's time for dessert."

"We're coming," Micah said. "Let's eat some pie, y'all. We've earned it."

Chapter 37

Hey, Gunnar, do you want to play football with us?" I asked after we'd eaten dessert. I wasn't sure why the tradition of physical activity existed on the day when everyone overate. It seemed like naptime was the only thing that made sense, but that wasn't happening.

"I can?" Gunnar asked, jumping up.

"Yes," I said. "I want you on my team on account of you being such a fast runner."

He cheered and, as if proving my point, ran out the door and into the Williamses' backyard.

"I guess that means I'm on your team," Andrew said to Micah. "Are you any good?"

"I'm the best," Micah said, following Gunnar outside.

"Nice. You're going down, Sophie," Andrew said.

"Kind of like that rock you tried to skip in the lake?" I replied.

"Um . . . yes actually. Were you meaning to back up my statement?" he asked.

I thought about it. "No, I was trying to insult your throwing abilities."

Micah picked up a basket of flip-flops by the back door, which she always used to mark out boundaries on the grass. "Next time just say: 'Well, you can't throw, so there,'" Micah said.

"I thought you were on my team," Andrew said to her.

"I am, but Sophie needed help with her smack talk."

"Since when?" Andrew asked, glancing at me. "You've been flinging the best insults at me all year."

I kicked at his leg as we walked to the grass. "I know! I've gone soft."

"I have a feeling that's not true at all."

We'd been playing for a while when the adults came outside, wanting to join us. They'd never done that before and I wondered what had happened inside to make sports with us seem appealing.

Mr. Williams answered my question when he said, "Jett has never played a game of touch football."

"Plus," Mom said, "he thinks it looks easy."

Gunnar had probably been making it look easy. He'd caught almost every throw I'd passed to him and was just as fast as I'd hoped. We were totally killing Micah and Andrew, much to Andrew's dismay.

"We'll take my parents!" Micah called out, waving to her mom and dad to join her and Andrew.

I gave Jett a once-over as he came to join my team. "Are you going to make me lose?" I asked him.

Andrew laughed.

My mom seemed to be assessing Jett as well. "We got this," she said to me, holding her hand up. I complied by giving her a high five.

"Sorry you felt like you needed to wear that dress," I said to her quietly.

"It's really comfortable."

"You never have to wear it again."

She laughed and pulled me into a side hug. "Love you, kid."

"Love you too."

I remained in my position as quarterback. It seemed to be Andrew's new goal, now that he had extra people on his team and didn't have to play receiver, to try to get to me before I could throw the ball. For the fourth time since the adults had joined us, I found myself trying to outrun him. Gunnar was being double-teamed by Micah's parents, my mom was illegally holding Micah to keep her in place, but Jett was open downfield.

I hadn't thrown to him once and he held out his hands and called, "Give it up, flower girl!"

I pressed my lips together and threw just as Andrew reached me. He picked me up and spun me around.

"Too late!" I called out to him.

He laughed and then paused, me in his arms, as we watched his dad catch the ball and run into the end zone.

"Ha!" I called out.

"It figures that my dad's a natural," Andrew said. "And that he's on your team."

Gunnar came running our way and slammed into me and Andrew, knocking us both down. Andrew landed on his back with a grunt and I landed back first on top of him, with Gunnar lying flat on me.

"We win!" Gunnar said, rolling off me, jumping up, and doing a lap around the yard to rub his victory in everyone's faces. I rolled off Andrew and onto my side to face him.

"You okay?" I asked.

"No air," he said, still on his back, holding his chest like he couldn't breathe.

I smacked his arm. "Good thing we didn't play tackle, wimp."

He stared up at the sky, a small smile on his face. "This is why people don't cater on Thanksgiving," he said.

"Why?"

"Because being with family is so much better."

I smiled, sitting up, and looked around. My mom was showing Jett how to hold a football. Micah was tickling Gunnar while telling him that she let him win. Mr. and Mrs. Williams were studying some weeds at the edge of the grass, his arm around her shoulder. We weren't all technically family, but I knew what he meant. Family was everything.

New Year's Eve Barn Dance

FORGET-ME-NOT

With a bloom of one centimeter or less, one might see how this tiny flower earned its name. But with its pretty blue color and self-spreading nature, which help it easily take over flower beds, it makes sure that it's pretty unforgettable.

Chapter 38

I sat in the flower van, close to hyperventilating. I didn't want to feel this way. I took a deep breath in through my nose and out my mouth, trying to calm myself down. I hadn't seen Andrew since Thanksgiving and I was getting myself worked up about seeing him tonight.

He had helped cater a few out-of-town events with Micah in early December, the business picking up speed, just like Jett had promised, and then Andrew and his dad had gone back to New York for Christmas. We'd been texting back and forth a little. I forced Micah to send him the camera I'd bought him for Christmas, saying it was from both of us, so he wouldn't read too much into it.

I pulled out my phone and read through our most recent text exchange.

Merry Christmas! Thanks for the camera, friend. I didn't know we were exchanging gifts or I would've gotten you something.

Like I said, I found it at Everything. You know I'm in there all the time. No big deal.

I thought Micah found it.

Right. We found it. She found it. When we were in there.

Well, it's amazing. I love it! Did I ever tell you that I wanted one almost exactly like this?

Yes, you did.

You make dreams come true.

How has your Christmas been so far?

My mom is here. It's weird.

You okay?

Yeah, actually. It just feels like a cousin visiting or something. Like, I know her, but I don't know her. You know?

I know.

I thought you might. Speaking of, have you talked to your dad since Thanksgiving?

He called today and acted like nothing had happened. I'm learning that's kind of how he is. Not good with confrontation. But the good news is that he's flying Gunnar out to see him during spring break.

Just Gunnar?

He knows I would've said no.

Would you have?

Probably.

I'm sorry.

Don't be. Take some pictures of Christmastime New York and text them to me. It will help.

He responded with pictures. Pictures of lights on trees and in department store windows. Pictures of a dog wearing reindeer antlers and a skinny Santa on a street corner. Pictures of people ice-skating and big red ornaments stacked on top of one another. And snow. Snow on railings and stairwells, and frosting tree branches.

He must've been all over Manhattan taking those pictures. Or maybe that had been one city block. I didn't know. The last picture he sent was a selfie of him on a rooftop somewhere, in a beanie, colorful lights behind him, a goofy expression on his face. I smiled as I looked at it now and then tucked my phone away with another deep breath.

It was no big deal. I was seeing Andrew. We were friends. And we had obviously proven we could continue to be friends even when we were in completely different states. My pep talk seemed to work on me and I climbed out of the van. Completely calm. I walked around to the back.

An explosion of blue and white greeted me when I opened the van doors. Forget-me-nots and baby's breath arrangements filled several boxes. The Barn always had some indoor and outdoor tables that we decorated. But most of the night was for dancing, with a live country band providing the soundtrack.

"When someone said this was at a barn, I was picturing something more rustic." Andrew's voice from behind me made my heart pick up speed again. *Breathe*, I commanded myself. I hadn't heard a car pull up so Andrew must've already been here.

"It's not *a* barn, Andrew. It's *the* Barn. I don't think it's seen an animal in decades." I finally allowed myself to turn, having proven I could talk like a normal person. Andrew looked . . . amazing. He wore his suit from the Eller-Johnson wedding and I had forgotten how cute he was. I don't know how. It felt like his face had been in my brain for the last month.

"Wow," he said, taking me in. I wore a sleeveless dress, the bodice fitted and silver. I had hand stitched little blue flowers onto the blue lace skirt. It flared and hit me several inches above the knees. "I . . . you . . ."

"What?" I asked, looking down and smoothing out my dress, suddenly feeling self-conscious.

"You look good," he finished lamely.

"This was one of the dress designs I sent off with my applications."

"Then you are going to be accepted for sure."

"I hope so."

"How have you been?" He stepped forward and gave me a side hug.

I thought he was giving me a full hug, though, so I turned into him, which made us both fumble with hand placement for a moment. I stepped back.

"It's like we've never hugged before," he said.

"Have we?" I asked, going over the last year of events in my mind.

"Corn maze?" he asked, seeming to have done the same analysis. "Should we try again?"

I laughed, but he wasn't kidding. He stepped forward and wrapped me in a hug, then rocked me back and forth dramatically. "See, I'm an excellent hugger."

I smiled and lay my head on his shoulder, returning his hug. He stopped teasing and gave me a real hug. He smelled good and felt even better against me.

This could not happen. I dropped my arms and turned back toward the van. "Will you help me carry some of these boxes inside?"

"Of course." He lifted one box and I lifted another and we carried them silently into the Barn.

"I think I picked the wrong job," Micah said when she saw me. "I want to be a babe tonight."

I laughed. "I thought you'd talked your dad into letting you dress up." I slid the box onto a table.

"Obviously not," she said, tugging at her polyester cater waiter pants.

"Where do you want this?" Andrew asked me, referring to the box he still held.

"Oh, just put it next to mine."

He did, and then left, probably to get another box.

Micah raised her eyebrows at Andrew's retreating form. "So? How was the reunion?"

"Good." Since Thanksgiving, Micah and I were closer than ever. I was so glad that we'd talked out our problems. We did have differing opinions about the Andrew situation, though. She thought I should just enjoy him while I could and then move on when he left. I didn't think that moving on from Andrew would be as easy as she made it sound. So my solution was not to get hooked on him to begin with. Friends. Friendship wouldn't lead to heartbreak. "We're good."

"Good? Just good? I know how you could make it great." She gave me a smirk. "In fact, I'm going to find myself a boy to kiss at midnight tonight. I don't care who."

"Really?" I said, surprised. "You don't have one highlighted and starred on your spreadsheet? Someone you need to interrogate first with questions of hometown loyalty?"

"I don't!" Micah declared. "I'm going to . . . let things just happen."

I raised my eyebrows, not completely convinced but willing to play along. "I like this plan."

"It's not a plan!" she argued. "It's a natural occurrence."

I noticed Lance then, carrying a big jar of mints to the back table. He glanced in Micah's direction.

I had a feeling Micah would not have a problem finding someone to kiss tonight. "Right. Very natural."

"It's New Year's Eve, after all," Micah was saying. "Remember when that one kid from Jasper kissed you last year and how mad you were? Did he have a name?"

"You're kissing people without names?" Andrew asked, setting another box of flowers on the table next to the two others.

"He had a name," I said. "I just didn't want to know it."

"I think you might have called him Jasper all night," Micah said.

"What about him?" I asked.

"I don't know, I was just thinking about that," Micah said. "That guy didn't let it happen naturally. I will not make that mistake. It must be mutual. A mutual kiss is the best. Take note of that, you two."

Andrew and I exchanged a glance and I tried very hard not to blush. I nodded toward the exit. "I'll go get the last box."

"I can get it," Andrew said, following me.

"Thanks."

"Look at that," he said. "You're actually going to let me."

"I know. I've come a long way." But I still followed him out. "So how much longer will you be in town?" I asked, hoping I sounded casual. "Has your dad picked out the next location for the mentorship, or whatever he calls it?"

Andrew picked up the last box and I shut the back doors of the van.

"Yes, he has. We leave next week."

My face went numb. "That soon?"

"Yes."

"So . . . where?" When I realized that wasn't a complete question, I clarified. "Where are you going this time?"

"Remember the wine lady from the benefit? She had a sister near Birmingham?"

"Yes." My hopes skyrocketed.

"It was almost her."

"But it's not," I said as I realized he had used the word *almost*. My spirits crashed back to earth.

"No. We're going back to New York because I told my dad I wanted to finish out high school in an actual school. So he found a candidate in Manhattan."

"You're right, there are no actual schools in Birmingham," I said.

"My dad probably doesn't think there are."

Andrew was still letting his dad dictate his life. Or maybe he wanted to go back to New York. It's not like he knew anyone in Birmingham. And he obviously had no reason to want to be two hours away from me for the last semester of our senior years. "You get to go to a whole five months of high school?" I asked.

"I know, it's what dreams are made of." We walked back inside and Andrew set the box on the table with the others. "You going to miss me, Soph?"

"How can I miss you?" I replied. "I only see you at special occasions. It's like you're a cousin or something."

Why did I say that? *Why?* That's what he'd said about his mother and I knew it and I said it anyway because I was being a jerk. And because he could've asked his dad to pick Birmingham. I said it because I *was* going to miss him. So much that my chest was aching and I wanted it to stop.

I didn't feel any better seeing that my comment had hit its

328

mark. Seeing the hurt in his eyes. "Right," he said quietly. "Like we don't even know each other."

No! I wanted to scream. *We do.*

It had been almost a year. Of course we knew each other.

Before I could say anything, a microphone screeched with feedback as it was plugged in. It was like a wake-up call.

"I better get to work," I said. "People will be here soon."

Andrew held up his phone. "Me too."

Chapter 39

Are you seeing this?" Micah asked as she refilled a water dispenser.

"Seeing what?" I said, trying to pretend I didn't know exactly what she was talking about. Because I *was* seeing it. Shelby Dickenson, freshman at Alabama State, obviously home visiting her family between semesters, had been talking to Andrew for the last hour. Not just talking. Laughing, and flipping her hair, and touching his arm. And I didn't blame her. She *should* be flirting with Andrew. He was not discouraging it and he was handsome and funny and smart.

"You know very well what I'm talking about," Micah whispered. "In two hours, at midnight, her lips are going to be on his if you don't do something."

"He could've picked Birmingham, Micah. So now I know how he feels about me."

She shook her head back and forth. "First of all, *he* doesn't get to pick anything. His dad does."

"But he acted like he didn't even want to go there!" I protested. "He wasn't even disappointed."

"Second of all," she went on as if I hadn't said anything.

"You are not a mind reader even if you pretend to be one. You have no idea how he feels because the two of you are dumb and won't talk about it. And now I've been so preoccupied with who you are obviously not kissing tonight that I haven't laid any groundwork with who *I'm* kissing."

"Wait, who are you kissing?"

She took me by the shoulders and turned me toward the far corner. A tall, cute black guy I'd never seen before stood watching the line dancing happening on the floor. His hair was cropped short and he wore a blue suit.

"I thought you weren't planning it. I thought it was going to happen naturally," I teased.

I started to worry. Where was Lance? He was going to blow this opportunity if he didn't step up his game.

"It was, until I saw him."

"Who is that?" I asked.

"Exactly!" Micah said. "I need to find out. Or rather, you need to go find out for me."

"I do?"

"Yes, and hurry. I have two hours."

"Okay." I started to walk over to the new boy when Kyle stepped into my path.

"Sophie, hi."

"Hi." I tried to look around him to see if my destination was still there. He was.

"Do you want to dance?"

"What?" My gaze whipped back to Kyle.

"Do you want to dance?"

"Um . . . Sure." I tried to tell myself I wasn't dancing with Kyle because Andrew was talking to Shelby Dickenson, but in my shallow heart, I knew that was exactly why.

It was a slow song and Kyle took me into his arms and we swayed for half a minute in silence.

"Your band isn't playing tonight," I said.

"They wanted a country band. We don't play country."

"True." We turned a slow circle. "How is Jodi?" I don't know why I asked it; the question made it seem like I was jealous or angry about what I'd seen over the summer when really, I hadn't thought about it again after that day.

"I learned dating a band member isn't good for the band."

"This is a lesson many bands have learned before you. Too bad you didn't do your research."

He smiled his lazy smile.

"Especially because Bryce liked her too," I added. "That was definitely a blowup waiting to happen."

"Yeah," he said. "I didn't know Bryce liked her . . . until later."

"Do you know who that guy in the corner is?" I finally asked, because Micah had caught my eye and was tapping the nonexistent watch on her wrist.

"Which guy?" Kyle asked.

We did another turn and I pointed him out.

"Oh, that's Damon's cousin." Damon was a kid in our grade and probably the best student in town.

"How old is he?" I didn't think that mattered at all to Micah, but I was curious. He looked a little old for her. Maybe I was just trying to find flaws with him.

"I don't know. I think he's in college."

"Okay, cool." I dropped my hands and started to leave.

"The song is still going," Kyle said.

"Oh, right." I'd forgotten that I wasn't talking to Kyle just to find out information about Damon's cousin.

The rest of the song went by painfully slow and when it was over, I mumbled, "See you around, Kyle," and left.

"Bye," Kyle said from behind me, sounding a little regretful.

Damon's cousin was walking away when I finally made it to his corner. "Wait," I called out and he turned. "Hi."

"Hi?" he said, uncertain.

I stuck out my hand, which immediately made me think of Andrew mocking me for my hand shaking. "I'm Sophie," I said, my hand still extended.

"Russell," he said, shaking my hand.

"Nice to meet you. Where are you from?"

"Birmingham."

"Where there are actual schools, I'm sure," I said.

He looked confused, understandably. "Uh . . . yes. I go to college there."

"I'm sure it's a great, high-quality one as well."

"What?"

"Nothing. Sorry." I put my hand on my hip. "Do you have

a girlfriend?" I was really off my subtle game tonight. Okay, maybe I was sabotaging this on purpose. Lance deserved a fighting chance, and this guy with his dreamy brown eyes and velvety voice had the ability to make Lance a distant thought.

"Not at the moment, no." He still seemed super wary of my presence. Probably because I was not acting normal.

"I'm sorry, I'm a friend of Damon's," I said, not sure if that would help at all. "He's your cousin, right?"

"Yes. Our moms are sisters."

"But didn't Mrs. Brown grow up here?"

"No, they grew up in Auburn, actually, which is where my mom still lives."

"Which is why you're here alone. Because Birmingham is fairly close to here, so you came to visit your cousin. I'm sure you could visit him all the time if you wanted. Every weekend if you desired."

Russell tilted his head to one side, looking more confused by the second. "I don't visit my cousin every weekend."

"But you *could*, hypothetically speaking."

"Sure . . . hypothetically speaking. It's about two hours away."

"I know! So close!"

"Sophie," Micah said, suddenly at my side. Or maybe not so suddenly. Maybe she'd been standing there for a while. "Are you yelling at this poor guy?"

"No, I wasn't yelling at Russell. Was I?" I asked him.

"You kind of were," he said.

"Oh. Sorry."

"Hi, Russell. I'm Micah." Micah did not put her hand out for a handshake. She just offered a gorgeous smile.

"Hi, Micah. You work here?" he asked, taking in her outfit.

"Well, this is what I like to wear out, but yes, I also work here. We catered the event."

"Oh, so you're working with Jett Hart, right? How is he?"

"He grows on you," I said.

"He's been great." Micah elbowed me. My cue to leave.

"I need to check on the . . . flowers," I finished, when my brain couldn't think of a better excuse to leave. I didn't wait to explain, I just left my friend to get swept off her feet by the dreamy Russell.

"Lance," I hissed, finding him in the crowd.

"What?" he asked, pausing with a tray in hand.

"Find Micah by midnight."

"Why?"

"Because it is imperative for someone to be happy tonight."

"Um . . . okay."

"Great. Thanks."

As I walked away, I decided that maybe I actually would check on the flowers. The crowd was a lot younger than at our normal events and some people couldn't help but mess with the arrangements. I started in the far back corner and did a slow walk around, adjusting a drooping flower here and an off-centered vase there.

When I was halfway around the room, a waving hand drew my attention. Caroline was standing by the far door. I cut across the floor to where she stood.

"How is everything going?" she asked as her eyes traveled down my dress. "That is gorgeous, Sophie. Are those little forget-me-nots?"

"They are."

"I love it."

"Thank you," I said, feeling a flush of pride.

"So I can't pull the cord tonight."

"What?" I asked, thrown off by her abrupt subject change.

"At midnight." She pointed up to the ceiling, and the net that encased hundreds of balloons.

"But you love to release the balloons," I said. She did. It was what she looked forward to from the day after Christmas on.

"I know. But my mother recently moved in with me. Did I tell you that?"

"Yes."

"Right. And she wasn't feeling well when I left and I worry about leaving her alone."

"Okay. I can definitely pull the cord. Where is it?" The location of the balloon release was guarded like a military secret. Caroline always said if she told anyone where it was, "one of those boys" would pull it early and ruin everything.

Her face went serious, denoting the gravity of this moment. "Follow me."

I did. Through the door and around the outside of the Barn and to a back set of wooden stairs tucked behind a padlocked opening that led to a loft area above the main floor. A half wall mostly hid the loft from the view of the people below. Caroline led me over to the far wall and, sure enough, draped over a hook was a thick cord rigged up to the netting over the dance floor.

"At midnight, you pull this," she announced.

At midnight, I would be standing up here, releasing balloons with the perfect view of everyone below.

As if reading my mind, Caroline said, "It really is the most exciting view of the night. You will love it. The energy is mesmerizing."

This was where Caroline had stood for the last however many years and I'd had no idea. Nobody would know I was up here.

I watched everyone now. Micah was still talking to Russell in the corner. She had him smiling and laughing. Lance seemed oblivious to everything but his job, which was probably why after a year of chemistry between him and Micah, nothing had happened. Andrew now had a drink in each hand and was heading back to where Shelby waited at one of the tables, running her finger over a little blue flower in a vase. Kyle was dancing with Lisa Marks from school and seemed to know how to talk to her.

Caroline slowly let her gaze drift along the expanse of balloons like she was missing out on the greatest experience of her life.

"I promise to do a good job," I said.

"I know you will. You and this cord have a date for midnight."

I patted the cord. "I can't wait."

Chapter 40

I ducked inside the kitchen and leaned against the nearest counter. Jett Hart looked up from where he was slicing lemons for the water.

"What's wrong?" Jett asked when I didn't move or say anything.

"Nothing. It's just crowded out there." Two people too crowded to be precise. I closed my eyes and took several deep breaths. "By the way, I found the perfect box for you. I was just clipping flowers at the shop the other day and we got a delivery and I swear to you it's the exact right size."

"A box?" Jett asked. "For what?"

"For your mixer. To replace the one I trapped a critter in."

"Oh." He sliced another lemon. "I already replaced that box."

"Oh."

My mind went back to that rainy, hot June evening. Sliding an overturned box across the grass with Andrew. Stepping on the glass, Andrew bandaging my foot.

Mr. Williams walked into the kitchen with a bin full of dirty dishes. "Sophie!" he said in his jovial way. "Aren't you as pretty as a peach tonight?"

"I never understood that saying," Jett said. "Are peaches meant to represent the pinnacle of beauty?"

"I think it's about the alliteration," I said, walking to the fridge and opening it. A burst of air cooled my hot face.

"I think peaches are beautiful," Mr. Williams said.

"I would say strawberries are the most beautiful fruit," Jett said.

"You see what I mean, that doesn't quite roll off the tongue," I said, my head in the fridge.

"How about as sweet as a strawberry?" Mr. Williams suggested.

Jett grunted.

"If we're going to talk about comparing things to beauty," I said, "we should probably stick with flowers and leave food out of it."

"Spoken like a true flower girl," Jett said, and I laughed. I would claim my flower-girl status proudly now. Flowers had saved my future.

"Is there anything I can help you find in there, Sophie?" Mr. Williams asked, joining me.

"What? No." That's when I noticed a jar of maraschino cherries on a shelf in front of me. "What are the cherries for?" I asked.

Mr. Williams picked them up and studied the label. "I don't know who brought them but Andrew added them to a drink earlier."

"What kind of drink?" I shut the fridge and leaned back against it.

"A Shirley Temple," Mr. Williams said. "Would you like one?"

"Um . . ." I sucked my lips in. "Yes, actually." I could handle the taste of cherries again. I actually liked them. Andrew and his kiss weren't going to take that away from me.

Mr. Williams whipped me up a drink, dropped two cherries into it, and handed it to me.

"Thank you," I told him. "What time is it?" I asked.

Mr. Williams looked at his watch. "Eleven forty-five."

"I better get to my post," I said.

It had cooled off considerably outside, but there were still people at tables and walking about the lit gardens that surrounded the Barn. But as I made my way to the back, I was all alone. I undid the padlock and climbed the stairs. I reached the far wall and sat down next to the cord on the hook. I tapped my glass against it. "Happy New Year, date," I said. I took another drink of my Shirley Temple. See, I could handle this.

I pulled out my phone. I had several missed texts from Micah.

Where are you?

Me and Russell have been hanging out with Andrew, distracting him from you know who. You're welcome.

Where are you?

I texted back: *I've been put in charge of balloon release.*

Her response was nearly immediate: *Lucky! Where is it?*

If I told you I'm sure I would immediately die. The ghost of the New Year would take me.

I thought a baby represented the New Year. Are you saying a baby would kill you?

Yes, that's what I'm saying. Hey, make Lance hang out with you too. He looked like he was going to work right through midnight. Everyone deserves to have fun for at least the first minute of the New Year.

Yeah, okay.

I was bad. Here Micah was trying to live plan-free and I was meddling. But I knew, with the heart of a best friend, that Lance was a better fit for her.

The band stopped playing and a voice said into the microphone, "Five minutes to midnight, y'all. We'll play one more song, so grab the person you want to dance into the New Year with, and let's fill up this dance floor!"

The crowd let out a whoop and then music vibrated the wall against my back. I detached the cord from the hook and sat, holding it tight.

Three more minutes.

I bit my lip and got to my knees, then my feet. I leaned an elbow on the wall and continued to sip my drink. The dance floor was crowded and it was hard to make out everyone from up above. But I could see Micah. She had Lance on her left and Russell on her right. Andrew was there too, and she was teaching the three of them the steps to a line dance. Shelby wasn't there and I scanned the room to find her. She was at the food table, grabbing a packaged mint from a large jar. We always had mints at the New Year's Eve Barn Dance. Micah's idea.

Two minutes.

I slipped out of my heels. My feet were killing me. The feet below stomped in unison as everyone did the jumping section of the line dance. I took my last swig from the cup. Only a few ice cubes and the two cherries sat at the bottom of the glass now.

"One minute!" someone yelled out.

Everyone cheered. My eyes went to Shelby, who looked around the room and began weaving her way through the crowd. Andrew looked around as well, like he just now realized he had less than a minute to find her. He stood on his tiptoes.

Micah leaned over and said something to him. He shook his head.

Andrew must've caught sight of Shelby because he squeezed Micah's arm and left her with Lance and Russell.

Thirty seconds.

It was so strange viewing all this from above. I could see them—Andrew and Shelby—on a zigzagging path toward each other, and I'd be up here witnessing what happened when they met.

The music stopped and into the microphone the singer called out, "Twenty, nineteen . . ."

The crowd started counting down with her. "Eighteen, seventeen . . ."

I tipped my glass to my lips and ate one of the cherries. Immediately the memory of kissing Andrew flooded into my brain. I looked at the cord in my hand. What was I doing? Was it really going to be me and this piece of rope at midnight? Was I really going to let Andrew just walk into Shelby's lips?

"Fifteen, fourteen . . ."

I took a deep breath and yanked on the cord. The balloons spilled out of the net and a surprised cheer emitted from the crowd followed immediately by popping balloons. *Pop. Pop.*

"Eleven, ten . . ."

I dropped the rope, left the cup behind, and ran down the stairs barefoot. I ran around the Barn and into the crowded room.

"Three!"

I couldn't find him.

"Two!"

Pop. Pop.

"One!"

I spun in a circle, greeted by only backs.

"Happy New Year!"

I pushed my way through bodies, trying to orient myself. Everything looked different down here and I didn't remember where Andrew had been. People were hugging around me. I ran into a solid form and realized it was Russell, lips locked with my best friend. The sight made my heart fall. I pushed off to the left and battled my way through the crowd and floating balloons.

"Lance!" I said, nearly running him over. "What are you doing?"

"What?" He seemed clueless.

"Nothing. Have you seen Andrew?"

Lance shook his head and I took off. I couldn't find Andrew. And I knew it was too late. I'd waited too long. Did I really want the next people I ran into to be Andrew and Shelby? I didn't need to see that.

I found my way back outside, around the Barn and back up the stairs. I downed the last cherry in the cup. I watched Lance weave aimlessly through the crowd below, occasionally picking up the remnants of the balloons, getting a jump on cleanup. The image depressed me. I turned to go.

Andrew stood at the top of the stairs.

My breath left me.

A slow smile spread across his face. "Happy New Year, Soph."

I took in a jagged breath.

"You're hard to find. And fast, by the way," he said.

It took me five large steps to close the distance between us and then I lost my courage. I stood, an arm's reach from him, frozen.

His courage was still intact. He wrapped one arm around

my waist and lifted me up against his chest. "I'm going to kiss you now," he said.

My toes brushed the floor and I nodded. He didn't need more permission than that. He brought his lips to mine. I slid my arms around his neck and kissed him back. He tasted like cherries. Or maybe that was me. I didn't even care; he tasted like heaven. I was kissing Andrew. And maybe he'd break my heart or be the great love of my life or maybe I didn't need to know any of that right now, I could just enjoy this. I could enjoy being pressed against him, feeling each breath he took, each move he made. It felt like I was floating on air, dancing in the clouds in a billowy silver dress. He lowered me to the floor but didn't let go, just pressed another kiss to my shoulder, then rested his cheek against mine.

"Have you been eating cherries?" he asked.

I smiled. "I'm sorry. I know you hate cherries."

"I love them now. So much."

I kissed his cheek, then looked at his beautiful face.

"I have a confession," he said.

"What?" I asked, still breathless.

He backed up a little and I realized his left hand was behind his back. He pulled it out, revealing a small blue flower. "I've had a relapse."

I tried to narrow my eyes in mock anger but it didn't work.

"But I know the girl who arranged them and I think she'll forgive me." He held it out for me. "Something beautiful for someone beautiful."

The line sounded just as cheesy this time around. But it also made my head float back in the clouds. I took the flower and brought it to my nose, then let it lightly brush against my lips.

He watched me intently. "Are you going to say anything?" he finally asked.

"Like what?"

"I don't know."

"Like, don't leave?" I asked.

"For starters."

"Like please talk your dad into taking the mentorship in Birmingham?"

"You want me in Birmingham?" he asked.

I nodded. "I want you here, but that's the next best thing."

"I thought you were heading for New York after graduation," Andrew said. "So I figured I'd better be there waiting."

Oh. "That's why you didn't push for Birmingham?" I asked.

"Of course." Andrew leaned closer to look at me. "You *are* heading to New York after graduation, right? I know you. You've realized you deserve to follow your dream."

He *had* figured me out. "I am heading for New York." At least that's what I hoped to do. I took a breath. "I'm not my father. Following my dream doesn't have to mean abandoning my home and the people I love."

"Of course not. You love this place," Andrew said.

I smiled. "I do."

He nodded. "So we're apart for five months. We can

handle five months. Let's give this thing a fighting chance," he said.

"This thing?"

"Us."

"Us," I agreed.

"It could work," he said, as if still trying to convince me. "We can text and call and send pictures."

I gave him a smile. "That does sound doable."

Andrew was quiet for a minute, then said, "I've wanted you near me since we sat in the back of an old boathouse together watching fireworks."

"You have? Huh. I still hated your guts that day."

He laughed. "I know." He reached out, took my hand, and brought it to his lips. "So when did it change for you, then?"

"I don't know. Maybe you getting so mad that Kyle was kissing someone else."

"I wasn't mad that he was kissing someone else. I very much wanted him to be kissing someone who wasn't you. But not if that hurt you. Not if you wanted it to be you."

"I didn't."

"Good. Because you kissed me that day."

"I know."

"And I haven't been able to get it out of my head since."

"Me neither."

"You were really good at hiding that."

"You too!" I protested.

"So . . . New York?" he asked, pulling me into his arms again.

"Are we being crazy? Is this impractical?"

"Who cares? Now is the time to fail spectacularly. We have our whole lives ahead of us to try again and again."

I smiled and closed my eyes.

"You're beautiful," he whispered. His lips brushed mine softly.

I melted against him. He was warm and solid. I could feel his heart beating a steady rhythm.

"You're quiet tonight," he said. "What are you thinking?"

"That I'm so happy."

"Me too." He pressed his lips to mine again. "Me too."

Chapter 41

That Barn isn't going to clean itself," Micah said. She, Andrew, and I had wandered the grounds as guests started to leave and had found a stack of hay six bales high and just as wide. Andrew had boosted us to the top and we now lay side by side (me in the middle), looking up at the bright stars.

"It might if we never go back," I said.

"I thought you said no animals live at this barn." Andrew patted the straw beside him. "What's with the hay?"

"People use it for weddings. Seating or decorations or . . ." I trailed off.

"You couldn't think of a third thing?" Micah asked.

"Can you?"

"I probably could, but I won't go there," she said.

"Where is your boy?" Andrew asked Micah.

"My boy?" she repeated.

"The one you were kissing earlier?"

"He was a midnight kiss, Andrew. Don't try to tie me down to someone I kissed at midnight."

"Oh," he said.

I smiled. That was a good sign for Lance. Micah had ended up actually talking to the beautiful boy and finding out that he didn't fit her criteria.

Andrew rolled onto his side and propped his head up on his hand.

"Do you know that Sophie yelled at Russell about Birmingham?" Micah asked Andrew. "And how close it was and how easy it would be to visit her since he lived in Birmingham?"

"You want Russell to visit you?" Andrew asked me with a grin.

"Yes, that's exactly what that was about." I threw a piece of hay at him. Then I threw one at Micah. "And that's not at all what I said, but whatever."

Andrew draped an arm over my waist and pulled me closer.

Micah stuck out her tongue. "I might need to get a boyfriend if you two are together now. I can't compete with this."

My eyes flitted to Andrew's, wondering what he thought of Micah proclaiming us a couple. He seemed to read my mind because he just raised his eyebrows at me, like a question. I pulled on his already-loosened tie, bringing his face down to mine, and I kissed him.

"Yep," Micah said. "I definitely need a boyfriend. You have any friends in New York?"

Andrew threw a piece of hay at Micah this time. "I thought I told you that I have no friends."

"Had," I said. "You need to start using the word *had* in that sentence."

"True," he said.

"Micah!" The sound of Lance's voice rang out through the crisp night air.

Micah sat up. "He probably needs me to help clean. See you two later." She hopped off the stacks of hay and went to meet Lance.

"I've never seen her so anxious to clean," Andrew said as she walked away.

"Yes, that's exactly what that was about," I said for a second time. "Cleaning."

"You don't think it was about . . . Ohhhh!" he said, realization dawning. "Good because I was kind of depressed when she kissed Russell."

"Me too." I sat up to see Micah and Lance talking as they walked to the Barn together. I smiled.

"When are you supposed to hear back from colleges?" Andrew asked.

"Between now and February. I'm hoping more on the now side because I'm nervous."

"I saw your designs," he said. "You have nothing to be nervous about."

I nodded. I was still anxious. But I was also more confident about my work than I'd been in a long time. "Thank you."

He tucked a piece of hair behind my ear and then traced my earlobe with his finger. "So. I hear there's this yearly Valentine's Dinner at the old folks' home around here."

"Yes, it's a tradition," I said with a shiver.

"Want to be my date this year?"

"I don't know," I said. "Things didn't end well for my last Valentine's date."

Andrew laughed and kissed my cheek. "I'm willing to take my chances."

"You'd come here for that? Don't you think you'll be working a completely different New York party?" I asked, running a hand along his tie.

"No. I have a date."

I smiled. "Okay."

"Let's go out this Friday too," Andrew said.

"What's this Friday?" I asked.

"Nothing. I'm starting a trend of seeing you outside of special occasions."

"How will that be?" I said. "To see each other just because."

Andrew pulled me close and together we looked up at the stars. "I think it will be perfect," he said.

Acknowledgments

Those of you who know me personally know that I am a raging extrovert! (No sarcasm needs to be applied to that opening sentence. It is true.) So for me, events, parties, holiday get-togethers, really *any* occasion is where I want to be! As you can imagine, this book was fun for me to write. A book of occasions. It had its unique challenge of needing to fill the reader in on what happened in between without slowing down the story too much, but I hope it worked. I hope you enjoyed following Sophie through a year of celebrations, a year of discovery, a year of love.

Thanks to my family, who support me through everything. My husband, Jared, and my kids, Skyler, Autumn, Abby, and Donavan. Like all families, we've been through ups and downs, and I'm just happy we have each other, always.

Thank you, readers, for sticking with me all this time. Or for just discovering me with this book. It means the world to me that you're reading my stories and talking about them online (or throwing them against a wall; either way they're getting some airtime). Thank you for your kind words to me over the years.

Speaking of years, I've been with my agent, Michelle Wolfson, now for seven! Lucky number seven. And believe me, I've felt lucky for all seven of those years. Here's to at least seven more, Michelle. You're the best.

Thank you to Aimee Friedman, my editor! You're an amazing editor and a lovely person. And I just genuinely enjoy working with you *and* hanging out with you. I think that's pretty rare (or I tell myself it is to make me feel more special), and I'm so grateful for it. Thanks as well to the entire Scholastic family: David Levithan (great idea!); Josh Berlowitz; copyeditor Kerianne Steinberg; Yaffa Jaskoll; Olivia Valcarce; Rachel Feld; Elisabeth Ferrari; Tracy van Straaten; Lizette Serrano; Emily Heddleson; and everyone in Sales. Clubs and Fairs, I love you! I know it takes a team to make a book, and I have a great one!

I also have a team of amazing women in my life, women who would be there for me in a heartbeat if I asked: Stephanie Ryan, Candi Kennington, Jenn Johansson, Renee Collins, Bree Despain, Natalie Whipple, Michelle Argyle, Elizabeth Minnick, Rachel Whiting, Brittney Swift, Mandy Hillman, Jamie Lawrence, Emily Freeman, Megan Grant, Misti Hamel, Claudia Wadsworth. Thanks, friends. I love you all.

And last but definitely not least, thanks to my amazing family. Chris DeWoody, Heather Garza, Jared DeWoody, Spencer DeWoody, Stephanie Ryan, Dave Garza, Rachel DeWoody, Zita Konik, Kevin Ryan, Vance West, Karen West,

Eric West, Michelle West, Sharlynn West, Rachel Braithwaite, Brian Braithwaite, Angie Stettler, Jim Stettler, Emily Hill, Rick Hill, and the twenty-five children and the (I lost track of the amount) children of children that exist between all these people. You're the best!

About the Author

Kasie West is the author of several YA novels, including *The Distance Between Us*, *On the Fence*, *The Fill-In Boyfriend*, *P.S. I Like You*, *By Your Side*, *Lucky in Love*, and *Listen to Your Heart*. Her books have received numerous accolades and have been named as ALA Quick Picks for Reluctant Readers and as YALSA Best Books for Young Adults. Kasie lives in Fresno, California, with her family, and you can visit her online at kasiewest.com.

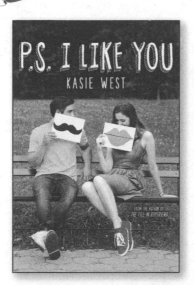

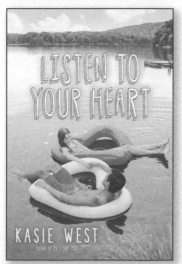